THE
SHATTERED GODDESS

THE CHANGELING AND THE WITCH

When an evil witch secretly substitutes her own son for that of a royal heir, she unwittingly creates her own greatest nemesis.

Condemned to a hole-in-the-wall existence at the bottom of society, the true heir must study magic to survive.

But when he discovers his own real identity, he learns that to reclaim the throne he must unleash a magic that will destroy his world!

"Compelling fantasy, intriguing characters."

Vicki Ann Heydron

**"Moody, haunting, persuasive...
a master storyteller."**

Mythprint

"Mood, pace, characterization, fierce imagery containing equal parts legend and fantasy, distinctly different."

Night Voyages

THE SHATTERED GODDESS

DARRELL SCHWEITZER

WILDSIDE PRESS
NEW JERSEY • 1999

WILDSIDE PRESS
PO BOX 45
GILLETTE, NJ 07933-0045
www.wildsidepress.com

For John Sevcik, who never
had to buy the Meaning
of Life from me for a quarter.

I think that all gods were men once, and, further, that they did not choose or seek out their divinity, but were swept along by events like twigs in a flood-swollen river, until at last the current became holy, and they lost sight of the shore of human mortality, and came into the light.

—*Telechronos of Hesh*, To Himself

A secret birth at midnight, and all the world shook.
—Othelredon, Miraculous Songs

All truth is revealed in dreams.
—Hadel of Nagé, On Fears

Chapter 1
His Name
Shall be Mystery

It was in the time of the death of The Goddess that the thing happened, when the fragments of her godhead were beginning to assume those unstable shapes called the Dark and Bright Powers. It was in an age of prodigies, of miracles, of signs and wonders in the heavens, when the Earth rolled blindly through those same heavens with no hand to guide it, that the old witch feigned death and caused herself to be buried. She had long since given up her name to the darkness because of her hatred for the holy city of Ai Hanlo, and for all the folk of Randelcainé. And so absolute was that hatred that she had forgotten the cause of her quarrel; malice grew in her like a living, consuming thing, until she was but an instrument in its vast and unknowable design.

No one mourned her passing. Priests were sent from The Guardian himself, the emperor of the country thereabout, to drive away what evil might linger over her corpse. Most citizens stayed in their houses and bolted their windows when the coffin was carried through the winding, narrow streets, down Ai Hanlo Mountain and through the Desert Gate. A very few looked out, and fewer still spoke, and a mere handful spoke against her, rejoicing in her demise. It had long been noted that this witch must have been a kindly old lady despite her dire occupation, for she had so few enemies among the living.

1

She lay in the darkness, listening, remembering. She smiled.

She noted the length of her journey, the incline of the way which banged her head against the inside of the coffin, the constant heaving and shaking as the bearers stumbled down a rocky hillside. As she expected, she was being taken to no cemetery within the city, but to a spot of unclean ground beyond its walls, away from any road, where those who drove refuse wagons through the streets at dawn were wont to dump their loads.

When her revenge was complete, they would pay for what they thought to be their last insult.

The grave was dug. She felt herself lowered into it, and then clods of dirt fell on the coffin lid with continuous thuds. A few incantations were muttered by the priests, and a reliquary containing a splinter of a bone of The Goddess was passed back and forth overhead. She could sense a tinge of its power, like centipedes scampering across her face, but she was resolute and did not stir.

After a time there was silence. She waited, feeling in her mind the turning of the Earth, the rising and setting of the sun and moon, until she knew that the appointed hour had come. Then she called out the name of a certain thing that dwelt somewhere beneath her. It was not even a Dark Power—no splinter of the evil aspect of The Goddess this—but merely an echo, a stirring embodiment of some vileness which crawled underground. She spoke its name, and it came to her.

The silence gave way to a sound like running water, but then it was more like the distant roaring of a furnace. The coffin shook. The earth around her trembled and grew hot.

There followed a stifling, acrid pause, after which something was scraping against the wood on which she lay.

The coffin bottom was pulled away in a series of furious yanks, and she was falling down, down, in a funnel of absolute darkness, but not alone. The burning, lightless presence was at her side.

She came to rest in a grotto. Dimly glowing blue stones stood in a circle about an oily pool.

Something crouched at the edge of that pool. In part its form suggested a massively muscled man, but the whole was nothing at all human. The lower half of the body was a riot of useless, misshapen limbs. The thing moved slowly, like a slug, its outline flickering all the while as if it were an illusory disguise the wearer was unsure of. Only the face was clearly outlined. Little bands of red fire glowed from every wrinkle and furrow in the creature's flesh, and there were many.

"I—have come—"

"For the reasons mentioned when last you summoned me." The voice was faint but clear, like a wind issuing up from the hidden depths of the Earth.

"Yes, for those reasons," the witch said, "and for the fulfillment of our covenant, as agreed aforetime."

"So be it then. Give me what is my due."

Without hesitation, using her long, sharp nails, she gouged out both her eyes. She only gasped briefly—"Ah!"—at the act, but she could not help but recoil as the payment was taken from her. Other hands touched hers in the semi-darkness, and she felt an intense pain, like fire but with less heat, as if acid had been poured over her outstretched hands.

"Now go," said the thing, "and all will be accomplished."

But before she could make a move the hands touched her ears, and the burning was inside her head. She could not even hear herself scream, but by the exertion of her lungs she knew that she was indeed screaming.

In absolute darkness and silence and agony, she crawled on her knees and her ruined hands back up the long, sloping shaft down which she had been carried. At last, when she feared that even the power of her hatred would fail her, she touched the wooden bottom of the coffin, where it had been discarded among some stones in a bend in the tunnel. She dragged it with her the rest of the way until she came to the splintery remains of the coffin, itself. She turned this on its side, so she wouldn't tumble out of it, and crawled back in. But the added weight dislodged it from its precarious position, and the whole mass, witch, coffin, and bottom slid downward a hundred feet or so in a shower of gravel until it came to rest in the bend in the tunnel. Satisfied, lying on her side, she edged the bottom over the opening as a kind of lid. Then she fumbled among her garments and drew out a little metal box. Within was a wafer. With delicate, desperate care, her fingers stiff with pain, she laid this wafer underneath her tongue.

At last able to relax, she shut her eyelids over the bloody sockets and exhaled one last breath.

Even as she did the change came over her. The effect sparkled brilliantly as it spread over her puckered cheeks and across her whole face, encompassing her head and racing down her body. She was turning into crystal. In scarcely a minute she was stiff and glittering inside her incongruous, ragged clothing, like some huddled sculptural grotesque wrought out of luminescent quartz.

These things happened in the time of the death of The

Goddess, when the Powers began to form, in the reign of The Guardian called Tharanodeth. They would not have been possible in a more ordered age.

It was somewhat later in the reign of Tharanodeth the Good that a child was born in the holy city of Ai Hanlo, in the imperial nursery, no less. Perhaps it is inaccurate to say that the child was born, for no one saw the act, and there was no mother to be had.

What actually happened was that a nurse came in one morning to feed the infant prince, whose fortuitous and much-prophesied birth had relieved much anxiety so late in The Guardian's life, and found *two* babies in the jewel-studded cradle. One offspring meant that the bones of The Goddess, which lay somewhere beneath the city, would continue to be watched over after Tharanodeth's departure from this life. *Two* surely portended a struggle for the honor of watching over those bones. War, wrack, and ruin. It took no profound political wisdom to see the implications.

And it was not just a case of a misplaced baby. Any fool could recognize this as a sign.

Eventually Tharanodeth was called, and he came, moving about the palace as he always did, surrounded by many retainers.

The old man looked down on the two tiny forms asleep in the cradle. He scratched his chin, as he was often seen to do when deep in thought, and at last said to one of his ministers, "Do you suppose my wife had twins, and didn't tell me about it?"

Flustered, astonished, the fellow tried to maintain his dignity.

"Blessed Lord, no! It cannot be!"

"I mean, she was still in pain after the first one was born. You'll recall how the physicians bade us all, even me, to leave her alone. Perhaps the other baby was in there, and came out later."

"Holy Guardian of the Bones of The Goddess," said the minister, "that is impossible. Your son is six weeks old. This other is newly born, and smaller and darker than the prince. They are not twins."

"Well, I didn't think so. What then?"

"*Evil!*" said Hadel of Nagé, a court magician. He was a short, wiry husk of a man with a pointed face and a huge moustache. Everyone called him The Rat.

"How so?"

"Dread sovereign,"—he never called a ruler that unless squirming to depths of flattery which would stagger the imaginations of most people—"as you can doubtless see in your

4

boundless wisdom, as you find beneath your dignity to explain because the nature of it is so obvious that even I, who am but a trickster, can perceive it, it is frightfully apparent that one of the Dark Powers visited here during the night. I fear it might have brought some contagion. But more concretely, I fear this thing which was the main object of its mission. No doubt the plan was to substitute this creature for the infant prince. But fortunately I was in my tower last night, reading aloud from the offices of my art, and this was no doubt sufficient to repel the monster before it could complete its task."

"How fortunate that you were watching over us," said Tharanodeth, visibly amused at the other's theatrics. "Pray tell, what now?"

"Please, I beg of you, take me seriously. If you kill this child, as indeed you must, you should cut off its head. Inside you will find only a stone. Let the body lie for a night and a day, and it will turn into a lump of weeds, which is all it really is."

The Guardian reached down and gently touched the back of his hand to the newcomer's side, feeling its warmth.

"Indeed."

"Yes, Lord! So it is!"

"No, this is only flesh and blood. Let the women raise this child apart from the prince, since it is not my heir. Still, it is under my protection."

Then The Guardian clapped his hands, a trumpeter blew a blast, a priest waved a bowl of incense around to purify the air through which Tharanodeth would walk, and in time to the ringing of silver bells held by half a dozen boys, the whole company left the nursery.

For a few minutes the two babies were alone. Servant women were sent for, but in the short interval before their arrival, something happened which no one observed, except perhaps those to whom it happened.

The stranger rolled over and began to convulse, as if something were forcing its way out of him. He opened his mouth to cry out, but the only sound was of a wind issuing up from measureless depths. A black, oily smoke poured out of the baby's mouth and hovered in the air over the cradle. Briefly it took the form of an old, hobbled woman without any eyes. Black hands groped for the mouth of the larger, paler baby, and, finding it, forced it open.

Instantly the prince was awake and shrieking, but the black hag leaned over and, losing all shape, poured down his throat

5

until all sounds were smothered.

When the nursemaids arrived it was the foundling child which was crying in furious terror, now that he was able to, now that the source of that terror had left him.

The prince lay still and stared up at them sullenly.

* * *

Tharanodeth's heir was, with all due ceremony, given the name of Kaemen Ai Hanlo ne Papeleothrim, that is, Kaemen (Bright Hope) of the city of Ai Hanlo of the house of Papeleothrim, for the fathers of the Good Guardian were of that clan.

The other child went without a name for many months, until Hadel The Rat chanced to be passing by the nursery late one night. He walked along a narrow corridor. To his right was the large, brightly decorated room in which Kaemen resided. Expensive candles let perfume into the air. Many women were in constant attendance.

To his left was a barred door. He lifted the bar and looked inside. He had heard of much consternation in the nursery of late, women going mad and running away, so the gossips said. Once he had directed a simple spell of seeing in that direction, in hopes of finding out what the fuss was about. But his spell had been repulsed by some unknown and powerful force, and he had awakened from his trance with two black eyes. This was why he had come in person, why he had opened the door.

He looked in on a dark, unfurnished room. At the far end starlight shone through a small, barred window. In the center of the room was a rough, wooden cradle in which lay the stranger.

Hadel gasped at what he saw.

The baby was awake and blissfully juggling balls of light in the air. They were the size of plums, bright as embers, but semi-transparent. Two tiny hands would come together, then part, and a glowing sphere would float upward about a foot, light as smoke. Then, as the magician watched, the ball would begin to sink. Those which fell outside of the cradle winked out of existence like soap bubbles. The rest were playfully swatted up for another descent. All the while more were being created. There was no end to them. Their light made the man's stooped shadow flicker behind him.

He approached the child, leaned over the cradle, and jumped back as a ball burst against his face.

"Teats of a desert nymph! I have never *seen* such a thing."

The baby was aware of him and began to cry. All the lights vanished.

The Rat scurried from the room, bolted the door behind him,

6

and ran as fast as he could to the Guardian, who had just then emerged from the vault into which only he might go, where lay the very bones of The Goddess. Servitors whose tongues had been cut out announced his ascent, since no voice may speak of such a thing. Blindfolded priests helped him remove his vestments, each of their movements part of a prescribed ritual.

Hadel stumbled breathlessly into the anteroom of the Holy Chamber, then remembered where he was, fell to his knees, and tapped a small gong on a stand nearby. Tharanodeth entered and looked at him sharply.

"Well, what do you want?"

Too frightened to conduct himself gracefully, the Nagéan blurted out all that he had seen, embellishing the tale with a few malicious laughs, words muttered in an unknown tongue by a child too young for speech ("But there's a lot of that going around," interrupted the Guardian.) and the faintly heard sound of *something* scraping its way down the wall beyond the barred window.

Intensely, passionately, recovering some control of his rhetoric, Hadel begged as he had months before, to be allowed to smother the little enigma before worst came to worst.

"You waste my time," sighed Tharanodeth. "Go away. This whole interview borders on blasphemy. You could not have come at a more inopportune moment."

"But, most dread lord," continued Hadel, "to have such a *mysterious* influence in your court can never come to good. I have sensed danger with my magic."

"Hmm. Has the brat got a name?"

"I...don't think so."

"Then his name shall be Mystery."

"What—?"

"Let him be called Ginna. In the speech of the hill people the word means 'mystery.' Ginna ne Ai Hanlo."

"No! Never! That cannot be!"

Tharanodeth grew angry. "What makes you so sure of what can and cannot be. *I* rule here. For the last time, no harm shall come to the child. I do not think him dangerous. If anything, he intrigues me. Now, if I were not as patient as those who sing my praises claim, *you* might not be safe from harm much longer. Have you considered that?"

Hadel's moustache quivered. His eloquence fled away. He was barely able to speak at all.

"I...only mean....I mean to say, that is, that I mean— meaning no disrespect—that if this...ah, *unusual* infant bears *Ai*

7

Hanlo in its name, well, it isn't proper. I mean, you don't know *where* the boy is from, and he might be of low birth actually. I mean—"

"You mean. So be it. Just Ginna then."

The Rat made the gesture of Blessing Received and backed out of the room, his head bowed, bumping into the doorway as he did. He was glad to have accomplished something, even if the squirming intrusion would have to live. It irked him to settle for second best.

Chapter 2
Like the Child

As the days went by, Kaemen turned out to be a veritable monster, the terror of his nurses, ill-tempered, foul-mouthed at an astonishingly early age, and wholly lacking the grace and moderation of his father. His teeth came in early. He learned how to use them. It nearly cost an old woman a finger.

Like the child, so shall the man be was a proverb of Randelcainé. Despite his name, he was not the bright hope of anyone.

Ginna was ignored for the most part. He was not brought to meals with the high-born children of the court, nor did he eat in the kitchen with the servants. Occasionally someone would leave scraps by the door of his room. He was not even taught how to keep himself clean until the stench disturbed Kaemen.

All were forbidden to enter that bare room. Rumor had it a deformed monster was kept there. Once the boy learned to walk, this was to his advantage. He was properly shaped, if undersized, filthy, and pale for want of sunlight. When he wandered about he was often not recognized.

At first the only places he knew were a few musty rooms, a corridor, and the entrance to Kaemen's nursery, beyond which he was not permitted to pass. He often heard cries and shrieks coming from the nursery, dishes crashing to the floor, and the bare feet of the servants padding back and forth. Those same feet would kick him whenever he tried to investigate, so after a time he learned to keep to himself.

There was a girl who came to play with him, who said she would pretend to be his big sister. She was very big, twice as tall as he. He didn't know her age, all ages being unimaginable, but she was much wiser than he. She taught him many new words, and how to count on his fingers. He decided he was most happy when she was around, and wished she would be around always.

But then she came no more. Months later he saw her in the hall, straining under a yoke from which two buckets of water hung. A massive woman twice her size walked behind her and glowered. He called her name, but she turned her face away. He never saw her again.

One day a bird came to his window, stood between the bars, and began to sing. It seemed to Ginna that this song was even more beautiful than any the girl had sung, and more mysterious for not having any words. This was surely the most wondrous creature he had ever encountered.

He stood on a stool and reached for it, but it vanished into the unknown blue void beyond, and then he had a new desire. He wanted to go where it had gone, away from things familiar.

He was three and a half then. He had heard of a world outside but knew nothing about it, and he was aware of his ignorance.

At the end of a certain hallway there was a huge door, too heavy for him to open. It was always kept shut, but sometimes someone was careless. Occasionally he caught glimpses of a stairway on the other side of it, spiralling down into someplace he had never been.

When the young prince bawled that his bathwater was too cold that night, and swore that he would have everyone flayed alive when he was a little older, Ginna saw his chance. There was much scurrying about, and two burly men came through the door with a new tub of steaming water. In their haste they left the door open.

Ginna found the steps too large for his short legs, so he went down backwards like a man on a ladder, dropping from step to step.

He knew he was in a tower from the way he was going down, down, farther than he had ever imagined he would go. The stairs curved away above him until he could no longer see the door. He had truly ventured out of his world.

At last the stairway ended. There was a damp stone floor at the bottom, which was cold beneath his feet. A lantern hung from above on a chain, driving the darkness away from a doorway. Over this were two portraits of the same woman, but in each she was different. In one she wore a long black gown sprinkled with stars, and held a serpent in either hand. Lightning flickered above her head. At her feet was a boiling cloud in which hundreds of writhing figures were visible: horned men, serpents, toads with the heads and claws of lions. He had never seen such things. The girl had told him about many animals and described them, but these went well beyond the range of her descriptions. Many were just shapes to him.

The other picture showed the lady in brilliant white, astride a dolphin. Or Ginna thought it was a dolphin. It looked vaguely like a fish, and he had seen a fish before, swimming in a bottle being taken into Kaemen's room. He was able to guess that the bright thing in the lady's right hand was the sun. In the left was a tree.

He liked the lady of the second picture more than the other. He smiled at her. He pressed his hands together, as he had done so many times before, and opened them. A bubble of light floated up where the lady could see it. The girl had always seemed happy when he did that. He hoped the lady would too.

Just then the whole place was flooded with light. Someone had opened the door.

Ginna tumbled back and looked up at the most mountainous individual he had ever beheld, who peered down at him impassively from beneath a winged helmet. He had a red moustache and a beard as big as a blanket.

"Well, by The Goddess, what have we here?"

Ginna spoke a few of the words he knew, but the man didn't seem to understand.

"You belong back upstairs, not down here." The giant bent over to pick him up, and he stared, not sure whether to be afraid or not. To please the man he made a glowing ball which floated into his face.

The man recoiled before it touched him.

"Witchcraft!" he gasped, and backed away hurriedly.

Ginna had wondered many times before why no one else made lights in his presence, but he'd assumed they were too busy, or didn't think him worth the bother. After all, they ignored him in every other way. It was the natural order of things, as far as he was concerned.

But now, for the first time, he understood that he was not like the others. Perhaps he was the only one who could do the thing.

Alone one more, he closed and opened his hands, and

watched the light bubbles rise, then slowly drift to the floor. A draft from beneath the door made them roll in the air.

A while later he made his way back up the stairs. Fortunately the upper door was still open.

* * *

Two years passed, and a serving woman came for him in his room and led him down those stairs again. It was an astonishing journey through many new corridors, and he caught glimpses of rooms vaster than any space he could imagine. There were pictures on the walls, often of the twin ladies, sometimes of men in winged helmets and armor, with battles going on in the background. He wanted to stop and look at everything, but the woman dragged him on. Thick rugs lay underfoot in some stretches, muffling sound. For the most part the way was deserted. Twice he saw groups of wholly unfamiliar people going off on unimaginable errands.

The greatest wonder of all came when they emerged into an open courtyard beneath a bright blue sky. He had never seen the whole sky before, just pieces of it through small windows. He planted his feet firmly and refused to move until he had gazed more fully at this spectacle, but the woman slapped him on the ear, grabbed him under the arms, and carried him.

He was left in a new place, so distant from where he had been that he never saw anyone he had known before. He was among keepers of animals and workers of iron, and fascinated to watch both. The furnaces crackled merrily and were splendid if one kept a safe distance from them, and the animals were more so. Horses were mountains of flesh on legs, but huger still were creatures called *katas*, which stood on their hind legs twice as tall as any horse. They were hairless, grey-skinned, with tiny forelimbs and even tinier seven-fingered hands, and small, narrow heads. He was never allowed near a *kata*, because they were rare and expensive and because one could smash him to mush with a flick of its tail, or so the keepers claimed. Where it joined the body, the tail was as thick as the man who warned him, and he was broad-shouldered. At the tip grew three spikes of white bone.

Ginna did not really know how to be a part of the society of stable hands and smiths. He didn't know what to say. Their children played incomprehensible games. So he stayed out of the way and watched most of the time, learning, peeking out of corners, until someone called him "The Mouse." The name stuck.

He was better fed and clothed than before. Like everyone else he wore a simple tunic, and like the other children, he went barefoot.

12

He saw no one else making balls of light with their hands, so he thought it best to do this only in private. He did not like to draw attention to himself.

Eventually he made a friend. She was half a year older than he. Her name was Amaedig, which means Cast Aside. She did not seem to have any parents, but wandered from place to place as he did, sleeping wherever there was room. She was not good looking, and her back was slightly crooked, but he found her pleasant to be with. They played together among the metal scraps, and sometimes climbed atop something to watch the men feeding slices of meat to the *Katas*, or even trying to ride them in a small, fenced-off yard.

After a while he swore her into secrecy with as terrible an oath as he could think of ("If I tell this secret, I hope terror and doom will come upon me, and my arms and head fall off, and extra toes grow out of my empty neck!"), then took her into a closet and showed her how he made light balls.

"Can't you do it?" he asked, as she gazed in amazement.

"No, but I wish I could."

"Then try."

She did. Nothing.

"How did you learn to do it?"

"I didn't. I always could. I used to think everyone could, and then I thought maybe only grownups couldn't, but now you can't either. I don't understand. Maybe I'm special."

More spheres floated up to the top of the closet.

"They're pretty," she said.

* * *

Ginna was seven when The Guardian first sent for him, and suddenly he was someone important. All faces were turned toward him. All hands helped as he was scrubbed and shorn and brought fresh clothing. All eyes looked after him as he was taken away and Amaedig ran up to him as he was leaving and said, "Will you come back? Will you?"

"I hope so," was all he could say.

He came back. It was the first of many visits. Tharanodeth was in his declining years by then, and he sent for Ginna often. When the boy was still small he sat him on his knee and sang songs to him, or bade him sing other songs back. They traded riddles. The old Guardian even read to him from an ancient book, which from the date marked on its clasp had not been opened for fifty years. It told of the deeds of the remote forebears of the people of Ai Hanlo, how they had come out of the mountains and out of the desert to found the Holy City, which stood in the middle

13

of a fertile plain in those days.

"It was a golden age," said The Guardian of The Bones. "Men were content then, and the Earth was calm. It was before the death of The Goddess."

"How did she die?"

"I don't know, my boy. I don't know. Does that surprise you? It has been prophesied that someone will find out, but all I can tell you is how it was discovered that she was dead. The age of peace ended. Suddenly all the world was in turmoil, even more than it is today. There were two suns in the sky and the land burned. Then winter lasted all the months of the year and it froze. The oceans froze too, but then they melted and rushed over the land. Invading hordes tore down cities mightier than our own. But this was not enough to let them know that The Goddess was dead. Pestilence, earthquake, and war had come before, No, it was discovered in this wise: a certain holy man, the holiest of all men living, who was sort of a guardian back before there were any bones to guard over, took a bone, an ordinary bone, the leg bone of one of his order who had died, and he wrote a message to The Goddess on it, begging for her help in the time of trouble. Then he cast the bone into a fire. The Bright Aspect of The Goddess could be made manifest through fire. But when he drew the bone out again, there were no cracks on it and the message was erased. No answers because there was no one *to* answer. By that he knew that The Goddess was dead."

"But where did The Bones come from?"

"That, young man, is a holy mystery, which only I may know. I can't tell even you. Now you are dismissed."

Another year passed. The manner of the visits began to change. Ginna was brought in secret to The Guardian, and told not to speak of what went on. So he confided only in Amaedig.

It was during his eighth year that he was ushered into the private chambers of Tharanodeth and he found The Guardian dressed in heavy shoes and a travel cloak, with a staff in his hand.

"We are going somewhere," the old man said. "We are going now, while I can still make the journey."

Ginna's heart leapt. So far in his life he had never been beyond the walls of the palace, and there was much within those walls he had never seen. Beyond the palace there was the lower city, beyond that—

He could not imagine what was beyond that. He had seen a little, but only from windows. It was very far away. So were the stars.

It was after midnight then, well into the stillest hours of the night. Ginna no longer dressed in fine clothes to visit The Guardian, and he was in his usual plain tunic, and without shoes. He was not ready for any journey, but he went. Tharanodeth took him down a long, winding staircase, through a secret passage, until they had descended for so long he was sure they were at the center of the Earth.

The stone floor was intensely cold beneath his feet. Damp slime squished between his toes. Then the floor ended and there was only rough stone. He trod gingerly.

"Get up on my back," said The Guardian. "I'll carry you."

He did, and the old man staggered and let out an "oompf!" but he carried him for miles. Once Tharanodeth looked up at the dripping stalactites and said, "We are no longer in the palace, but underneath the city itself." Then the way sloped down sharply. "We are at the heart of the mountain," he said. A long while afterwards, as they began to move up again, he said, "Now we are just barely in sight of Ai Hanlo. We are well beyond the walls."

It was still dark when they emerged into the open air beneath the stars. The moon was bright and nearly full, and the old man pointed to the west, where it was nearing the horizon.

There stood a mountain revealed in the moonlight, surrounded by barren foothills and topped with crags and sheer cliffs. But all over the mountain, like ivy growing on it, were towers and walls, terrace after terrace of tiny houses more walls ringed with towers from which pennons flew, and at the foot of the mountain still more levels of houses with a thicker wall encompassing the whole. Two huge gates were visible. Atop each tower, spread all the way up the mountain, watchlights burned, and there were lanterns in many windows. The lights were a natural part of the city just as the city seemed a natural outgrowth of the mountain, and the sum of all seemed an enormous beast with glittering scales and a thousand eyes, crouching beneath the moon.

Tharanodeth set Ginna down, and bade him look for a long time. They stood there until the moon set.

"Now that you have seen the city of Ai Hanlo from the outside, as it sits upon Ai Hanlo Mountain, you will understand what I mean when I tell you that our ancestors did not *build* the city when they came here from far away. They carved its foundations out of the flesh of the stone."

He pointed to the golden dome on the summit.

"Behold. That dome and the towers surrounding it comprise only that part of the palace which is visible from this side. And yet there is enough there for you to spend your whole lifetime

exploring and even then you could not know it all in its fullness. And around the palace is the city, through which you could wander all your days, and still some of its ancient secrets would remain hidden. Yet consider how small they are seen from this distance. Just one mountain surrounded by hills, beyond which are wide plains and other lands. Now come. I want to show you something."

He took the boy on his back again with difficulty.

"You are supposed to be underweight. Have you gotten heavier without my permission?"

"No," said Ginna meekly, too overwhelmed to be aware of the levity.

They traveled for hours over the sloping, rocky ground. Constantly Ginna looked back at the wonder of the city, and slowly, as he watched, the curvature of the terrain hid it from him. To be out of sight of Ai Hanlo was wholly incomprehensible, like being adrift between life and death. And yet there he was.

The eastern sky was reddening in front of them. In all directions nothing was visible except stones and scrubby underbrush.

Tharanodeth stopped and set Ginna down.

"Stand here and look," he said. "Look, and you'll see the Earth as it always was, even before the death of The Goddess. I come here sometimes to reflect, when the toils of my station are more than I can bear. I come out here to where it seems that mankind and all his works have made no more impression on the Earth than the passing shadow of a cloud. I tell myself not to worry, to face what I must face with courage and dignity, for nothing matters ultimately. I come out here to watch the sun rise."

And they stood still as the glow in the sky increased and all the secret colors of the desert were revealed. Formerly dun brown hillsides suddenly flashed orange and crimson. There were furtive yellows and even a wink of blue. The colors and the long shadows cast by the stones shifted and flowed like a long, soft cloth being dragged across the land.

Ginna was sure he had never seen anything so beautiful.

"There is much more," said The Guardian, and he took him on his back again.

It was well into the morning when they came to that ridge which had been a mere line on the horizon. As Tharanodeth made his way up the incline, one hand on his staff, the other behind the boy's knee as he carried him, he turned his face from left to right and back.

There were mounds of crumbled stone all around them.

"You are in a city of ancient mankind," he said.

"Where?"

"Here. In every direction. This is why we waited till dawn. At night the ghosts of the inhabitants would howl in our ears."

Ginna did not know if he was joking or not.

When they topped the rise, Tharanodeth said between labored breaths, "And here is another city."

Ginna got down, stared, and gasped.

All the way to the horizon, towers taller than any he had ever seen filled the land. They were hollow and broken off at the tops. Each had hundreds of empty windows. Sometimes slender bridges stretched between them. Sometimes these were broken halfway, and sometimes the towers themselves were little more than suggestions of shapes in heaps of rubble.And at the feet of them were shells of countless lesser buildings, all nearly buried beneath the talus of fallen masonry and sand. A few stranger shapes, taller than anything else, flickered over the city like shadows cast by a candle in a drafty tunnel, not substantial at all.

"It is one of the dead places," the old man said. "I have heard that there are even larger ones elsewhere. This was a city as we cannot imagine a city, built by men we can scarcely think of as men. Surely The Goddess admired them. One legend has it that they created her, or some other one who came before her, to watch over the world after they were gone. No one can ever know what magic they possessed, or even what spells linger in a place like this. If you think our little mountain is vast, consider this. An immortal could spend all his days here and never examine it all."

"But the people who built this? Where did they go?"

"I have taught you to read, Ginna, and I have a book I must show you sometime. It is by the philosopher Telechronos, who said that the ages of existence are like the times of the day. The cultures of the Dawn rose and built their cities, and those people imagined themselves to be all of history, and indeed they were in a way. But when their cities were as the mounds you have seen among the hills, when they moved no longer and their eyes were closed, then came the Morning, when works were mightier yet. In the brightness of Noon mankind climbed yet higher, attaining other realms and other worlds even. What you see before you is a city of the Afternoon, when the heights had been scaled and the spirit of man rested in the warmth of the sun."

The boy was silent. He thought for a minute, puzzled.

"But if this is so, where do we fit in?"

"Our place in the procession, the book says, is toward the end. We are creatures of the twilight. No more impression than the shadow of a cloud shall we leave behind, when both Ai Hanlo and this you see before you are dust. But while it stands, we can at least admire the corpse of something greater than ourselves. *The spirit has passed from man,* said Telechronos."

"But what comes after us?"

"If there is another age, I think it will begin a whole new cycle. Perhaps there will be a place for mankind in it, perhaps not. I think even the laws and shapes of things, and the passing of time will be entirely different. In fact there is a curious prophecy— Telechronos himself made it when he lay dying. With his last breath he told of seeing a shining face looking down into his, saying that when *at last one understands himself,* the end will be the beginning and the beginning the end and the new age will open."

Neither of them said a word as they returned to the city. Tharanodeth was too exhausted to carry him, so Ginna walked. He cut his feet on sharp stones but never complained. After a while the old man leaned on his shoulder. They rested often. After a long time, when both were faint from thirst and hunger, the towers of Ai Hanlo rose above the dry hills. It was nearly evening when they found their way into the tunnel, and the sun had set before they returned to The Guardian's chamber. When they got there people were knocking on the outer door and ringing bells, calling out, "Dread Lord, Noble Sovereign, urgent news. Pressing business."

"It's always urgent and pressing business," sighed Tharanodeth. "Whenever I go away it piles up like water behind a dam."

He let the boy out through a secret way, then went to face his courtiers. But just as he opened the door he fell down unconscious and they carried him to his bed, letting the affairs of state pile up even more.

* * *

When he was twelve, Ginna saw Tharanodeth for the last time. The Guardian had not sent for him for several weeks, and he was disturbed by the silence. There was no message. But then The Guardian's man came to him and nodded, and he knew how to go and where. He found the old man lying in his bed, and for the first time Tharanodeth seemed truly old to him. His long white beard seemed scraggly, no longer smooth and fine; his face was shrunken and pale; his bones were like a stark wooden frame over which a thin blanket of flesh had been draped.

Charms made from the skulls of men and animals hung from the bedposts. An intricately carven staff of polished ebony leaned against the wall where it could be easily reached.

The boy looked at the staff with dread. He knew what it was. "Yes, it is for my last journey," said Tharanodeth. "I have my walking shoes on, too." He pulled up the blanket so Ginna could see them.

"Please...don't...."

"Die? Please don't die?" the Guardian laughed softly. Then he sighed. His breath was wheezing and tired. "I'm afraid none of us have much control over that, any more than we can prevent our epoch giving way to another. Telechronos said that. He said it all, the old windbag. But listen to me, my friend. Yes, you *are* my friend. Guardians aren't supposed to have friends. They can't. Everybody wants something, or spies for this faction or is in the power of that lord. It is like a cave of spiders, each spinning webs to entrap the rest. He who sits aloof, beyond all that, is the most alone. I have only you. You are the only one who is not tainted by intrigue. That is why I have tried to keep your comings and goings a secret. Of course a few people know. But they'll keep quiet for a while yet, I hope."

"But, why me?"

"There had to be someone. I think I would have gone mad without you. Some guardians have, you know, although their subjects interpret their madness as holy ecstacy. And why not you? You are mysterious enough to hold my interest. Yes, very mysterious. I think there is more to you than the eye can see."

"What? How am I so mysterious?"

"Who were your parents?"

Ginna was left speechless by the directness of the question. All he could utter was a babble of half-formed words. He sat down on a stool by the bedside and stared at his friend for a while in silence. All around him flickered scented candles, set there to attract the Bright Powers and drive off the Dark. Some sputtered. This and the old man's dry breathing were the only sounds.

With a great heave The Guardian sat up, turned, and took the boy by the shoulders. He stared intently into his eyes.

"You didn't have any parents," he said. "You know that much already."

"I was...found."

"But do you know *where?*" Ginna shook his head.

"In the same cradle with that horror of a son of mine. You didn't know that, did you? Did you know that everyone said you were bewitched? My magician wanted you killed. He's a fusty old buzzard, but he means well, so I think he really felt there was a danger to me. But I said no. I saw a destiny in you. I don't know what. These things have a way of working themselves out.

But something special."

Exhausted at the strain of sitting up, he let go of the boy and dropped down onto his pillows.

Moved near to tears, wanting to open himself as fully to Tharanodeth as he had to him, Ginna did something he had never done before in The Guardian's presence. He folded his hands together, then opened them, then folded them, until he had made a dozen balls of light and juggled them. They drifted slowly, none of them brigter than the candles. When he stopped they fell on the bed and the floor and winked out.

"Then it is true. You are magical."

"I can do what you just saw. When I first came to you, I was afraid to. After that, I guess I never did."

Tharanodeth smiled. "I never asked you to."

"It's as easy as talking or moving my fingers, but I don't think there's anyone else who can do it. I don't know what it means."

"I had really hoped you would," said The Guardian, staring up at the ceiling, where the two aspects of The Goddess looked down on him. "I am going into a far country, from which I shall never return. They say that when we depart thence, when we walk the last long road, if we are brave and true and avoid all the perils, we come to paradise, and sit there listening to The Musician play beautiful songs for all of eternity. But this is uncertain, for no witness has ever come back to report it. I am afraid. I will tell you that much. I had hoped you could provide me with some insight, some comfort, some secret gained through your magical nature. Something. Have you ever had visions?"

Ginna spoke slowly, very carefully. "I have had dreams. You are usually in them. You are very wise and you lead me. Sometimes we walk in the dead city among the flickering towers, and I can see the faint outlines of the buildings as they looked when they were new. There are people hurrying back and forth. We try to talk to them, but they don't stop. To them we're invisible."

"Then whatever secret is in you has not yet come out. Perhaps it shall when I am gone. That is why I fear for you."

"For me?"

"Yes. If I could have things as I want them, you would be my heir and rule all of Randelcainé after me. But I have made it clear from the start that you are not. I said so in front of witnesses when you were found, and for a very good reason. After I am dead, you must keep that quality which had endeared you to me. Stay out of politics. Don't seek position or fame. Don't get to know the right people. If you are part of even a little intrigue, a tiny strategem, you are changed forever. Do you understand why I was so careful to disinherit you? If you had any claim to the throne, how long do you think you would be allowed to live? Kaemen has his followers already."

"What shall I do, after—?"

"Just live. I hope you can do that. Then, if there is a destiny hovering about you, it will be fulfilled. If not, you'll still be happier." He took a ring from one of his fingers and gave it to Ginna. "Wear this always. It will tell people that anyone who harms you will face the curse of my ghost. It is my last command to you that you survive. See that it is carried out."

"I love you," the boy wept. He leaned over and put his head on the old man's chest. He sobbed without restraint.

"I love you too." Thin, pale fingers with skin dry as parchment stroked his hair. "I don't believe guardians are supposed to love anyone. We're supposed to be beyond all that."

Someone knocked on the door to the chamber.

"Holy Lord," came a voice. "Are you awake?"

Ginna sat upright, stiff with terror.

"Go quickly," whispered the old man. "It's one of my accursed doctors. Very skilled, utterly useless now. A bore. You wouldn't want to meet him."

The boy left the bedside without another word. He drew aside a tapestry, pressed on a stone, and left the way he always did.

* * *

Shortly before dawn, Ginna lay awake atop a heap of straw in his room in one of the short, squat towers overlooking the *kata* stables. The quiet of the night was broken only by the occasional snorts and whines of the beasts and the far off cries of the watch.

He chose to be alone then, but it occurred to him that most of the time he was alone anyway without any choice. Courtiers and soldiers ignored him as just another urchin. The stable folk, the trainers of the *katas*, the smiths, and the serving women were always polite. They tried to act naturally around him, as if he were no one special, but he knew, he could secretly sense that they were a little in awe of him and a little afraid. He sometimes overheard snatches of whispered conversations. He was, after all, so often led away by men of purpose and bearing. Someone was showing him more attention than he would normally merit, and trying to hide the fact. He was, rumor had it, part of some intrigue, perhaps a child of high rank being hidden until some danger was past. But the gossipers could never possibly imagine the truth, that he was being summoned by The Guardian himself, that he

22

was Tharanodeth's friend.

His friend. It occurred to him that he had only two friends in the world. He knew so few people. He had been educated only by Tharanodeth, and spottily, learning whatever it had moved the old man's fancy to teach him.

Tharanodeth and the girl Amaedig, whose name meant Cast Aside. And now Tharanodeth was dying. But he could weep no more. He had exhausted his supply of tears that evening, and there was only a hollow ache within him.

"Ginna."

He sat up with a start. The straw rustled. He peered breathlessly into the gloom. The world was absolutely still. Something had shut out all the sounds of the night.

"Ginna."

"Here I am." His heart pounded with bewilderment, then terror, then joy when he recognized the voice, followed by terror again. It was impossible that he was hearing that voice now, in this place.

"Ginna."

Tharanodeth stood in the doorway to the room. He had the carven staff in his hand and he wore a travelling cloak and his walking shoes. His face shone brightly, as if a lantern were held up to it, and yet there was no lantern.

"Ginna, I am on the road now. It is a long way. Goodbye."

"Wait! Where are you going? Don't go!"

The light went out like a candle extinguished. The boy leapt up and stumbled out into the hallway which was filled only with the echoes of his shouting.

It was very dark every way he looked, and when he fell silent the night was still.

He walked the battlements until dawn in search of his friend, hoping for another glimpse, but he asked nothing of the few people he met. They couldn't help him. He dared not tell them what he had seen.

The new day found him in a wide, high hall. The sun touched the blue glass of the skylight, flooding the room with color. On opposite walls were hung portraits of the bright and dark aspects of The Goddess. One, clothed in midnight, remained dark. The other, astride a dolphin, glowed with the brilliance of the sunrise.

Remembering when he had first met her, he placed his hands together, then parted them, and a ball of light rose up for The Goddess to see.

Suddenly trumpets sounded. Cymbals clashed. Many metal-shod feet tramped. Two huge doors swung wide in front of him, and suddenly the room was filled with people. First came the trumpeters, then a squadron of soldiers in full armor, with richly decorated shields and banners trailing from their spears. Drummers drummed. A line of boys Ginna' age rang bells and chanted. Countless courtiers, lords, and ladies followed, all in their richest attire. In the midst of them was a chair on a platform, held aloft by eight burly men.

Ginna was so bedazzled by this intrusion that he just stood there in the middle of the floor, gaping.

"You there! Brat! Get out of here!" A captain in a scarlet cape and winged helmet came forward waving a sword.

"*No. Let him stay. Let him be the first to congratulate me.*"

Ginna looked up to see who had spoken. Everyone else looked up too. When *that* voice was raised, all others fell silent. He recognized the pudgy, pale figure on the platform, even though he had not seen him in years and certainly had never seen him like this, dressed in vestments which were black on one side and white on the other, and holding a golden staff in his hand.

It was Kaemen. He was only a month older than Ginna, but now he was the new Guardian, the holiest person in the world.

The great mass of people divided and flowed around Ginna like a stream around a boulder until the chair of Kaemen drew near him. Then the bearers set it down.

"Come forward," said The Guardian, his girlish voice cracking in an attempt to be deep and commanding.

Ginna didn't know what to do. Court etiquette was wholly strange to him. He had never spoken to a guardian in *public* before, or even with any noble lord.

He fell on his knees, keeping his eyes to the floor.

"You may kiss my hand," said Kaemen. "Yes, Ginna, I know who you are. They say you are magical and were sent to bewitch me *when I was a child.*"

"Oh no! I wouldn't—I could never do that—*Dread Lord!*"

"Of course you couldn't. But you tried and you failed. Now it amuses me to see what you will do next."

"Holy One! I would never do anything. I didn't! Please forgive me!" Ginna desperately hoped he had said the right things. Apparently he had.

"You may kiss my hand and look upon my face. Consider yourself greatly honored."

Hastily he made one of the few court gestures he knew, that of Blessing Received, and to be sure he repeated it twice more. Then he raised his head, and took Kaemen's sweaty, soft hand in his own and touched it to his lips.

The Guardian was doing his best to look on impassively, to demonstrate that this inferior did not concern him one way or the other, but he could not completely hide his astonishment when he noticed that Ginna wore Tharonodeth's ring. And Ginna could not fail to see that flash of pure hatred on his face, even though he recovered almost at once.

Kaemen's eyes were blue voids, revealing nothing.

The whole of the day and much of the evening were filled with the coronation of the new guardian and the funeral of the old. Countless rituals had to be observed, and officials, called Masters of the Act, oversaw each with scrupulous care. Kaemen alone was able to descend into a certain vault, while his attendants sang a hymn which could never be sung on any other occasion and were accompanied by instruments which could accompany no other song. He was the only one who could bring forth a certain reliquary containing a splinter of bone of The Goddess, and of all the living he alone among them was permitted to touch the inestimably holy corpse of his predecessor, to open the mouth, place the reliquary within, and close it again. This one act, with all its prayers, pauses at preordained stations, and pantomime re-enactments of the highlights of Tharanodeth's reign, took hours.

Ginna was relieved that The Guardian let him go on his way after that first encounter. He watched the proceedings from a tree at the back of the crowd. The whole population of Ai Hanlo was present, this being the only time when the folk of the lower city were allowed within the forbidden precincts. He had never imagined there could be so many people alive in one place.

Tharanodeth lay on his bier with his travelling cloak wrapped about him, his death-staff in his hand, and his walking shoes on his feet. And yet Ginna knew that his friend had departed the previous night and was already well along his final, perhaps endless road.

He was left behind with his only remaining friend, Amaedig, and with Kaemen, who might be ignoring him for the moment, but had certainly not forgotten him.

Chapter 3
The Bright Hope

As far as Kaemen was concerned, what was wrong with the world was that there were *so many* disgusting people in it. Vile, obnoxious, stupid, every one of them. And then there were the lesser sort—soldiers, servants, common folk. They were just beasts, animals, oafs. Oh, they could give you the time of day and blather about trivia, but they were animals nonetheless.

"Yes, my lord," this and "Yes, my lord" that. They knew how to grovel, which was only proper, but they didn't mean it. He knew they all hated him. They were out to see him dead. He was sure of it. They had been working against him for a long time.

His earliest memories were of screaming for food or when he'd wet himself in his cradle, and the idiot nurses *wouldn't come.* He'd screamed himself hoarse. It was amazing, he told himself when he was older, that he had any voice left at all.

His idea of a perfect world was one in which everybody was dead except himself, and there weren't even any squawking crows to peck those millions of eyes out. Just rotting corpses—no, just bones. He would stroll among them and kick the skulls around like balls, and then pause, and his laughter would shatter the silence.

Anything would be an improvement over what he had to live with. Once he had come back from spending an hour in the cemetery, contemplating the way things should be, when a veritable army of nurses surrounded him, fluttering like silly birds.

"Oh *there* you are, little one!" they said. "You *shouldn't* wander off like that. You *mustn't* get yourself dirty playing among those *ghastly* gravestones. Ugh! The *slime* and the *mold*. You'll get them into your *brain* if you don't take *care* of yourself! Come away now. It's time for your *bath*. Scrubba-dub-dub, won't that be *fun?*"

He wanted to say that perhaps there was something to be said for slime and mold after all, but didn't. They dragged him into the palace, past sneering, snickering priests and courtiers, and they even stopped to talk to that sanctimonious asshole he had for a father. ("Oh, he's been out in the dirt again, Holy Lord, and isn't he a morbid child; I don't know what to do with him, and if he were not your son I'd say—I mean it's his nature, but—" "You must be patient with him," said Tharanodeth, but of course he didn't mean it, the smiling hypocrite.) When they got him into his own chamber (That *other* boy, who had all the personality of a flowerpot, was across the hall babbling and juggling balls of light.) they peeled off his soiled clothing, stirred the bathwater to foam up the soap, and lowered him in.

It was cold! He shrieked and kicked and bit one of the women on the hand until she screamed. They were trying to freeze him with that accursed water, then drown him under the suds. *Cold!*

"Now, now," cooed one of the nurses. "The water wouldn't have gotten cold if you hadn't run off like that. We couldn't find you."

"Who brought it? *Who?*"

"You know who. The two big, strong men who always do. Konduwaine and Tiboth."

"Then it's their fault. *Kill them!*"

All the nurses stood back in surprise. He took the opportunity to leap out of the tub. His naked body was already turning blue. He was shaking all over.

"Kill them! Kill them! Kill them!" He grabbed a stool by one leg and banged it against the floor until the leg broke off. He brandished the leg like a sword. "I want them dead! Throw them in the furnace and burn them up. If I can't be warm, they'll be very warm."

"Little Lord," said one of the women. "We can't do that. It isn't right."

He remembered who he was and stood up straight, trying to cut a commanding figure. Even young as he was, he knew how

27

ridiculous he looked. For years afterwards he played the scene over again in his mind, multiplying the indignities he had suffered.

"I shall be guardian one day," he said. "I am only a little child now, but when I grow up, unless you do what I say, *I shall flay you alive!* Go!"

He waved his arms and made a face. They all retreated from the room in confusion. He put on his dirty clothing, just to spite them. After a while they came back, trembling, and the one who had contradicted him said, "We have done as you ordered."

Liars. He knew they were all liars. He had to find out for himself. He went over to the flue and sniffed. Then he smiled. At last they had done something right. There was flesh burning down below. Two different men brought a new tub of water in, and it was hot enough this time.

But *later* he saw the culprits working in another part of the palace. He had been tricked. Someone had thrown a heap of old skins into the furnace, and that was what he had smelled.

The most frustrating thing about the whole affair was that when he found out, and complained to his father, the old fool refused to execute Konduwaine and Tiboth.

That was how they had always treated him when he was small. As he grew older, things hardly improved.

No one understood him. No one. He often dreamed of being underground in a dark place, where all he could hear was water dripping. In his dream he tried to move, but his limbs were like stone. He had the distinct impression that not only was it dark, but that he was blind. Time in his dream did not pass the way it did in waking life. He could lie there for days and days, buried and unmoving, and he would return to the world to find that only a few hours had passed.

Once he told Hadel the Rat about it and got back some gibberish about disbalanced vapors in his stomach. "Must be something you ate," he'd said. "Here, put this powdered herb in your drinks for a while." But Kaeman wasn't *that* stupid. He threw the poison away secretly. Later he cursed himself for being exactly that stupid. He should have saved it and fed it to Hadel first, then the nurses, then Tharanodeth.

And there were times when he knew he was not dreaming, when a lady stood by his bed. She was absolutely black, more like a bottomless hole shaped like a bent old crone than a living creature, and she would lean over him, sink her fingers like blades of ice into his brain, and he would hear her voice inside her head.

"When you are lord, everything will be as you want it to be," she said, and that was comforting, but she went on to add, "I will be with you."

Sometimes she said things so terrifying he nearly went mad with the horror of them, and his inability to confide in anyone added to the burden. Afterwards his head would always hurt, and he could never tell anyone why, and he knew that the idiots around him were secretly laughing at his pain, even if they didn't understand it.

Finally there were those rare intervals, impossible as they might have seemed to him in retrospect, during which he had known calm. The black hag did not always whisper inside his head. Sometimes she went away entirely. Perhaps she was asleep. Then he was free for a little while. It was then that he looked at the people around them and noticed how they smiled without malice, and he saw other children playing among themselves. He envied them. They had mothers who cared for them. His was always so distant, so rarely seen, always followed by a train of gaudily-dressed ladies fluttering fans in front of their faces. He could hardly remember what she looked like when he was older. On top of all her other offenses, she had proceeded to die when he was six.

In these strange moments of weakness he wanted more than anything else to have a real friend. He would wander about the palace crying, asking everyone he met, "Will you be my friend? *Truly* my friend?"

Of course they would smile and say, "But Little Lord, we *are* your friends. Everyone loves you."

Later the black hag would tell him how they all hated him, and he saw she was right. The pains, the dreams would come again. The frigid hands would dip into his skull and pull his spirit out, then carry him away into a midnight land of empty houses and crumbling castles, where bestial, grotesque things crawled and tittered among the ruins. He would open his mouth to scream and darkness would come pouring out, spreading like thick oil until it smothered the whole world.

Only then would there be complete quiet. Only then could he rest.

And because no one understood him, because he was alone with no one to turn to, because he hated those around him so bitterly, there could be no defense against that darkness, and, as the years went by, he gave himself over to it absolutely.

Chapter 4
The First Vision

"Amaedig, what is it?"

"Someone is coming. A man in a red cape."

She peered through the crack between the shutters, then opened them an inch for a better view. It was midwinter, the rainy season, and the air was chill and wet at midday, sky slate grey. Both Amaedig and Ginna were fifteen this year, and they had been living in this drafy apartment overlooking one of the countless courtyards of the palace—it seemed *every* room overlooked a courtyard—for three years.

He joined her at the window.

"It's one of The Guardian's messengers."

"Master, shall I go and greet him?"

He looked at her, disappointed.

"You forgot again."

"Oh—yes."

"As long as no one can hear us, you don't have to go through that silly 'master' business. You know perfectly well that you are my friend, and I only asked for you as my servant so we could be together when I was moved here."

"Sorry. It gets to be a habit. And you're of a higher caste, and maybe The Guardian's half-brother, or so they say—"

His disappointed look became a glare, somewhere between anger and a show of hurt. One of his greatest fears was that he *would* come to a high station, and be dragged away from those few people who had been kind to him.

"I'm sorry," she said, and even as she did her right hand went halfway into the gesture of Repentance—thumb and little finger up, turned sideways and back straight—before she caught herself.

"The truth of the matter is," he said in a low voice, "I wouldn't want to be related to this guardian in particular—"

There was a thunderous knock on the door. Amaedig ran from the window and raised the latch.

The messenger stood in the doorway, holding a polished disc of stone in his hand. He would not give it to Amaedig, but when Ginna approached, he surrendered it immediately.

The boy turned the thing over in his own hand and stared at it blankly, then looked up at the messenger, puzzled.

"It's an invitation, you little idiot!" the man snorted. "You are invited to The Holy Guardian's banquet in the great hall this evening, an hour after sundown. It is a great honor. Be grateful."

"Tell The Guardian I am indeed grateful and honored," said Ginna slowly.

The messenger turned on his heel in a smart military manner and left, even before Ginna could think to make the sign of Blessing Received. He made it to the fellow's back as he vanished down the winding stairs outside the apartment.

In truth he considered himself commanded, and he was afraid. Yet there was some thrill to it. He felt anticipation. All the lords and ladies of the court would be there. He did not know any of them, and from what stories he had heard of plots, counter-plots, purges, and intrigues, he didn't want to get to know them, but still they were exciting to watch, like a flock of dangerous, gorgeous, strutting birds.

"Shall I get your best clothing ready, Ginna?"

"Yes. Please do."

At least the dinner would bring some variety to his life. He knew it was safer being tucked away in a corner and ignored, but this didn't make his days any less tediously featureless. He was willing to sacrifice safety for variety, even if it meant a chance of being noticed by The Guardian, who even now was being secretly called Kaemen the Sullen and Kaemen Iron Heart.

So it was eagerly, although with some trepidation, that he put on the clothing Amaedig brought to him, the bright blue and red knee-length shirt of water-silk, the tightly fitting hose made from the soft inner skin of the *kata*, his wooden-soled, beaded slippers which were the most awkward things to walk in but the height of court fashion, and finally a cloak of plain brown cloth with no insignia on it denoting rank or honors bestowed.

"I wish you could come too," he said.

"What would I do there, among all those high-born people?"

"A good question. What shall I do? I think you're better off, having your station clearly defined."

They sat for a while making small talk, waiting for the hour to come. They stared out the window, watching the sun sink over the tilted rooftops. Then it was time for her to draw water from a nearby well, as she did every evening, and she left him. He paged through some poems he had copied out of a book in a library he had only discovered the week before.

He thought about that library, and the strange old man who presided over it. He had found it in an alleyway he had never noticed before. There the librarian sat, frequently all alone, like an extension of the dust that covered everything. It was always twilight in there. Only a single lamp burned. The books were all bound in heavy leather and linked to the shelves by long chains. You could take them to any desk if other scholars and most of the furniture didn't get entangled in the meantime.

So he'd sat in there, straining his eyes, making copies of some strange verses which seemed to foretell the coming of a new age, when everything would be different and there would be unfamiliar gods in the heavens. The book he copied was written in an ançient script, in a sort of dialect. There were countless allusions in the text which were opaque to him, and many words he did not know. He couldn't be sure he understood even the vaguest outline of the meaning. He wasn't wholly dissatisfied with his life, but he did wish he were better educated. Whenever he tried to discuss anything with the librariam he was met with a barrage of more opaque allusions which told him nothing more than that he was only half literate and very ignorant. According to the old man there were two varieties of people in the world, venerable sages, who were usually several centuries dead, and everyone else, who were only distinguished from animals by the way they smudged and dog-eared book pages if not watched with unfailing vigilance. So Ginna learned little from him. He did not understand what he was reading. But there was nothing else to do while the hour of the banquet approached, so he read.

He was sure he was neither a sage nor venerable.

* * *

When at last the time came, a great gong rang out from the highest terrace of Ai Hanlo, and Ginna climbed to the entrance to the great hall. The moon had not yet risen. The sky had cleared.

The stars and the flickering light of torches made the dome glow a ghostly golden.

All around him were hundreds of other folk dressed in bright costumes, many with gaudy plumes on their hats, headbands encrusted with gems, and flickering, iridescent cloaks and gowns. Many were carried in litters borne by servants more finely garbed than Ginna was. Some were escorted by soldiers in gleaming silver armor carrying ceremonial pikes of clearest glass. He felt out of place among them all, plain and awkward. He hoped he was inconspicuous. When he had watched others do it, he handed his stone disc to a watchman who stood at the entrance, and went in.

He found himself in the room of the blue skylight. Huge flaps in the dome had been turned back, exposing the blue panes, letting the starlight in. There was such a crowd now, most of it taller than he, that all he could see clearly was that skylight. Oil-burning lamps hung from the roof. Braziers flickered atop pillars. Torches lined the walls and colorful paper lanterns were strung overhead on wire.

He was jostled this way and that by brightly draped bodies. Sometimes, when he was in the clear enough to see what was going on, he would notice signs and gestures passing back and forth, an upraised hand, a pause, a lady's fan before her face, a certain turn of the head. It was as if a second language was being spoken around him, or a whole series of languages, layer upon layer, understood only by the speaker and the spoken to, with all others deliberately excluded.

Eventually he wormed his way to a table along one of the walls, on which various appetizers were spread out. He paused, watching other people take the food, to see of some ritual were involved, but they seemed to be just helping themselves, without regard to rank. So he took one of the little fishes which curled back and caught the stick which impaled it between its teeth. He also took a sweet bun. As he did he noticed a bowl of punch which was bubbling and swirling all out of proportion to the number of times the dipper was used. He lean over and peered into the pink liquid.

As he had suspected, something was swimming in it.

A scaly, manlike little head popped up and spat punch into his face. He leapt back, astonished, and collided with an elderly lady.

"It means hurry up and take some punch," she told him. "The spirits never agree with you unless you drink quickly."

"The spirits?"

"Yes, the sprite in the bowl, which prevents it from ever

being empty, Haven't you ever—? Oh, I see. . . ." She had noticed the lack of rank indicated by his clothing. Discreetly she submerged into the crowd.

He turned back to the punch bowl, but found his face smothered in the perfumed ringlets of a massive beard belonging to an equally massive man in the uniform of a general of The Guardian's armies.

"You there! Watch where you—"

"Excuse me, noble sir!" There was no room for any gesturing.

The man looked down at him and smiled, and the fearsomeness of his appearance seemed to vanish in the winking of an eye.

"You seem ill at ease here, young man." He held out his hand. The boy took it. The grip all but crushed his fingers. "I am Kardios ne Ianos, commander of the Nagéan Legion, at your service. And you?"

"Ginna."

"Of what house? Ginna who?"

"Just Ginna." He blushed and looked down at the floor to hide his shame at not being anybody.

"But then how—?" A recognition flooded over the man. He called another military figure over, and some ladies. "Look," he said, "it's Ginna, the magic boy they talked about years ago."

"We've heard of you," said the officer.

"I was sure you were entirely mythological," said one of the ladies flatly.

"Are you really magic? Can you perform some wonder for us here?" asked Kardios.

"No. I'm not really magic. I'm ordinary."

"Come, come," said a wiry man with a hooked nose, bending over him. "When you were—er—born, they said you could call up fiery demons by clapping your hands."

"Well I can't. I'm sorry."

"You can confide in us. We won't tell anyone. No need to be shy about it."

"But—"

A trumpet blew, followed by a hundred more. Drums thundered. Cymbals clanged. The mumbling roar of the crowd was stilled.

The Guardian entered the room, held aloft on a throne set on a platform on the shoulders of eight bearers, as he had the last time Ginna had seen him in this room.

The crowd divided like water before the prow of a boat, and The Guardian passed through. Ginna caught a glimpse of him between the shoulder of Kardios and the nose of the wiry man. Kaemen was paler, more pasty-faced than before, and growing fat. His almost white hair stuck to his sweaty forehead beneath the black and white peaked cap he wore. He held the golden staff of office in his right hand, as he apparently did on all public occasions.

Ritual greetings were given. The Guardian pointed his staff at the crowd and moved it from left to right in a slow arch. All present raised a hand to acknowledge the received blessing. Ginna hid behind the bulk of the general, hoping to be as inconspicuous as possible. He was sure somehow that those pale eyes were searching for him.

For more than an hour after this, Kaemen sat atop a dais above the heads of the multitude, surveying the room, apparently deep in thought, waiting for a certain moment, or so it seemed to Ginna.

"He must be about to announce something," said one of the ladies. It was obvious to everyone that they had been summoned for some purpose. People talked in hushed tones, every other glance directed at the seated Guardian. Ginna took some comfort in the way Kardios stood there, drink in hand, as ill at ease as he himself felt.

At last The Guardian rose, thumped his staff for quiet, and every face was toward him.

"Let the woman Saemil come forward," he called out.

The silence broke into whispers of "Who?" and starched clothing rustled as people milled about and stood on tiptoes, trying to see what was happening. Ginna noticed movement nearby, heads turning to his left then following something. Bodies stepped back, pressing upon one another like a rippling wave. Someone stepped on his foot and he squirmed free. Now he was in front of the massive general, behind three short ladies in feather-covered gowns, and he could see clearly.

An elderly woman stood before the throne. She looked familiar. When she turned slightly, in a kind of twitch, he recognized her. He had known so few people in life that he never forgot a face. She was one of the nurses who had overseen his earliest years. He remembered how she approached him fearfully at first, but after a while developed a completely uncaring attitude, as if he were no more animate than a lump of dough in the hands of a cook. She was also one of the ones who had constantly dashed about, wringing her hands in worry, trying to please the infant who had grown into the boy now gazing down on her from the seat above.

36

She raised her hand and made the sign of blessing received, first and fourth fingers upraised, the others held under the thumb, the hand moved in a little square.

"A blessing indeed," said The Guardian. "Woman, you have lived for the last three years because I forgot about you, but just this morning I remembered. I hope you will accept my apologies for the delay."

The Guardian made a sign none of his office had ever made in public before, that of forgiveness humbly begged, and he smiled viciously as he did.

"Your Holy Majesty is...of course...joking...Oh, what a splendid joke!"

She forced a weak laugh.

"*No!*" He stood up and out of his seat, something else no guardian ever did. "My Holy Majesty is *not* joking. I am in *complete* earnest, and I declare you to be a traitor, a bearer of ill will against me. There are many here who hate me, and your death shall be an example to them. By my command, you shall not leave this room until you are dead."

"What do you mean? No, you can't...."

Two soldiers pushed their way through the crowd. They wore no finery at all, but were dressed in simple leather tunics. Long, many-thonged whips hung coiled from their belts. They seized the helpless nurse and ripped her clothing off, until she huddled naked before the court, whimpering.

"I can't believe this is happening? What is happening?" said one of the women standing in front of Ginna.

"We must all be drunk and dreaming," said the hooked-nosed man. "No son of Tharanodeth would ever do such a thing."

"He has gone mad," said Kardios. "The dark side of The Goddess is in him."

With a loud snap a whip struck the old nurse's bony back, leaving bloody stripes when it was drawn away. This made the whole experience real, more vivid than any bad dream. Another whip, in the hand of the other solider, descended. She grunted, then screamed, and began to crawl across the floor on all fours. She rose to a sitting position, and one of them lashed her across the face. She screamed again, feeling her eyes, then groped about, obviously blind.

Her screams were not the only ones. The women in the crowd screamed at the sight. Some fainted. Men looked away. Others gazed at the terrible sight, the faces stoic marble masks. These, Ginna knew, would survive the longest in the days to come.

He desperately wanted to be elsewhere. He wanted to look

away, but dared not.

Behind him, someone was vomiting.

He looked to one door, then another. All exits were guarded by soldiers whose pikes were not ceremonial or made of glass. He had to escape, but could not. There was nowhere to go. He edged backwards until he pressed against the refreshment table. Almost without knowing it, he took a glass of punch and gulped it down, then another, and another. He had only brief glimpses of the dying woman now. Most of the people in front of him were taller, but when a lady in a plumed headdress shrieked, covered her face, and began to push to one side, this created an opening, and he was afforded a full view of the huddled, naked form and the bloody smears on the tiled floor all around it. The whips rose and fell with mechanical precision.

He couldn't taste the punch as he drank it. Only unconsciously did he know what he was doing. This was the only way out. He usually avoided such excess, but now the alcohol was making itself felt. The room reeled around him. He was very warm. The people around him seemed to have become a mass of sweating, milling, frightened animals.

He found himself studying Kaemen intensely. The Guardian leaned forward in his chair, surveying the scene with rapt fascination. What was happening to his face? Ginna wondered why no one else seemed to see it. The pale blue eyes were gone, replaced by black pits which spread slowly across the cheeks, eating away the flesh. Eventually there was only an oval darkness where the face had been. Then there was another face, outlined in fiery red in that darkness, a hideous old woman who, or so it seemed to his dizzy imagining, was somehow nourished by the pain and fear, drinking it all in.

Even that face grew soft like melting wax and disappeared. The blackness extended outward grotesquely, until it was nothing human at all. It was the head of a wolf, no, a bottomless abyss, a rip in the fabric of the world in the shape of a wolf, growing out of the front of The Guardian's head.

All other eyes were on the two floggers and their victim, who now lay still.

Didn't anyone else see?

The wolf was flowing up out of the boy's corpulent body. Like a stream of black ink it poured down over his lap and onto the steps which led down from the throne. Then, finding its feet, the wolf scampered to where Saemil lay.

Again there was a rift in the crowd and Ginna could see through. The wolf was lapping up the old woman's blood. The executioners didn't seem to notice and went on with their work. On the throne Kaemen sat, his face gone, his head hollow. Ginna's knees buckled. He fell against the table. Grabbing wildly for support, he struck a tray and sent it clattering to the floor. For an instant he was kneeling, his head and one hand against the edge of the table. Then he pitched forward and rolled under it, onto his back, vaguely aware of a vast forest of legs extending in three directions and a wall blocking the fourth.

* * *

For a long time after that there was nothing but warm haze. Slowly it cleared, until he could see every detail of the great hall. It was empty now, and dark. The crowd had departed. The corpse of the nurse lay sprawled on the stone tiles, atop, curiously enough, a mosaic of the dark aspect of The Goddess like the one on the opposite wall.

He was not quite alone. Kaemen still sat on his throne, still leaning forward. His face was still gone, his head still hollow. But the darkness was stirring inside, slowly rising. It began to pour out of the opening, over his chin, like an underground river suddenly emerging out of a cavern, spilling down the steps and onto the floor. There seemed no end to it. It gathered around the carcass and splashed over it in oily waves, spreading to all corners of the room. Toward Ginna. He wanted to rise and flee, but his body would not respond. In helpless terror he watched the stuff ooze toward him. He counted the squares of the tile as they were covered one by one. The floor was almost entirely hidden, and still the stuff came forth from The Guardian in great gouts.

It was not a substance at all, but a lack of anything. A total void, a dark, limitless emptiness erasing the world.

It touched him on one shoulder, then all along one side. He was numb and cold, so cold. The waves washed over him, covering him until only his face was above the surface.

All sensation faded. He lay there, staring up at the underside of the table for a long time. He had no way of telling how long. It seemed as if his body were gone, and only his face remained. He concentrated. Yes, he could feel the air on his cheeks, and something else. A tingling. A sense of floating.

His face was becoming detached from his head. He could feel it peeling off, flapping as the fluid darkness found its way underneath. The cold was inside his brain now, stabbing, killing. His face drifted free. His awareness seemed to go with it. He saw the underside of the table whirling around, or so it seemed. In fact it was he—his face only—which was turning, spinning like a leaf in a swollen stream. The waves caressed his cheeks from beneath.

39

His vision shifted as he rose and fell with the current.

He was in the center of the room, near the dais. The black fountain of Kaemen's head had not slacked off in the slightest. The level of the flowing void was rising, carrying Ginna's face with it, past the throne, toward one of the huge brass and wood doors, which stood open. He floated into a corridor, then dropped roughly down a flight of stairs, somehow never capsizing. He was sure that if he did, if what remained of him were touched by the blackness, he would cease to exist altogether.

For an endless time he drifted through deserted rooms and passageways in the palace, until he emerged through a window into a courtyard. The level was still rising. He was lifted up, up, over a wall, past a roof. In the periphery of his sight he could make out a featureless expanse of blackness spreading to the horizon. The sky was clear and filled with stars, but their light did not reflect off the surface. He caught a glimpse of the golden dome of the palace, the highest point of Ai Hanlo, just before it was covered over.

The whole world was flooded. He floated alone. He was somehow aware that he would float for a time, then slowly dissolve, and blackness would rise to blot out the stars, filling the universe. No one would be there to witness the end. He was the last.

The experience of floating was vastly unpleasant, like falling slowly into a bottomless pit of cold air, but all his feelings were dulled. He blinked again and again, trying to remain aware, but the last of his senses were slipping away.

He was conscious next of a hump of land rising above the ebon sea. On it the black wolf stood. The current drew him toward it inexorably. The wolf leaned over, ready to blend in with the greater nothingness. Just as its snout was over his face, he saw it rise on its hind legs and begin to change. It was becoming the hideous, bent old woman whose face had replaced Kaemen's momentarily. The old woman no one else could see.

Still, like the wolf, she was no more than a black outline, a pit without a bottom, but somehow she seemed two-dimensional. Only in profile could he see the hooked nose that almost touched her chin and the wild hair that hung in a matted tangle. When she bent over him as the wolf had, her face was a blurry oval.

"Flesh of my flesh," she tittered. "My receptacle, my useless, empty vessel through which my revenge was begun, what am I to do with you now?"

Ginna tried to speak, but no sound came out of his mouth. Instead the blackness spurted through the opening from underneath. He was sinking. The cold spread over his chin, up his cheeks, toward his eyes.

The black hag crawled to the edge of the little island, hung on with both hands, and raised a foot to stamp him down under the surface, but paused.

The last thing he saw was the sky beginning to lighten. She looked even darker in contrast to the dawn.

* * *

His eyes blinked open. An overturned tray lay by a table leg, a few inches from his face. Astonished, he felt his body to assure himself it was whole. Painfully, stiffly, he rolled over. He could see all the way across the room. The throne was empty. The corpse of the nurse was gone. The faint light of early dawn seeped through the skylight.

He crawled out from under the table and staggered to his feet. His head hurt as if split by an axe.

He was more disoriented now than he had been at any time before. He knew where he was and when, but was unsure of anything leading up to that instant. How much had really happened? What had he actually seen, and what was delirium?

In the center of the room, before the dais, he found the brown stains of dried blood spread over the image of the dark half of The Goddess. There was also a fistful of white hair and a strip of leather which had come off one of the whips. Here and there across the floor were broken drink glasses, a dropped veil, a trampled plume, a handkerchief, a cap, a walking stick. A large crowd had indeed been here, as he remembered it, and had doubtless departed in a hurry.

When he made his way outside, the world seemed too familiar, too real to have contained such a thing. He looked out over the lower city and the road beyond it. The sun was coming up. A trading caravan from some remote land was approaching Ai Hanlo along the great highway that led to the River Gate.

The cool morning breeze made him shiver. His wooden-soled slippers were awkward and uncomfortable, so he took them off. The paving stones were hard and cold underfoot.

He passed members of the night watch making their last rounds. He had seen them all his life, but now, for the first time, they frightened him. They were all his enemies. He did his best to hide any emotion, but was scarcely able to prevent himself from screaming and breaking into a blind run.

When he got back to his room he found Amaedig asleep in a chair. She had tried to wait up for him.

Chapter 5
The Second Vision

Hadel of Nagé, The Rat, had aged more than his years. He was now very frail, very thin, with a face like wrinkled parchment. His moustache was a white-silver brush, somewhat less copious than it has once been.

He paced back and forth on the carpeted floor of his study with his head down, his shoulders hunched, the almost iridescent blue robe of his office flapping loosely.

At any other time Ginna would have examined the study with rapt fascintion. There were so many marvels in it: a large water tank containing a whole empire of half-human, half-fish creatures no larger than one's thumbnail, stuffed specimens of curious beasts which no longer walked the earth, including the fabled *glimmich* which was reputed to have frightened dragons to death, but which looked so innocuous on top of a bookcase that the boy figured that any dragon frightened by such a thing deserved to be extinct; there was a book which read itself, whispering its words and turning its pages as if alive, allegedly quite capable of driving someone mad who didn't know the spell to close it; a stone fallen from a star; a scroll containing the names of all the rivers of the world, with which the traveller might halt their flow or even make them go backwards if it suited his purpose; a skull that spoke; a mushroom that could never be placed in the same spot twice; and much more. It was a veritable museum of the odd, the quaint, and sometimes the terrible. The only safe tours were guided ones. Unattended visitors frequently did not leave, nor did they remain behind in any recognizable form.

But at present the two of them paid no attention to anyone but one another.

The magician looked trapped. He constantly glanced from side to side, as if watching for spies or enemies.

"He can't hear me," he said. "I put a silencing spell around the room. Or he *shouldn't* be able to hear me. But I have a feeling that somehow he can."

There was a moment of silence.

"Who can hear you, Eminence?"

"Are you as stupid as you look, boy? *Him.* The Guardian. No one is safe from him. You know perfectly well who I mean, idiot!"

"Your pardon—" Ginna hastily made a sign.

"Oh, stop waving your hand at me! Did you know I wanted you smothered as an infant? I told Tharanodeth it would be for the best. But did he listen? Did he take me seriously at all? No, no, he did not." At this Hadel's anger seemed to pass, and he sounded weary, defeated. "No one listened to me until it was too late. If I am to educate you—and you know why you are here, why you are my pupil, don't you? This morning when I went to give The Guardian his lesson, he waved me away saying, 'Don't bother me any more, you silly old fool. Give lessons to the pigeons on the roof, or else to that creature Ginna, which was dumped in my cradle. Waste your hot air on him.' So here you are. I think you are preferable to the pigeons."

Ginna smiled slightly.

"I fear for you, young man. I really do. I'm sure *he* plans to make some use of you, something so vile he won't do it himself, or else he is waiting for some slip, the slightest excuse to execute you."

"But why, Eminence, do you care what happens to me, when you wanted me smothered?"

"Even I can be wrong, can't I? If I am to teach you anything, and I guess I shall, since there is nothing else for me to do in these last moments of my life—no, I don't expect to escape him for very long either—I suppose the first thing I should explain is that there are two kinds of magic in the world: shallow magic, and deep magic. Everything I do is shallow magic. Mostly tricks, illusions, maybe a short-term prophecy, that sort of thing. Deep magic moves the whole world. It involves vast forces and powers. Yes, the Dark and Bright Powers are part of deep magic. They live by it and are controlled by it. All deep magic flows from The Goddess, and since her death there has been little of it to speak of, and all that scattered and irregular. But like The Goddess, it is dark and light, evil and good. It's just as well that no one controls it all, because the possibilities are endless."

"Then what is there to be afraid of?"

The magician stopped in midstride, then pulled up a stool next to the one on which the boy sat. He leaned toward him, until his nose and moustache were uncomfortably close, and Ginna could feel his breath as he whispered intensely.

"Listen to what I say very carefully, and never repeat any of it. When you were found in the cradle with Kaemen, I went into a trance to find out what the thing—that is, you—portended. My spirit left my body and I could see things far differently than I can now. I saw only spiritual things clearly, with material shapes, the walls of the palace for instance, no more than vague outlines of light and shadow. I was walking through this flickering world when I came upon an intensely black, huddled shape. It was an old woman. She was crouched on the floor by the cradle. As my spirit approached her, she looked up at me and I saw how hideous she truly was. Her eyes were gouged out, and little red fires burned in her sockets. She laughed at me, and exploded into a cloud of black shapes, some of them like herself, some not human at all, many no more than puffs of smoke. They were all around me, their numbers rapidly increasing. They were the Dark Powers. I am sure of it. They clustered around that cradle like bees to sweet sap dripping from a tree. Suddenly I was no longer in that place, and I had a vision of the world covered entirely with darkness dripping like oil from the body of that woman. She loomed huge over me, chanting some prayer or invocation in a language I could not understand. And as I watched helplessly, new continents and cities rose out of the midnight sea, all of them irreparably strange and evil. It was not a place in which mankind could live. The Dark Powers were fruitful and gave birth to more monstrosities. One of them shaped like the old woman walked right through me. I was suffocating in her nearness. When I turned and looked back I saw her shiny, dog-like teeth through the back of her head, and an eye glared at me from her hair. It was then I perceived that she had no feet, but instead it seemed her body was balanced on two serpents standing upright. Her legs were ropy, scaly affairs, wriggling along. As I watched, her outline became less definite. It flickered, and melted into the blackness at my feet.

"I was suffocating, I tell you. I couldn't breath the air. I tried to rise out of my trance state, and I felt myself floating up from that level—it's like a box within a box within a box and you have to get out of all of them to wake up. Every time I did the hag was there, pressing her frigid hand over my face. When at last I escaped, it was because she let me go. She was only toying with me. 'You shall live to bear witness to the coming of my dominion,' she said at the very last. Then I found myself right here, in this room, lying on the rug, and you'll never know how glad I was to see the place, and to be alive. But I was terrified also, because I knew that Ai Hanlo was filled with deep magic, and it hadn't issued from the bright aspect of The Goddess.

"Of course I thought you were the focus of it. I could never probe the nursery with a seeing spell, I was repelled. But now I understand that it was *Kaemen*. I was wrong. That's obvious enough from the way things turned out."

For a long time the two of them sat there, digesting what had been said. The only sound in the room was the faint blast of bubbly trumpets. There was a war going on among the fish-men in the tank.

When Ginna was at last moved to speak, he told Hadel of the experience he had had the night of the banquet. The magician listened with a grim face, and finally said. "I suspected as much. You too are magical in some way. I think I understand why Tharanodeth wanted you to live. Somehow he sensed you were like an egg, with something inside you that hasn't hatched out yet."

"He—" Ginna cut himself off. He didn't want to tell about his last conversations with his late friend.

"That is why you are able to see such things. You are sensitive to the spiritual, as I am. The ignorant would say you have witch-sight."

The boy thought about his past. He was not yet sixteen, and still it seemed that his life stretched behind him like an ill-defined, shadow-covered road. There was no apparent beginning. When he considered it seriously, he had no idea who he was or where he had come from.

Hadel seemed to be ahead of his thoughts, waiting with an answer.

"When I was unable to probe the nursery, I went up there to have a look, and I saw you in that little room they kept you in, juggling balls of light—"

Ginna let out an involuntary yelp.

"Yes, I know about it," continued Hadel. "Now shut up and listen. When I was on that floor of that tower, I felt a tingling all over. That meant magic, but nothing defined or focused. I felt it even when I was in the room with you. I have a theory that the evil which is now upon us came through you, or in you."

"No it didn't! I would never—"

"Hush lad. Can't you keep quiet when I tell you to? I only let you know any of this because I don't think there's any hope for any of us. So what is there to lose? Anyway, you'll recall how the woman in your vision—I'm sure it was the same one *I* saw—called you her 'empty receptacle'? I think that's it. A spirit can't survive outside of a fleshly body very long, and it certainly has no power outside of one. So you were created, brought to the palace somehow, and the spirit passed out of you and into Kaemen, like fluid being poured from one jar into another. That is my guess. That's why you were found beside him. You were discarded when it no longer needed you. But then, I don't know. The tingling may have been more than just magical residue. There were those lights."

"I can still do it," said Ginna. He was not afraid to demonstrate. The whole experience had been overwhelming, to be called suddenly into the presence of someone who had always been a distant and sometimes menacing figure all his life, and now have all these things spilled out. Was it truly because the world was coming to an end with evil to reign thereafter?

He folded his hands together, separated them, and a glowing sphere floated gently to the ceiling. Hadel watched it carefully all the way, then looked down at the boy again after it popped.

"Remarkable. Again."

He made another one. Hadel placed his outstretched hand above it, directly in its path. As soon as the ball touched his palm, it winked out of existence.

"Amazing. Now this time, you do as I just did."

He obeyed. He felt nothing as the thing touched his hand, rolled to the tip of his fingers, and continued upward.

"I want to see something else. Lie down on the floor. Get as low as you can, and make another."

This ball slowed as it neared the ceiling, then began to drop. Ginna made another, and another, and began to juggle them, lying on his back on the thick carpet.

"Hmmm...." The magician tugged on his moustache, deep in thought.

Ginna sat up.

"I don't know what they are," he said. "When I was little I couldn't understand why everyone couldn't do it."

"Never mind that. Now this time, let the thing go, but catch it.

46

Make a cage with your fingers. Don't crush it, but don't let it get away either."

When he held one of the balls captive, Ginna said, "Why is it I can touch them and you can't?"

"Because you're different, boy. Now be quiet." Hadel turned as he sat, opened a trunk, rummaged through dusty books and parchments, and took out a large magnifying glass. He spat on it, then wiped it clean with the hem of his robe.

He examined the glowing ball through it. As he watched, as Ginna watched also, the thing grew less bright and seemed to expand slightly. The boy wondered why he had never tried this experiment on his own. The answer was that as a child he hadn't thought of it. As he grew older, and became more aware of his abnormality, he was less inclined to exercise this ability, or whatever it was. He had never known what it meant and desperately hoped it meant nothing.

He was wrong. Hadel gasped in astonishment at what he saw.

"It's an image of the world! I'm sure of it. I can see faint little continents and oceans coming into being. If it were bigger, if you held it long enough, if your powers were refined and developed, it might be... *real*... big enough to live on...."

The magician stood up and back away in awe. Ginna, surprised, let his hands come apart. The glowing shape drifted to the ceiling and burst with an audible pop.

Suddenly frightened, nearly weeping, he asked, "Eminence, who am I?"

"I—I don't know, but you're not just an empty jar. Not a discarded receptacle. Your power is real and very great. It isn't residue. Who are you? The question is *what* are you. I think if you knew what you were doing, you could become almost... *a god!*"

"No! This is all crazy!"

Before either could say more, the room began to shake. Both let out yells of astonishment and fear. Ginna staggered to a window, unbolted the shutters, and looked out. The whole palace was trembling. Plaster and stones fell. Tiles slid from rooftops. Dust rose in clouds. People were scurrying about like ants in a hill someone had kicked.

He turned and saw the magician lose his footing and fall against his desk. The magnifying glass slipped from Hadel's grasp and shattered. The talking skull tumbled off the bookcase and into the water tank, gurgling, crushing coral towers.

"Stop!"

"It's not me! I'm not doing it!" cried Ginna. "You must believe me!"

"Help me up, will you?"

The floor swayed and heaved.

He hurried over and pulled the old man to his feet.

"I *know* it's not you," Hadel said, grasping the window ledge. It's *him*, Kaemen. You are the vessel emptied. He is the one filled to overflowing with dark wine. Now—I know what makes the earth shake—he is doing something even I did not imagine him capable of. How can I say what he is attempting? *He is making the bones of The Goddess stir!*"

Chapter 6
Lessons

"As long as you are here," said Hadel the Nagéan one day, "I might as well teach you how to read."

"But I already know how to read," said Ginna. "At least a little."

"Fine. Good. Then read this." Hadel handed him a book. A passage in it had been marked:

In the beginning, the seed of the Earth sat motionless in the void of Unbeing. From that seed a god emerged, and walked completely around it in three strides. With the first he created the air, with the second the seas, with the third, land. In the fullness of time this god died, and a second rose out of the scattered dust of his corpse, walking over the sea and onto the land, his head high in the air. The Earth had grown larger since the birth of the first god, and the second circled it in four strides, with which the seasons were divided from one another, winter, spring, summer, fall, as the humor of the god changed. Next came a goddess, who took the dust of the first god and the bones of the second unto herself. She set the Earth spinning; she placed the crown she wore in the sky to be called the sun, dewdrops from her hair to shine as stars; she gave birth to men and beasts, and when she died a new deity arose out of her remains, out of mankind, and out of the beasts. The world grew larger with each age in the lifetime of each god, each goddess, each one which was both god and goddess, *each cycle burying the past, until time encrusted the original seed, layer upon layer, like the skin of an onion.*

Ginna looked up when he had finished.

"Well, do you believe it?" Hadel leaned over his desk, his moustache twitching. He had never looked more rat-like.

"I don't know." The boy didn't know what to say. Those strange poems he had copied said somewhat the same thing as the passage he had just read, only this was a lot clearer.

"Well, it's best you don't. I have a theory of my own, namely that the world festered in a dung-heap for aeons upon aeons until parts of it became animate and began to write books on the subject. Which of course means that you and I and everyone in the world and every thing in the world is just a piece of sh-e-e-e-i-tt and there's not much more to be said...."

He sat back in his chair behind his desk and laughed a dry, hoarse laugh like bits of old leather being rubbed together.

The boy didn't know what to say. It was a very strange moment.

"Remember this profound truth," said Hadel. "It's comforting when you're depressed." He laughed again and waved Ginna away.

* * *

"As long as you are here," said Hadel on another day, "I might as well teach you something. Look at that."

He pointed to his desk. Ginna saw only the unusual clutter.

"Look more closely."

Now he saw a tiny flower, a violet such as might be brought from the riverbank during the wet season. It was growing out of the wood of the desk top. Then there was another, and another, and grasses sprouting between them, until the whole desk had been transformed into a grassy knoll.

Ginna looked to Hadel in amazement and saw the old magician standing in a clump of wild rosebushes.

Something caught his eye, and he whirled about. There were trees stretching away as far as he could see. He was standing on damp, soft ground covered with dead leaves. He turned around again in time to see the remnants of the study waver and disappear.

He was in the middle of a dense forest. It was the most magnificient thing he had ever seen. The greatest marvel of all was directly above, an infinity of green, branches blocked out the sun. He had never before believed the tales of such forests, which travellers claimed grew to the north, beyond the borders of Randelcainé.

All sense of direction was lost, but there came a gurgling sound from where (he thought) the window had been.

"Is it water?" he asked Hadel, then flinched inwardly at such a stupid question.

"Yes, but if you find it, don't drink. If you do, you'll stay here forever."

"What?"

They pushed through some underbrush. The forest floor rose into a little hill and fell into a valley beyond. Still he didn't see any stream.

"You're still in my study," said Hadel, "but if you partake of anything here, you won't be."

"Huh?"

Suddenly something slammed into Ginna's face. The forest was gone. He was back in the study, rubbing his nose where he had walked into a wall. He felt around with his tongue to see if any teeth were loose.

"Well, I hope you learned something. You have experienced a very important distinction. Shallow magic is illusion, but if you go too far into it, you become illusion too."

"Huh?"

"Aren't we articulate today? Ginna, I only obey The Guardian's command, and I impart to you whatever I can, be it magical lore, history, writing, or good manners. In general I try to make a presentable human being out of you. Sometimes I fear it will be a long, hard struggle. I'm too old for this sort of thing. That's enough lessons for now."

* * *

Traitor! Spy! Liar!" Hadel the Nagéan screamed one day. "The Guardian knows everything we have said. What did you do, write it all down and give him a transcript?"

"*No!* You must believe me! I didn't tell anyone!"

The Nagéan rose from behind his desk. The boy stepped back at his approach. But there was no anger in the other's face. It had drained out of him in an instant.

"I believe you," Hadel said, embracing his student, trying to hold back tears. "I believe you, and because I do, I know you are in grave danger. I can educate you no longer. Somehow Kaemen knows everything we do, everything we think. I fear he spies on us by more than mortal means. If you told him nothing, how could he have known? This morning one of his men—no, his *creatures!*—came to me. He mocked me. He repeated some of the things I have confided in you. Then he gave me this message."

The old man separated from the boy. He gave him a piece of

paper which had been on his desk. The handwriting was a crude attempt at formal court calligraphy. The seal of The Guardian was on it. The text read:

> Hadel of Nagé, rightfully called The Rat—
> Vermin, you chatter too much. See to it that
> you never speak again.

"He wants you to kill yourself," said Ginna dumbly. "He is ordering you to die."

"He is ordering me to silence myself, which is not quite the same thing. But I'm not sure what there is to live for, except to fulfill the prophecy the black woman made in my vision and see the end come. The Dark Powers will smother Ai Hanlo before long."

"Is there anything we can do?"

"There is nothing I can do, but I'm not sure about you. Seek the lady of the grove and the fountain. I wish I could be more specific, but if I were, our enemy would find out. I am sure he can hear us even now. You undertake the gravest risk being with me, listening to me. Don't do anything to anger him. Try to stay alive. Now I must obey his command."

"No, please don't. There must be some way."

"There is. Get out."

"What can I do without you?"

"Whatever is *within you*" Hadel smiled briefly at the play on words. "Wait till the egg hatches. Ultimately, my friend, you must rely on yourself alone. Now go."

Ginna wept as he left the room. He closed the door behind him and stood at the top of the flight of stairs which would take him down, out of the magician's tower, into one of the countless courtyards. He could not bear to go. He sat down and pressed his ear to the door.

For a long time he heard nothing. Then there was a grunt, the sound of papers and books falling from Hadel's desk, and a pained gurgling.

"*Stop it!*" He threw the door open and rushed into the room.

Hadel, seated at his desk, looked up at him. Hastily he dropped something into a drawer and closed it. He took a pen and paper and scribbed a note. Ginna took it and read:

> With a long, thin, very sharp knife, I have
> reached down my throat and cut my vocal
> cords. Thus I obey the order of The Guardian.

He dropped the note and stared at the Nagéan in horror. Hadel gurgled again, coughed up a mouthful of blood, and fainted, head down onto his desk.

* * *

The days that followed were grey. The sun refused to show itself. The sky never grew brighter than the color of steel. Chill winds blew out of the desert, bringing festering, dark clouds with them.

The Powers were gathering in Ai Hanlo. Ginna was sure of it. He didn't know if anyone else could see what he saw, but he could tell that people were afraid. All Amaedig would say was that she felt uneasy and the weather was bad. She would be better when it was. But he noticed that there was no laughter in the world anymore. He had always enjoyed sitting on the battlements, listening to the jokes and songs of the people in the market place in the lower city, but now they went about their business in sullen silence, all eyes averted from the walls above. In the palace itself, men and women passed one another in the corridors without a word. At meals they whispered and made signs.

He was almost sure that they too saw shadows when there was nothing to cast them, and recognized the menace in the angry sky. He wondered if others had experiences like the one he had one night while returning from the library.

He had come across a dark passageway he did not recognize. Wondering if it might not be a short-cut to the level on which his room was located, he entered it. Bare brick walls curved endlessly past heavy doors, all of them barred. Faint flickering light came through slits in one of the walls, from torches and lanterns beyond.

At last he reached a stairway leading upward. A torch was set in the wall at the base of it. The scene didn't look right, and he paused until he had figured out why. Slowly he realized that with the torch there, there should have been light, and long shadows cast up the stairs. But the flames were not very bright, and only the bottom three steps were visible, the rest shrouded in impenetrable blackness.

He put a foot on the lowest step. Something stirred above. The sound was like an enormous rug being dragged across stone. He stood on the second step and the thing moved again, drawing away from him. On impulse he leaned forward and plunged a hand into the blackness. He felt a rough, dry surface. It yielded slightly to the touch.

Suddenly the blackness recoiled from him like a living creature, revealing the fourth step, the fifth, the sixth, stirring up enormous amounts of dust, which stung his eyes. He reeled back down the stairs, then recovered, and for some reason he could not fathom grabbed the torch and pursued the thing until he came to a doorway at the top of the stairs. It led into a corridor. Looking around, he knew where he was: near one of the kitchens, not at all where he wanted to be. The place was dark and empty, but the light of his torch cast normal shadows. Everything seemed in order.

What had he seen? The impression came to him afterwards of an enormous black snake slithering away at his approach.

He went back down the stairs, torch in hand, along the winding tunnel until he emerged into the opening beneath the murky, overcast sky. He made his way back to his quarters by the normal route. But even as he did he chanced to look up at the golden dome of the palace. It seemed to glow faintly against the night.

He saw something. He was sure of it. There could be no doubt that dim, winged shapes like enormous moths, some of them without any clear outline and little more than drifting patches of darkness, were gathering at the top, around the skylight.

"We have got to leave the city," he told Amaedig that night. They sat in their room, in the dark. They had no candle. He closed his hands together and made a ball of light.

"You've been saying that for a week now, ever since poor Hadel did what he did. But *where* shall we go, and *how*?"

"I don't know. But we're in danger. Everyone is."

"Yes, I know that," she said quietly. "But it is *because* the danger is here, coming from The Guardian himself, that you can't get away. The soldiers would never let you go, even into the lower city."

"Me? Just me? You too. Listen: now that Hadel can't talk anymore and no one is allowed to see him—I went there and there's a guard in front of his door—and now that all this has happened... you're the only person I have left. Everyone else is afraid to talk. The Goddess knows I wouldn't want to talk to Kaemen, although I am sure he would want to listen, particularly if I were on the rack at the time. So when I go, will you come with me? Please? What good would it do you to stay here?"

"Of course. *Of course.* I will. I wouldn't have too much to do without you around. Someone would make me into a drudge."

He thought she smiled, but the room was too dark to see.

He lay awake with her for a while, saying nothing. He juggled balls of light in the air. After a while they slept.

* * *

On a chilly morning they stood in the Place of the Lion, one of the many rooftop gardens, now neglected, in the middle of which stood an image of the animal carved in green stone.

"I wish," said Ginna as he ran his hand over the beast's mossy paw, "that the two of us could climb on the back of this lion and make him leap over the walls and carry us away to some distant land or another world. Hadel said there were many worlds where men lived once, up in the sky. I don't know if they're still there, but if this lion were alive, I'm sure he could cross the gap between them."

"An old woman told me that once they were alive, but only when a guardian willed it. He and the courtiers would play a game with them, using the animals as pieces and the whole palace as a board. They moved between the squares like this one. But that was a long time ago."

"Since then the lion has been stuck here, like us."

The two of them walked to the edge of the garden. Looking over the parapet, they could see the whole lower city spread out before them like a map. Nearby, before the Sunrise Gate, were crowds of mendicants, many of them gathered from the most distant lands of the globe, waiting for some residue of the holiness of The Goddess to touch them and drive their afflictions away. Many were raised naked on platforms, high above the crowd. Even from a distance, Ginna could tell they were shivering in the wind beneath the grey sky. A priest was standing on a wall, his arms upraised, blessing them. This, Ginna knew, was actually a duty of The Guardian, but one nowadays neglected more often than not.

Elsewhere, some streets were alive with traffic, some empty and silent. Smoke rose in a long, thin column from somewhere near the outer wall. Beyond that, nothing. Tilled fields. A few low hills. A highway leading to the horizon. The glistening ribbon of the Endless River, which was reputed to circle the Earth and flow back into itself, like the Worm of Eternity. Then there was the desert, engirdling the horizon. Maps had always shown Ai Hanlo to be the center of the land of Randelcainé and Randelcainé to be the center of the world. All roads, all rivers, all mountain passes led ultimately to the Holy City. Other places were colored patches on parchment, some having names, some not. Some were depicted only with abstract symbols.

Ginna realized that he knew absolutely nothing about the world outside. He was sure he could find his way through the streets of the lower city somehow, and perhaps by some trick or pretense get out one of the gates, or be lowered over the wall in a basket like some hero in an old tale, but what then?

If he were living in some fabulous old tale, he was sure these things would take care of themselves. But life, he had discovered, was seldom so neatly planned out.

"I wish something would happen," he said after a long silence.

Amaedig stood beside him, fidgeting with a clump of ivy. "Don't," she said.

"What?"

"Don't wish something would happen. If it does, you probably won't like it."

"But I feel so smothered here. Somehow *he* is watching all of us, and waiting, and making us wait for whatever he plans to do. Hadel said he was making the bones of The Goddess stir. We have to leave but I'm afraid to. Think of it. You and I, what do we know? How do we get food except from a kitchen? There aren't any kitchens in the deserts. And people say there are unformed things out there, creatures not like anything we know, slowly becoming something wholly new. Hadel once said the world gradually tranforms itself, and one day mankind will no longer be at home on it when it's done. Some places are more changed than others. We don't know how to survive out there."

She sighed with resignation. "We've been over this before. Either we go or we don't. We have to decide."

"Hadel also told me to seek the lady of the grove and the fountain. I don't know if he way laying a charge on me or giving advice or what. He couldn't be any more specific. Who is she and where is she? There's no mention of her in the knowledge books, and I was afraid to ask anyone."

"*Look*" she whispered. "Down there!"

Something was happening at last. About twenty feet below them a man ran along a narrow pathway between the base of the Place of the Lion and the palace wall. His dull green gown billowed as he puffed along. He was one of the clerks from the Guardian's archives. Why a clerk should be running anywhere, Ginna could not guess. He had once been to the place where the records were kept, and found it to be inhabited by withered old men who wallowed in dust and scratched on parchments until they went blind.

For such a one to be running was a veritable miracle. Surely the world was turned upside down. He scurried past where the boy and girl leaned over to watch so rare a spectacle. He held a scroll in one hand.

Then he stopped and fell forward, an arrow in his back. Ginna and Amaedig drew back, still watching, but concealing themselves. The archer, one of The Guardian's special troops, calmly walked into view, bent over the corpse, and pried the message out of stiff fingers. Other soldiers joined him, looked at the paper, and all of them hurried off.

"I wonder what is going on," said Ginna.

"Let's find out."

They were halfway down the stairs leading from the roof garden when they heard shouting nearby, followed by the clanging of metal on metal. A clash of arms. With unspoken agreement, the two of them hurried back up the way they had come, looking around for a place to hide. They settled on crouching among the overgrown shrubbery behind the stone lion.

Now all they could do was attempt to piece together what was happening from the sounds they heard. A series of trumpet blasts came from the direction of the great dome. It was useless to look in that direction. A squat tower blocked the view.

The fighting nearby died down almost at once. Several horses clattered along the path below. Then, a distance off, there was another trumpet blast, followed by screams, the neighing of horses, and silence for several minutes thereafter.

Swords sang their song on shields and helms. The line came to Ginna from an epic poem he had once read. In the old days, when The Goddess still lived, there were heroes on the Earth, and great deeds were done. Now stuffy old men were shot in the back and all Ai Hanlo suffocated with fear and expectation.

There was another brief combat somewhere beyond the squat tower. Also, there came sounds of commotion beyond the outer palace wall, from the city of the common folk below.

What was going on was obvious enough, in a broad sense. Neither of them had to say it. A palace revolution was taking place. Someone, more brave and able than they, was trying to overthrow The Guardian.

It was only after they ventured forth from the Palace of the Lion, after the struggle seemed over, that they found out who won, and it was only when the golden dome came into view that Ginna learned something else, equally important, although it did not seem so at the time.

When he saw the dome, he stopped and stared up at it, a look of horror on his face.

"What is it?" his companion asked. "What do you see?" What he learned in that instant was that he was as different from other people as Hadel had said and he himself had always suspected. The dome looked normal to Amaedig. But to *his* eyes it had

changed. Beneath the overcast sky it stood, its gold entirely gone. Blackness poured out of the top, covering the dome entirely, washing down over the palace. It would fill up the world, he knew. This was the end, or at least the beginning of the end. The winged shapes hovered thicker than ever. The running blackness bubbled and gave birth to more of them. By the thousands they fluttered and scampered down the rooftops, into courtyards and through windows.

"You there! Stay where you are!"

The vision flickered away. The dome was golden once more but neither of them had a chance to look at it. They were surrounded by soldiers with swords drawn and spears leveled.

"Come with us," one of them said.

"But we haven't done anything," said Amaedig.

"Orders."

They were prodded and poked along. Others joined them. Eventually a large mass of captives, over a hundred in all, were ushered into an unpaved yard Ginna knew from his days of living near the *kata* stables. It was an exercise yard for the *katas,* and also for horses. There was nothing but bare, trampled ground.

Now a group of laborers and stable hands, under the close supervision of the palace guard, were digging holes and bringing pieces of wood into the yard. Ginna felt sick when he saw the wood. He knew what it was for. Many stakes would be erected here and people would die on them. As the others understood what was happening, women screamed, men shouted, and the soldiers had to club several people senseless to get the crowd again under control.

They all stood there like pigs in a stall, waiting for slaughter.

After the work had gone on for quite a while, Amaedig whispered to Ginna, then had to kick his shin to get him out of his stupor. His face was pale and blank, like hers. She was struggling to hold back tears.

"It doesn't make any sense. *Why us?* If he wanted to kill us all, why here, why now?"

"I'm sorry," said Ginna.

"Sorry for what?"

"For not deciding to leave earlier. This is our last day. If we'd left, we might have lived a little longer."

"Or we might have been eaten by some monster in the desert. It's not your fault. There is nothing you can do now."

"I don't know what to say."

"Neither do I. Isn't that funny?"

She pressed his hand in hers and held on tight. Her eyes were closed. He looked up at the darkening sky, trying to avoid the sight of the stakes or the golden dome beneath which The Guardian lived.

Tharanodeth. More than anything else, he longed for Tharanodeth. If the Good Guardian were still reigning, none of this would be happening. It would only be a nightmare, from which he would be awakened by the touch of his friend. The world had been ordered in those days. There was still goodness left when Tharanodeth was alive. All of it had died with him, all hope too.

A frigid wind blew, whistling among the rooftops and battlements. A tremendous tempest seemed ready to blast forth, but it never did. The whole world was waiting. Clothing flapped. Laborers and soldiers shouted back and forth. The air grew deathly cold. Ginna, dressed only in a light tunic and baggy trousers, and barefoot, shivered with more than just fear. Amaedig had on a simple smock and thin slippers. The two of them pressed together for warmth.

Hours passed. It seemed the task was deliberately prolonged to make the waiting a special, exquisite torture.

It seemed that they had been there all day. Ginna's bladder told him hours had passed. Like others who felt the need but were not allowed beyond the wall of spears surrounding them, he relieved himself upon the ground. Since he was about to die, good manners didn't seem to matter.

Suddenly many feet were approaching in a measured tread. Another gate, opposite the one they had entered, swung open, and a squadron of The Guardian's personal troops, the plumes on their helmets taller than those of the regular soldiers, paraded into the yard in perfect formation. Trumpets blew. Drums beat and bells rang, announcing the coming of The Guardian himself. In came the Lord of Ai Hanlo, Kaemen, Protector of the Bones of The Goddess, carried aloft on his throne as for a state occasion. Behind him were more soldiers leading a long line of exhausted prisoners chained together, with only a few additional troops bringing up the rear.

Those already in the yard looked at one another with astonishment and some trace of hope. Ginna's heart leapt. Amaedig squeezed his hand so hard it hurt.

The Guardian was brought before them. Trumpeters on either side of him blew a series of blasts in a special pattern, indicating that he was about to speak.

He put a horn to his mouth to project his voice.

60

"All of you hate me," he said. "All of you are wicked, impious, and unworthy subjects. I should execute you all out of a sense of justice, but my justice is tempered with mercy, and I shall spare you, but only so you may witness the terror of my wrath and learn from it, going away humbled and obedient thereafter."

"We're not going to die!" one man near Ginna began to babble. Someone gagged him. But relief swept over the crowd like a tangible thing. Several of the women fainted, and some of the men. The guards, who had been pointing their spears at the mass of people, now held them upright. A few stood around the periphery of the crowd, but others went to assist The Guardian's troops in the work that followed.

In numb, helpless horror Ginna watched as the chained prisoners were stripped naked and nailed to the stakes by their hands and feet, then further secured with more chains. These were the ones who had tried to save Ai Hanlo, but failed. Some screamed. Others endured in stony silence and hopeless resignation. He recognized one man. It was Kardios, the general.

Someone bumped into him.

"Well, what do you think?"

He turned to face a man he did not know, but whose manner showed him to be no prisoner. Even in the state he was in, and loathing the act of speaking, the boy knew what words were required of him if he were to survive.

"How. . . fortunate we all are that these traitors were caught. Before they could do any more harm, I mean."

The man smiled. "By the way, who is the lady of the grove?"

Ginna gaped at him, speechless.

The other chuckled and went away, not waiting for an answer.

The stakes were placed in the holes and the earth around the base of each made firm. The victims hung there, bleeding slowly, upside down. It must have taken an hour to get them all in place.

The Guardian spoke again.

"See what happens to those who hate their lord!"

Now the soldiers began dipping hides and sheets into a pot of pitch some of them had fetched. These they wrapped around the legs of their victims. They moved from stake to stake with ladders. This also took about an hour.

It was definitely well into the evening now. The sun was setting somewhere beyond the clouds, where the world was still unsullied. The sky overhead was black.

Torches were lit, but not just for illumination. As he realized what was about to take place, there was a sense of dissociation, as if he had fallen into utter madness and none of this were happening in the real world at all. The Goddess herself, even in death, would not allow it.

And yet a soldier ran from stake to stake with a torch, igniting the pitch. The silence of the condemned was broken. They screamed like mindless, agonized animals. They writhed and tore at their bonds. Some yanked their extremities off the nails in great gouts of blood, but the chains held them. Columns of black, dirty smoke rose into the night sky. The air was thick the the smell of burning pitch and flesh. There was nothing to be heard but the screaming. All the trumpet blasts, all the drums, all the earthquakes in the world's history could not have drowned it out.

The ultimate horror was that the victims would not die quickly. The flames burned upward, away from their vital parts. They would suffer for hours or even days before death came to them.

It was like Kaemen's feast, only worse. People fell to their knees and covered their eyes. They reeled back. They raved at the impossibility of it all. Screams from the spectators joined the others.

Something in the minds of Ginna and Amaedig snapped simultaneously. Holding one another by the hand, they pushed their way through the dazed crowd and ran to one of the yard's two gates. Soldiers stood before it, spears crossed. Their minds working as one, they turned to the right, to where a tree grew against a wall. Without hesitation they let go of one another and made for it. They began to climb, heedless of anyone else. If a thousand archers had drawn bow against them, they would have climbed on. They stumbled onto the top of the wall, ignoring the glass and iron points which tore at their feet. Half jumping, half tripping, completely unaware of what was below, they went over.

The ghost of Tharanodeth, the magic of Hadel, or some other benevolence must have been looking out for them. There were countless places where one could fall to certain death, but here, ten feet below, was a slanting tile roof of a building of the lower city, leaning against the wall of the upper for support.

Sliding and tumbling, the boy and the girl slid to the edge in an avalanche of tiles and fell again. Something ripped the right leg of Ginna's trousers all the way up the thigh. There was a sharp pain. He was caught and flipped over head downward. Thus delayed for half a second, he was not the first one to plunge through the thin wooden roof below. It was Amaedig, buttocks

62

first. He followed her, arms outstretched to break his fall.

He came up spitting out wheat. They were in a granary. For a moment, neither seemed able to move. Then they fumbled about for a door. Amaedig found it and the two of them tumbled out in a shower of grain onto a threshing floor.

"Well," said Ginna. "I guess we have decided to leave. We can't get back into the palace now."

"They'd kill us for sure. Your leg—are you hurt?"

He was bleeding, but slowly, from a slash which ran from his knee almost to his waist. Near the hip the wound seemed deeper, so he tore a strip from his ruined trousers and tied it over that spot. When he stood up, the leg was reluctant to support him. It was painful to put weight on it.

"We have to get out of here," she said. "We can't stay."

They opened a door into the street outside. First looking up to see if anyone was looking down over the wall, they hurried away as fast as they could, glancing from side to side in breathless dread. Ginna leaned on Amaedig's shoulder and hobbled along. His injured leg was bare. Both of them wore the brightly dyed clothing of the palace, which alone was enough to make them conspicuous. She had lost a slipper.

Fortunately what few streets they passed through were deserted or nearly so. No one challenged them. Those few folk they passed huddled in dark corners and doorways and paid them no heed. Either because of the emergency, or simply out of fear at being in such proximity to the inner city and the death-gluttonous beast within, the common people shunned this district.

But they could not go far. Once they were sure there was no immediate pursuit, shelter was the obvious goal. The houses leaned over the unlit streets until the roofs almost touched overhead. Ginna and Amaedig could scarcely see where they stepped.

Pain and fatigue were taking their toll of him. For the last few yards, she was almost dragging him.

She pushed aside a board and slipped into an opening, pulling him in after her.

"In here."

A powerful, foul stench rushed over him.

"What is this place? It smells."

"Shut up. If it smells that bad, maybe no one will look for us here."

They lay there that night, quietly, in the close, filthy air.

Chapter 7
Journeys

Hours passed slowly. Ginna and Amaedig slept fitfully. Every time he dozed off, Ginna would see the burning victims and remember, or perhaps slightly imagine the face of The Guardian as he leaned in his lofty chair, watching the spectacle with intense delight. The screams would rise and rise like a storm in the desert, like an endless deluge, like the thunder of a never ending avalanche, and the boy would awaken into the foul, stuffy room. He hoped he hadn't cried aloud in his sleep. Sometimes, when he woke, Amaedig was awake. Sometimes not. Once he put his hand in hers and held her tightly.

After a long period of wakefulness there came a new terror. There was a stirring farther inside the building. Someone was coming. He heard footsteps, a mumbling voice, a latch being lifted. There was no time, no chance to escape. He lay there breathless, eyes wide in the darkness.

Suddenly light shone through cracks between boards. A door opened, swinging inward. A fat man with a curled beard entered, lantern in hand. The light reflected off his balding head. He put the lantern down on the floor, pulled up his nightgown above his waist, and began to urinate into a pit dug in the dirt floor. Now Ginna knew what gave the place its distinctive character.

When he was done he picked up the lantern, turned, and stopped. Ginna froze, hoping against all reason that he hadn't been spotted.

"You have to be crazy to sleep in the shit house."

Ginna stumbled to his feet.

"Please sir, you must help us...."

Amaedig was standing beside him. She elbowed him in the ribs. He lost his balance and fell against the outer wall.

"*What he means to say* is that you must help us if you know what's good for you." She spoke as authoritatively as she could. "We are on a secret mission for The Guardian himself."

Ginna could see the man's face only dimly, but he was sure there was a flash of hatred on it, which gave way, also only for an instant, to fear before becoming an expressionless mask.

"Surely," the man said, "the Holy Lord Kaemen, all blessings be upon him, provides better quarters for his agents than—"

"Idiot,' said Amaedig, "there are only two things you must understand. First, the mission is a secret. Second, certain traitors have made it difficult for us. If you are not one of them, you will do what we ask."

Ginna limped forward and held out his right hand, on which he wore Tharanodeth's ring.

"It has The Guardian's seal on it. Look."

The man held his lantern close and squinted.

"So it is. A thousand pardons for my rudeness, Lord and Lady, but I didn't know—"

"Never mind that," snapped Amaedig. "Show us out of here."

They were led through a creaking, unlit corridor, into a wide room. Ginna's feet hurt so badly he was afraid he'd faint. It was only then that he remembered the glass on the top of the wall.

They were motioned to be seated on a bench. The man disappeared up a flight of stairs, taking the lantern with him.

Amaedig let out a deep sigh. "I hope he believed me." Her voice cracked with fear. "What else could I do?"

"I was too afraid to do anything."

"Well, once I got going, I kept on. Like the way we fell. We couldn't stop once we started."

"Are your feet cut?"

"Yes. Quiet! Here he comes again."

The man returned, accompanied by a round-faced, middle-aged woman who also wore a nightgown. Both of them moved about the room, checking that the shutters were all tight, and then the man took two candles out of a drawer, lit them from his lantern, and set them on a table near the bench.

"That's a nasty cut you have there, young sir," said the woman, once there was enough light to see by. "Here, let me get

you something for it." She opened a cupboard and took out a jar.
Ginna watched apprehensively as she smeared a sticky substance over his leg. But as she did, the pain in it subsided.

"Please, my feet too."

She fetched a bowl of water, washed the mud off his feet, put
salve on the wounds, and bandaged them. The man did the same
for Amaedig.

"We'll do anything we can for you," the man said, "us being
loyal subjects and all."

"Bring us common clothing," said Amaedig, "and bags to
carry provisions, and provisions to carry in them. Everything we
need for a long journey. Include a jar of that medicine. And a good
knife for each of us."

Both of the man and his wife paused.

"Don't worry! You'll be amply paid when we're done!"

"Yes, good mistress and master," the man said. "My name is
Pandolay Marzad, by the way, and this is my wife Tuella. I am a
metal smith by trade, and I—"

"Never mind that. Get on with it."

So the two of them hurried off to gather what was needed.

"Artisans," whispered Amaedig when they were gone. "We're
in luck. If they'd been of a higher caste, they might not be in such
awe of someone from the palace. If he'd been the captain of the
lower city watch—"

"Won't they report us?"

"Maybe later, when they think about it. But they're too afraid
now. We'll be gone by then."

"Where?"

"Anywhere. Out of the city."

Pandolay Marzad and Tuella returned.

"Our son is away," said the smith. "He is larger than either of
you, but some of the clothes he has outgrown might fit."

So Ginna and Amaedig both dressed in male attire, which
struck him as just as well, since any search party would be
looking for a boy and a girl instead of two boys. They wore the
brown, loose-fitting trousers of the common folk, a bit baggier
than usual for being the wrong size, somewhat soiled grey tunics,
white cloaks with hoods, and high leather boots. Each was given
a sack which hung at the waist by a strap, in which were dried
meats, fruit, and bread. Each received a full water bottle and a
long, heavy knife in a sheath of reptile hide. Tuella gave Ginna the
jar of salve.

As he changed, Ginna tore another strip from his ruined
trousers, replaced the bandage on his leg, and gave the garment to

the woman.

"Burn it when we're done," he said. He handed it to her with his right hand, making sure she saw Tharanodeth's ring, hoping that like her huband she would not be expert enough, or the light would not be good enough, for her to tell it was the token of the previous ruler, not the present one.

By this time birds were singing under the eaves on the eastern side of the house, heralding dawn. Faint, grey light showed between the shutters. Far away, on the wall of the inner city, a soldier blew a blast on an immense bronze horn which hung suspended on a chain.

Pandolay and Tuella served them a meager breakfast, then saw them to the door.

"Thank you very much," Ginna said. "We're grateful for what you've—"

Amaedig stepped on his foot very deliberately.

"You have done your duty," she said.

"We hope we have, honored sir and madam," said the smith. He looked at Ginna oddly, but when the girl's eyes met his, his face was a mask again.

"You have to act the part of their superior," she said as soon as they were out of earshot.

"But now—"

"Yes, now we look like ordinary people, and must act ordinary. But then we were emissaries from The Guardian and had to be convincing. Ginna, I grew up inside too, but I think I know a little more about the world than you do, so just follow my example. All right?"

"All right. What do we do now?"

"Lose ourselves in the side streets. I'm not sure if those two really believed us. They may be running for the soldiers even now."

They walked through a series of narrow alleys, passing beggars still asleep in doorways. People were stirring in some of the shops. A yawning boy crossed their path, two buckets of water hanging from a yoke on his shoulders.

The city was awakening.

Ginna looked up and saw the golden dome against the dull, slowly lightening sky. He remembered how it had looked that time he and Tharanodeth had gazed upon it from the outside just at dawn, and how different things had been in those days. The old man had talked of plots and factions and intrigues, but nothing touched Ginna. There was no immediate danger. Now enemies were everywhere. Peril lurked behind every closed door and shutter. It was as if he had drifted from a pleasant, secure dream of distant memory into a nightmare of shrieking terror, thence into the waking world which was scarcely better. Hadel had described breaking out of a trance as escaping from one prison inside another inside another. It was like that. Which one were they in now?

In time, as the streets filled with traffic and the shopkeepers unfurled their canopies, Ginna realized that Amaedig did not know her way around as well as she thought she did. And she admitted it. She had, once or twice, been into the lower city on various errands in the company of serving women, but the corners and lanes were all alike to her.

"It looks a lot easier when you're up on the walls," she said. "You think you can just walk straight to the Sunrise Gate because you can see it. But there's a maze in between."

They dared not ask directions, lest they draw attention to themselves. Ginna noticed something he had not previously been aware of. The folk of the lower city had their own secret language. There were occasional words he did not understand, but he had listened to the common people from the walls before, so there were only a few. But he wasn't prepared for the gestures. The various castes, merchants, artisans, newscriers, beggars, and the like had a whole vocabulary of signs they made between one another and among themselves, just like the nobility did, only the gestures were different. This was yet another reason for not approaching anyone. Although they had never been anywhere else, they were strangers in Ai Hanlo.

Once they did confront a company of soldiers marching in strict formation, spears pointed upward, and they scrambeled to get out of the way, both trying not to betray themselves in their fear, but in this they were like everyone else. All the people were afraid of the soldiers and hid their faces from them, only to speak in contemptuous tones when they passed.

"Butchers!" hissed an old woman, pointing to the ground, then crossing her fingers. "Unnatural sons of dogs!"

"They had a feast in the palace yesterday," said another. "A real roast."

"The Powers preserve us," said the first, making another sign.

"What good will that do? The Powers are on the side of the monster."

Ginna and Amaedig hurried away. Ginna had no doubt who "the monster" was. How had Kaemen shown his true nature in the lower city for all the world to see? He didn't pause to find out.

They wandered through the city for much of the day. They drank from a public fountain, conserving what water they had in their bottles. When they came to a street of food vendors, it occurred to them that the smith and his wife may have equipped them for a journey, but still they had no money. It was time they got on with their journey.

At last they came to a large open area filled with people and booths. Beyond it was one of the four immense gates of the city, hanging open on its huge hinges, guarded by a dozen soldiers in unadorned helmets and breastplates and armed with spears. Most of them were leaning on their spears, looking bored. In the middle of the open space a hundred or more people were securing burdens on the backs of camels and pack horses, while three men in tall, conical hats raced back and forth on *katas*, shouting orders.

Ginna watched them with fascination. It was the first time he had ever seen anyone riding one of the creatures, except for stable hands breaking them in. They almost danced with fluid grace. He noted how people kept well clear of the spiked tails.

"This is our chance," whispered Amaedig. "We'll join the caravan."

When the man in the red hat waved to the other two, who wore blue, and one of them clanged a pair of cymbals, the camels lurched to their feet and the caravan began moving through the gate. The leader leaned down from his *kata* and handed a small purse to one of the guards, who waved the company on. Ginna and Amaedig made their way to the edge of the crowd and joined the procession, walking on either side of a heavily loaded horse, steadying its cargo as many other attendants did. No one seemed to notice them. They stared straight ahead as they passed the guards, neither letting out a breath until they were through. Then they looked over the tied bundles and chests, exchanging reassuring glances.

They had gone out the River Gate, near where the Endless River turned east for a while above the city before continuing south. With the leader and his two lieutenants on either side, the caravan snaked down the long highway from Ai Hanlo, as Ginna had seen many do before, watching from the battlements. Around him were the barren foothills of Ai Hanlo mountain. There were shepherds tending flocks on the slopes. After a while, further down, they came to fields of grain irrigated by water wheels on which men ran in place to make the water flow. For a while they were quite near to the river bank and Ginna watched the boats gliding by with great interest. They had never been more than specks to him before. Then the road took them away from the river, to the northwest, out of the foothills and onto a vast, empty plain.

Every now and then he glanced behind to see the city, like the crouching beast he had once imagined it to be, but now diseased and terrible. Slowly it sank behind the hills, and the hills themselves sank until they were no more than faint brown shapes. At last only the golden dome was visible beneath the sullen, off-white sky.

The caravan stopped once for a rest, and Ginna and Amaedig ate of their own provisions. Still no one seemed to take notice of them. The travelers, they learned from overheard conversations, were from many parts of the city and even from other cities. They journeyed for different reasons and represented different concerns. Most of them did not know anyone beyond their own specialized group.

When they started moving again, Ginna looked back. Ai Hanlo was still in sight. When they stopped again at sundown, it was not. He felt an intense relief at this. It was frightening to be beyond his world, completely in the unknown, but at the same time it was hard to believe, out here, that such monstrosities as Kaemen could exist and have any power. It was as if the infection from an Ai Hanlo given over to the Dark Powers had been drawn out of his system by the distance.

When he thought of medicine, he remembered his leg and feet. It was the first time he had thought of his cuts all day. They had ceased to bother him. Now that he was aware of them, his feet did seem to ache, and his leg was a little stiff, but he was no cripple. Everything seemed right with the world.

Each component group of the caravan gathered into a circle around its own fire and prepared supper. Ginna and his companion were willing to eat alone, but they saw that no one else did. Everyone joined one group or another. As they stood apart, people gave them puzzled glances.

Quickly they attempted to join one of the circles, but were repelled.

"You're not of the Brotherhood of Yellow Sashes! What do you think you're doing? Begone!"

They joined another, and the words were in a strange tongue.

"*Etuah namiyani! Navouran imborath!*"

The meaning was clear enough.

Finally they discovered a cluster of people who did not dress alike, who did not drive the same sort of animals since most had no animals to drive, who were not all of the same caste, guild, or order.

Here no one objected when each of them took a wooden bowl from a stack and dipped into a central pot of stew. They ate in silence, picking the meat out with their fingers, drinking the broth.

"You don't belong here, you two," someone said.

Ginna and Amaedig carefully put their bowls down and looked up at the speaker, a wiry man seated across from them, with a face burned brown by sun and wind and grey hair shot through with silver. He wore a lute slung from one shoulder.

"In my travels," he said, "I quickly learn who belongs and who doesn't. You don't. I have an eye for these things."

"We can explain," said Amaedig.

"I— I—" was all Ginna could get out.

"Be at ease," said the stranger. "We're all odds and ends here. I am Gutharad, a minstrel obviously. I have been one for many years. I like the life. I confide this to everyone I meet because it is true and because before long I'll be gone and won't care what they think of me. I like it because I can wander from place to place with no cares in the world beyond my belly and my sore feet. But you two are not like that, I sense."

He leaned forward until they could see his face more clearly in the firelight. There was a twinkle in his eyes; the corners of his mouth were at the threshold of a smile.

He sat back and laughed.

"The both of you have all the troubles in the world on your backs from the look of you. Don't stare like that. Your eyes will pop out and fall in the fire. *Hiss! Sizzle!*"

Everyone was looking at them. It was impossible to tell if the others were puzzled, angered, amused, or what.

Ginna turned to Amaedig and Amaedig to Ginna, each of them wordlessly pleading, *do something.* At last Ginna spoke.

"We're—I mean, I am—the apprentice of a magician, and this is my servant. My master sent us to find someone for him. A lady. She's called the Lady of the Grove."

"Yes," said Amaedig, nodding. "That's it."

Gutharad rolled his eyes upward in mock awe. "Oh, a mighty sorcerer is among us! Pray spare us from your magical wrath...."

"I am a *real* magician," a man in a black gown snarled. He stood up to an impressive height. His face was grim and lined. He wore a pointed beard which he was always stroking, and held a carven staff in his left hand. The flickering firelight made his face seem carven too.

He walked to the center of the seated group, planted his staff at arm's length, still holding it, and staring at it. Silence fell over all present. The sounds of other groups came to them through the gloom.

"The Dark Powers pluck at my beard even now. They are all around us. I can sense all things magical. What kind of magic do you possess, boy? I see no deep sorcery in you."

"Oh sir, I am but a mere apprentice, and my master taught me nothing of deep magic. Only a little bit of shallow."

"Well then, what can you do? You must be a slow student not to have progressed further at your age."

Ginna remembered one of the few tricks Hadel had taught him. He closed his eyes, made a sign with his fingers in the air, spoke a word, and opened his eyes again. A bush of white roses was growing out of the ground at the magician's feet, winding around his body for support. Every few inches a new flower opened.

The audience applauded. The magician stared at Ginna with haughty disdain, spread his arms apart, and the roses vanished. Without another word he went to his former place and sat down.

"Why don't you show us more?" someone said.

"Yes, entertain us."

"We'll let you stay."

So Ginna stood up. The minstrel had said he confided in strangers because they didn't know him and before long he would never see them again. There was nothing better to do than follow the implied advice and let the secret out.

He folded his hands together, opened them, and a glowing yellow ball floated into the air. He made a dozen of them, one by one, and by the end the first ones were beginning to fall. One drifted into a man's face. He swatted at it, and was astonished to see it vanish like a bubble. Ginna juggled the rest awkwardly, not having had much practice of late, but it was an intinctive thing, and before long he was doing it well enough, without thinking. Only two more evaded his grasp and burst. Everyone watched him with interest and in silence, even the magician. When he stopped, there was more applause. He bowed politely and sat down.

Gutharad moved over next to him.

"That was very good," he said. "I have never seen anything quite like it, and when someone shows me something I haven't seen before, I'm glad to have them with me. You shall be welcome into our midst, young—"

"Ginna."

"Ginna. Ah yes. How appropriate, since you are mysterious.

Yes, I know the hill tongue. And what are you mysterious about?"

Now Ginna reconsidered telling all his secrets to a stranger.

"I try not to be. Really. I'm just like anyone else."

"Not everyone makes bubbles of light with their hands."

"It's just a trick. My master says I have a talent for it."

"I saw him teach it to him," Amaedig said.

"And you, young lady, is there anything mysterious about you?"

"No, I am just ordinary too."

"Ah, despair! How ordinary the world is getting. Before long everything will be boring and there will be nothing for me to sing about and I'll die. What a tragedy, the last minstrel perishing forgotten...."

"The magician isn't ordinary," said Ginna. He was beginning to feel at ease with this friendly man. He laughed, but oddly the minstrel didn't.

"Lower your voice when you talk of him. That one is from Zabortash. A most sour and unpleasant fellow. They all are down there."

"Down where?"

"In Zabortash—my, my, you do have a lot to learn. You are not widely travelled in this world, even for your years."

"No, I have never been beyond the city before. Or, I mean, only once, and not this far."

"The city? Now Ai Hanlo is a famous and holy place, and people come there from all over, but to call it the city betrays a decidedly provincial outlook, my boy."

Ginna fidgeted with his knife handle, then his boot laces. "I can learn," he said.

"Actually you are very fortunate to have so much ahead of you yet. I, who have travelled so far for so many years, am in danger of becoming jaded."

"Yes, I suppose so." Ginna thought glumly of the events of the past few days, and it occurred to him that much of the world would doubtless be filled with horror. But now, he hoped, he was safe for at least a little while.

"As I was saying about Zabortash, it's far to the south, where the land is so hot it has melted into mushy swamps. The air is so heavy there that everybody carries it around in buckets, and when they breathe they stick their head in and go *gulp, gulp, gulp.*" Gutharad opened and closed his mouth, imitating a fish. Both Ginna and Amaedig smiled. Despite his own advice, the minstrel had not lowered his voice much. Several of those who overheard snickered. The man in black stared at them grimly.

73

"I was sailing into Zabortash," said Gutharad, "on a ship loaded with this and that, mostly that, with a bit of this, and a pinch of something else—hearers of stories don't like to be encumbered with such trivia as cargo listings, you understand—I was sailing into the great, greasy, smelly, overheated city of distant, tropical Zabortash, when one of the oarsmen called out to me, 'You there! Honeymouth'—that's what they called me down there in the south—'Play us a song or we throw you into the harbor for the crabs to eat.' So I asked for requests, and overwhelmingly they all wished to hear *The Generous Mother*. You may know the song. It's about a wife who's cheating on her husband, who keeps coming home drunk. He sees her lover's horse at the door, but she tells him it's a cow her mother generously sent. The lover's boots are chamberpots, and so on. But he stays out one night sober and watches the house. He sees the lover slipping out the back door very, *very* late. He asks her who it was and she says it was a poor traveller from Zabortash who was lost and asking directions. Well, I had never been to the south before, and I didn't know any better, so I went into the next verse."

The minstrel took his lute in hand, strummed, and sang:

> *Oh many a day I've travelled*
> *A hundred leagues and more,*
> *But a Zaborman who can last till dawn*
> *I've never seen before.*

The magician stood up, grunted something under his breath, spat into the fire, and stalked off.

"See, what did I tell you?" said Gutharad. "A sour bunch the lot of them. No sense of humor. It turned out half the crew of the ship had remained sullenly silent throughout the song. *They* hadn't requested it. They had no appreciation for music. They also couldn't take a joke. They were Zabormen, every one."

"What happened?"

"What do you *think* happened, boy? A riot broke out. The ship wallowed from side to side and almost tipped over as they fought. Somebody hit me with an oar. I had to swim ashore, though the crabs didn't eat me. But I ruined a perfectly good harp, which was what I played in those days."

Several people began to yawn and stretch.

"And these days," said the minstrel, "I am old enough to have need of sleep, so I think that shall be all of my tales for tonight."

* * *

The caravan approached the land of Nagé. Gutharad touched

Ginna on the shoulder and pointed to three small hills which rose out of the dusty plain like the backs of whales rising from the sea. The minstrel told the boy what a whale was, and pointed out the similarity in form.

"When we are beyond them, we are in Nagé."

"My teacher came from this country. He never said much about it."

"A silent bunch, these Nagéans, but very learned, I assure you. It is a perfectly respectable place to be from, unlike—" he looked over his shoulder at the sullen magician who followed them—" Zabortash." The minstrel chuckled, lowering his voice to a whisper. "I must tell you my *other* Zabortash story sometime. It'll put hair on your chest, boy. I think it would do the same for you, young miss, if it didn't curdle your innards entirely. Did you know that they don't, ah, make babies down there the way the rest of the world does it? In Zabortash they have to be different. I think it comes from gulping air out of buckets."

"*How* do they do it?" asked Ginna in a hushed tone.

"Yes, tell us," said Amaedig, less solemn, more amused. "Go ahead and put hair on my chest if you can."

"Keep your voices down, both of you! We can't allow ourselves to be overheard." Gutharad rolled his eyes upward, then glanced back at the magician, who led a pack horse and marched on in regular, deliberate steps. The expression on the man's face was one of contempt for a noisome insect which happens to be out of reach at the moment. Ginna looked back and saw him, and felt a tinge of unease.

"Is it possible," he said to Gutharad in complete earnest, "that babies *are* made in other ways in countries beside Zabortash? In other countries I mean."

With a broad grin the other leaned close and said, "If you and your friend here swear to absolute secrecy, I will tell you the greatest, the strangest, the *ultimate* truth."

"Oh really?" snickered Amaedig.

"Yes, young lady. The secret and the meaning of life. I wouldn't settle for second best in such a case."

"Then tell us. We swear." She made a gesture and Ginna copied it. The minstrel waved his hands in complex patterns which he seemed to be improvising as he went along.

"Now that we're through swearing, come closer." He put his arms around both of them, holding one on either side. His lute jangled as he walked, making hollow sounds. "Listen, and listen well. This is the wisdom to end wisdom, the secret of all secrets."

They both leaned very close, and he told them.

"Some people...will believe...*anything!*"

He threw the two of them aside and stood there, bent over with laughter. The caravan swerved around him, while Ginna and Amaedig stood and stared. Drivers cursed. The magician looked away as he passed. The three of them had to run to regain their place.

Gutharad was less talkative the rest of the day. Ginna thought that he might be somewhat embarrassed at leading them on like that. He was a good man, and very funny sometimes, but not seemingly of the sort who would make fools out of his friends deliberately.

Late in the afternoon they passed one of the Dead Places. There were no ruins, no solid shapes. Faint draperies of light flickered and waved against the grey sky, stirring up dust. In the periphery of his vision Ginna sometimes saw towers or walls, and once a fantastic procession of winged and plumed figures keeping pace with the caravan, but whenever he turned to look at them directly, there was only empty land stretching away into the distance. He saw waterfalls of blue and red light rushing forever into the earth. Something like a ship but large as half of Ai Hanlo drifted near the horizon.

"I think the builders of this place are still here," said Gutharad. "I don't think they were ever flesh and blood at all."

The three caravan masters on their *katas* rode up and down the length of the company with rods in their hands, shouting for all to keep moving, striking anyone who stopped to gaze.

"They have a point. I have heard that if you wait here till sunset, the place becomes so beautiful in the darkness that anyone who keeps looking at it goes mad."

Later the perspective somehow changed. They passed a crucial angle, and all at once the flickering lights, the dim, half-glimpsed shapes, the burning waterfalls all winked out and they were alone with the natural desert once more.

By nightfall they were well beyond the three hills. The caravan masters had been driving everyone hard. All made camp quickly, then dropped to the ground exhausted. Supper was served. After a rest Ginna and the minstrel performed. Later, when Amaedig was away to relieve herself, the two of them sat looking into the darkness.

Ginna spied lights moving up the slopes of the hills.

"What's that?"

Gutharad stared for a minute and said, "It might be a very stupid band of robbers showing off their position, but I doubt it. No, no...look now."

Some of the lights had risen above the tops of the hills and were floating in the air.

"The Bright Powers," said the minstrel. "I don't doubt it now. They congregate on the hills like that sometime. It's best to stay away when they do. Supposedly they assume human shape to dance and play strange music. If you hear it, you are bewitched and drawn to them, clear out of this world."

"And?"

"Maybe some get back. Did you ever wonder where lunatics come from?"

"There's a story I've heard, about another minstrel, like yourself, only more my age. His name was Ain Harad and —"

"Of course, of course. I know that story. Sometime I'll perform my version of it. You must admit he didn't come to a happy end. To this day he sits on top of the world, playing and singing away. Poor wretch. Imagine how hoarse his voice must be by now."

"But he lives forever."

"No, in the version in my repetoire he lives only until the universe is remade and there is a new goddess, or god, or the like born. That's not forever. It's the power of the guardian who sent him where he is. They can do that sort of thing. Guardians are the most powerful magicians in the world, you know."

"Yes," said the boy quietly. "I know." He said nothing more.

"What's the matter?" said Gutharad after a while. "You seem glum suddenly."

"I was thinking of something."

"Well don't. If you forget your troubles and just go where your feet take you, you'll be happy. That's the real secret of life. Not that load of camel crap I fed you this afternoon."

Ginna forced a smile. In mock seriousness this time he asked, "Do they really, ah, do it differently in Zabortash?"

In similarly facetious solemnity, Gutharad replied, "When you are old enough to understand those things, young man, I shall tell you, but not before. Now it is the time for all sensible souls to get some sleep, lest they lie around in the daytime and the vultures take them for corpses and dig in."

They sat up for a short while longer. Amaedig rejoined them and watched the lights on the hills.

* * *

In Estad, the Nagéan capital, whole groups left the caravan, natives returning home and others who had business there. The rest camped in the middle of the great square. Much trading was done with the folk of Nagé, all of whom wore identical robes of plain grey, explaining when asked that anything else would be vanity. News was circulated and tales were told. Gutharad sang and, later, when a high-caste citizen requested it, chanted endless verses of a slightly turgid ancient epic about a hero wandering across the darkened, barren face of the Earth, seeking the great black pyramid in which his beloved dwelt. The adventure took place in the far past, in another cycle before the birth of The Goddess. More than that no one knew. The poet who wrote it had dreamed it for a year and a day while he dwelt in a cave alone, rising from his sleep only to write the verses down, never eating or drinking, and dropping dead of hunger and thirst as soon as he was done. Everyone listened attentively when the epic was recited. There was a strange beauty to it, despite the archaic stiffness of its language.

Later Ginna and Amaedig slept together in a tent, and he told her what the minstrel had said about happiness. That night, as they lay alone and all Estad slept around them, they touched each other as man and woman for the first time, and they spoke in whispers afterwards.

"I want to go on like this forever," he said. "The two of us and Gutharad if he'll have us, just going wherever we want, not bothering anyone or being bothered. Wouldn't that be wonderful?"

"Yes, it would."

"So let's forget about Ai Hanlo, about everything." He yawned and dropped off to sleep.

Chapter 8
Now that the Light of Reason Fades

Shouting and horns blowing woke them. They crawled out of their tent into the dim, grey dawn and found themselves surrounded by men and women scurrying in all directions, gathering goods into bundles, loading burdens on animals, and filling waterskins from the fountain in the middle of the square. The caravan was making ready to depart. Ginna and Amaedig folded their tent and joined the rest.

Gutharad walked up to them, less in a hurry than most of the others. His pack was on his back; his lute hung from one shoulder; and he looked ready to go anywhere.

"Good morning," he said.

"Good morning," said Ginna. "Why are we leaving in such a rush? I thought we were supposed to stay in the city for several days."

Amaedig looked from side to side. "These people act like they're scared. They don't smile or sing as they work."

"I don't know for sure," said the minstrel, "but there's a good chance they *are* scared. Nobody tells me anything, but my guess is the caravan master wants to be on his way before bad luck catches up with him."

"Catches up? From where?" Ginna asked.

"From the way we came. Come here, the two of you." He led them up a stairway which mounted a wall. Even at this height the towers and outer wall of Estad blocked much of the view, but they could see the sky to the southeast and make out part of what seemed to be a dense black mass hanging over the world in that direction. Overhead the sky was as unpolished steel, but one could make out movement as darker and lighter wisps of cloud moved before each other. The blackness in the distance was featureless.

"It isn't smoke," said Gutharad. "If it were, all Randelcainé would have to be burning to produce so much. You two wouldn't have noticed—" he winked and the boy blushed; Amaedig remained stonily unperturbed— "but last night that quarter of the sky slowly became as you see it now. The moon was up, dimly showing through the clouds, which made the sky brighter. But when it got over there, it vanished suddenly, well before it should have set. That was at the fifth hour. The thing is expanding. It's coming this way. That's why everyone wants to get going. I'll wager there won't be any moon in Estad tonight."

"What does it mean? A storm?"

"Storm? Why, my boy, you don't have to be a master astrologer to know a bad omen when you see one. Or maybe it's a portent. But it's obviously bad. It's as if all the color in the universe, all the light, were being sucked out."

"Or like an infection spreading," said Amaedig.

"Yes, like that."

"Is there any cause for it? Any reason?"

"No idea, but I don't like it."

"Nor do I," said Ginna slowly. He could find no other words. He had many ideas, but they were too terrible to express.

In silence the three of them came down from the wall and rejoined the caravan. Amaedig hurried off to return the tent to the camel-driver they had borrowed it from.

The caravan assembled and moved quickly through the streets, out a gate, and onto the plain. As soon as they were a little ways beyond Estad, the immense black stain covering the southeastern sky was in clear view. Few looked at it. Most kept their eyes fixed ahead.

Ginna held Amaedig's hand tightly as he walked. He felt glad to be going away from the anomaly, and he desperately wished that his fancies of the previous night could come true. Now more than ever he wanted to wander like Gutharad, carefree and footloose, through all lands. But with a sinking feeling he knew he was deluding himself. He knew that the darkness would not go away, that the sky would not clear. Footloose wanderers were reputed to sleep under the stars. He had seen no stars for quite some time.

Like the others, he averted his gaze from the strangeness. Few spoke. The only sounds were the jingling bells on the camels and the occasional whinnies of the horses. Once a pack horse went berserk and reared up out of its master's grip, its cargo tearing loose and scattering over the ground. There was much shouting and the men astride the *katas* trotted quickly to the scene, but the company as a whole merely rerouted itself, like a stream of water flowing around an obstruction. When Ginna passed by, the excitement was over. The horse had been slain with a lance and several men were gathering up the spilled goods.

The sun did not rise that day. After a time the sky overhead seemed slightly brighter, but there was no warmth in that brightness. The air was chill. A dry wind blew. Ginna held his cloak tightly around himself.

When the caravan began to move again after the noon meal, some of the drivers began to sing, but there was no joy in that song. They went through it like a chore and stopped after a while.

At night encampment Gutharad and Ginna performed together before an unresponsive audience. The boy had learned to time his golden balls to the minstrel's music, and the results were sometimes amusing, sometimes spectacular, but no one was in the mood for it.

"What a waste. What a shame," muttered Gutharad as they sat around a fire afterwards, chewing on some of the meat from the butchered horse. "In a proper city with a proper crowd, we could have made a fortune just from the coins they'd throw up on stage."

"I'm not sure anything in the world is proper anymore," said Ginna glumly.

"Oh, come on now...."

"You yourself said the sky, the way it is now, is a very bad sign."

"I know I did, but is it the end of the world?"

Someone bumped into Amaedig, who was seated on the other side of Gutharad, all but walking over her.

"*Blind oaf!*" she snarled.

All three of them looked up at the man, who turned briefly toward them. All three caught their breaths. The face was pale and almost featureless, with mere suggestions of eyes, nose, and a mouth. Ginna was not sure if there were any ears. The flesh looked like putty.

When the stranger was gone, they stared at one another in silence.

"He hasn't been out in the open air very long," said Ginna after a minute.

"A disease? Was he a leper?" asked Amaedig.

"Leprosy isn't like that, believe me," said the minstrel. "I've

seen it, but...we'd best see what is going on. I have a hunch...."

They rose and hurried among their fellow caravan members. The groups were seated around their fires as usual, but just as they came near one a man rose to greet a newcomer who was clad in an ankle-length black robe.

"Ebad Andoram! Is it possible? I haven't seen you in years!"

Another similarly garbed figure approached and another man stood up, slack-jawed with astonishment.

"Spoochka Li! I can't believe it!"

This was happening all over the camp. Men were on their feet, shouting and greeting familiar faces. Some recoiled from the unnaturalness of it all. And then there came a scream.

"You! *But you're dead! I saw you die a year ago!*"

Ginna, Amaedig, and Gutharad grabbed hold of one another. Each of them drew out their long knives in an unthinking, simultaneous action.

As if the scream had been a signal, chaos erupted. There were other cries as the frighteningly familiar strangers leapt upon those who greeted them. Ginna saw a man fall to the ground nearby, wrestling with his adversary. Companions came to his aid, slashing with swords. Any mortal man should have been cut to pieces, but the enemy tightened his grip around the victim's throat until his hands crushed the neck to a pulp and the head rolled off in a spout of blood.

The slayer rose to his feet and confronted the swordsmen. Now his face no longer resembled any friend or associate. It was a blank oval. The hands sprouted sharp claws. With a single swipe a swordsman fell, his guts slipping through bloody fingers. Another hooked a man under the chin and the front half of the head was gone, the faceless corpse a staggering fountain of blood before it finally fell. Everywhere men were shouting, fighting, praying, fleeing, dying. Many were trampled as animals galloped in all directions, mad with terror. The Zaborman magician stood his ground, waving his arms, conjuring furiously. Swords passed through the attackers without resistance, but those hands were solid enough. Some of the creatures had bony blades growing out of their elbows, knees, and feet. Those were solid too.

Ginna, Amaedig, and Gutharad ran without making any attempt to fight. They didn't know where they were going, but as one, holding hands, they raced through the camp. When something lurched against them, they slashed with their knives, turned, and fled in another direction. The night was filled with motion, with silhouetted figures flickering back and forth in front of campfires, with flames from slipped lanterns licking up the sides of tents, and with screams. Yet beyond the periphery of the unsteady, garnish lights, the night was dark indeed.

"*Ginna! Ginna! Don't run away! Come to me!*"

He knew the voice. He knew the face. It was the old nurse, the one Kaemen had killed. Now she was alive, running toward him, a broad smile on her face, arms outspread.

His mind froze. His body lurched. His feet slipped away from under him for a moment as the others dragged him away.

They caught glimpses of the blank-faced figures as their flesh dissolved away, revealing flowing masses of blackness beneath. All resemblances to human beings ended, but the new forms were just as deadly. Something like an oily, half-liquid snake poured out of a sleeve, and a gown dropped to the ground empty. The thing wrapped itself around a woman who had stumbled. She screamed. Over all the noise, Ginna could hear her bones snap.

Without hardly knowing it, they had reached the edge of the camp. They plunged into the night and soon the screams and the burning were far behind. Still they ran until they came to a stretch of white sand. Here, because the ground was lighter than the sky overhead, they could see a little bit, enough to make out large boulders and to tell they were still three.

Amaedig sobbed and hugged Ginna. He was beyond all emotion, numb with terror. He felt sick. He wanted to vomit. He felt like his blood had all run out and he was standing weak and hopelessly empty.

"*Quiet!*" hissed the minstrel.

Something as large as a castle wall, yet serpentine was moving in the void nearby. The pale whiteness of the sand was slowly covered over as it approached.

Ginna and Amaedig screamed together, and they were running again, without thought, without sight, without any place to run to. It seemed to the boy that he had always been running, that he had always been in the darkness, in some bad dream where one is running, running, running from unseen terror, but feet are stuck, legs mired in quicksand *it...is...impossible ...to...move....*

There was no sound, not even screaming.

Suddenly he was snapped back into concrete reality: the gravel underfoot as the patch of sand ended, the chill of the night air, the burning in his lungs as he ran, ran—

Two limp hands were dangling from the sky, the fingers tapping gently against his face like a bead curtain.

They hung there. He was still running. Warm blood poured

down over him, the stream keeping pace with his flight. His mind refused to believe, refused to accept the paradox—

He collided with something solid which dropped out of the sky in front of him. It landed with a thud. He tripped over it, and fell in a screaming, mindless tangle of limbs. He slashed with his knife until somehow it was no longer in his hand.

Amaedig was with him, screaming. She crawled over him, her arms around his neck, screaming mindlessly in his ear, as if she ludicrously wanted a piggyback ride.

A lute banged in a hollow clangor of strings as they fell on it.

Choking, straining under the weight of Amaedig, he forced himself into a kneeling position. And then, for no reason as rational as a desire for light, but merely because in a hopeless situation nothing else made any more sense, nothing heroic or stupid or even instinctive, he folded his hands together, willed the thing to be so, and unfolded them. A glowing ball the size of a walnut drifted slowly upward. He made another, and another. Like an inscrutable figure in a prophetic dream he created them, letting them fall onto the ground for a while, and then he began to juggle them.

His mind was completely detached from all this. It was an unreal vision of something which could not be. For a flickering instant he was self-aware, and he thought, *this is what death is like, to be suspended inside an eternal now. This is the last thing my mind conjures up, and here I am, like an insect in amber.*

His hands, moving of their own accord, continued to juggle, and the darkness around him paused. The immense, encircling shape paused. Man-shaped things which padded as they walked came no closer. They did not recoil out of fear. It was no panicked retreat, but more of a *recognition* followed by a deliberate withdrawal. After a time it slowly registered in his mind that they were gone.

He juggled in the silence of the night, not even feeling the weight of Amaedig on his back, until at last his body collapsed out of exhaustion. He fell over backwards, onto Amaedig, rolled off her, and the two lay side by side for a long time.

He awoke later, trembling and dizzy, in a faint twilight that could have been either dawn or dusk. The blackness now filled three quarters of the sky. Only from the northwest did any light come. In that direction he could see the end of the great plain, and low, rolling hills outlined against a grey sky the color of slate.

He was on rough, rocky ground. He untangled Amaedig's arms and sat up. His legs were beneath those of another. He beheld the corpse he had fallen over and somehow half wriggled under. It was headless, but by the clothing he knew it. He also knew the smashed lute beside it.

"Please no...not you...."

Amaedig stirred. "Huh...?"

Tears streamed down his face. He staggered to his feet, bent over, and took her by the hand. With his other hand he covered her eyes. He helped her up.

"If you never do anything else I say, please, please, do this one thing. Don't open your eyes. Don't look. I'll guide you."

Slowly they made their way through the stones, towards the hills. When they were far enough away, he uncovered her eyes. She did not look back, nor did she ask what he had prevented her from seeing, but by the despair on her face and in her voice the few times she spoke, he knew that she understood.

The day didn't seem to get any darker or brighter. They trudged in silence for a long time. The whole earth was still and cold around them. There was no wind to sway the sparse tufts of grass. They came to a stream and drank from it, their slight splashings the only sound. The water flowed sluggishly. No fish swam in it. No birds flew overhead.

At last they found a grove of scrubby trees. There they paused to rest. Ginna turned to Amaedig and she to him and both tried to speak, but only babbling sobs came out. They fell into each other's arms, weeping. After a while, they slept.

* * *

Sleep never came to the Lord Guardian of the Bones of the Goddess. Kaemen remained awake all night, every night, drifting through the dark hours like a shark at the bottom of the sea, restless, relentless, hating.

He lay in his chamber alone, in the bed Tharanodeth had once occupied. The magical emblems, talismans, and charms had all been removed. Where there had been two images of The Goddess over the door, there was now only one.

He watched the progress of Ginna and Amaedig. For a long time he had known that if he chose to put himself in the right sort of trance, he could see through Ginna's eyes, hear through his ears, and feel what his body felt. He had never told anyone, because there was no one worth telling. When it occurred to him to taunt Ginna with it, just to frighten him, the black hag inside his head told him to never, never contemplate such a thing. Her teeth were clamped in his brain. Her jaw was a steel trap. The pain would be terrible before he died, if he dared disobey her. So he kept his secret to himself, and, before his great labor began, the keeping of it was the most important task she had set for him.

He watched. He had been amused at the boy's first shy caresses, that night in the tent in the square in Estad. The girl's response disgusted him. The two of them coupled like filthy animals. They reminded him of worms wriggling in the mud.

He heard their conversation. They would wander forever, would they? He thought otherwise. They were straying from their course. Hadn't that drooling idiot any sense of responsibility? What about Hadel's last, mysterious, melodramatic legacy? Oh yes, Hadel. He still moped in his chamber. A nuisance and a bore. Some exquisite and novel way to get rid of him would eventually be found.

But enough of trivial amusements. There were important things to be done. The black hag's words hammered in his mind over and over again, *Who is the lady of the grove? You must find out. You must find out.*

Therefore he followed Ginna and Amaedig. If they found this "lady," so would he. Now he sensed them among the stunted trees, asleep in one another's arms. It was so tender, so ridiculous. He laughed, and the sound was strangled in Ginna's throat, coming out a choking gurgle. He laughed again, still in his trance, his mind focusing on the matter at hand. Saliva ran down Ginna's cheek.

He heard Amaedig stirring. He felt her arms withdraw along the boy's pathetically bony sides. Then came her voice.

"Are you awake?"

Concentrating, he forced Ginna's eyes open and beheld her leaning over him in the murky twilight. She jumped back in alarm. He followed her, turning the eyes in the sockets. He couldn't move the head.

She leaned close. It would have amused him intensely to spit at her right now, but he couldn't control Ginna's mouth either. Doubtless his face was slack and expressionless. He wanted to spit, to speak an obscenity. One reason he hated everyone in the world so much was that he was always being denied these little pleasures.

Realizing that he had learned all he could, and that if he persisted, he might wreck the delicate operation of his scheme, he closed Ginna's eyes and withdrew, leaving him in natural sleep.

* * *

Ginna rolled and moaned. He awoke, sat up, and hugged Amaedig tightly, but was bewildered when she began to scream and struggle. Almost too quickly for him to see it, her dagger was out, slashing at him. He grabbed the hand that wielded it, caught the wrist, and twisted until she let go, but not before the blade went up his sleeve. He felt a sharp pain, but he took no notice of it.

"Let me go! Let me go!" she shrieked. He wrestled with her until he was on top over her and held both her arms to the ground.

"What's the matter with you? Have you gone mad?" And he felt a sinking feeling that yes, she had, and now he was alone. He might as well just fall on the dagger and end it all. He couldn't go on without her.

"You're not Ginna! You're one of them!"

He let go of her and stood up. She rose and stared at him with wide eyes filled with hopeless terror. She did not run, but merely cowered, as the prey of some flesh-eating beast might do when the chase is over and the end has come.

"What are you talking about? Look!" He pulled up his sleeve. His right forearm was slashed from the wrist to the elbow. It was only then that he realized how much he was bleeding. He began to feel dizzy. "They don't have any blood. . . ."

"Oh. . ." She put her hand to her mouth, as if to apologize ridiculously, and then she fell to his feet, as if all strength had drained out of her, and sobbed, "I didn't know. Please forgive me. Please." Then, because her mind could bear the situation no more, she fainted.

He looked down at her, not sure what to do, but then the pain of nis wound and the nauseous imbalance that bespeaks a loss of blood came over him. His head was light. He sat down. It was hard to put forth any effort. His fingers were weak and clumsy, but somehow he managed to cut strips from his cloak, and bind up the wound, using his left hand and his teeth. When he was done, he put the dagger into his empty sheath.

Then, because he felt very weak, he lay down, his head on her lap. The semi-darkness of the grove faded. The trees became indistinct blurs. He slept. When he awoke once more it was totally dark. Night had come. He wondered if it would end, or if the world would go on like this forever. Tharanodeth had spoken of the twilight of mankind, its final night. Had he meant it more than figuratively?

Amaedig stirred. He heard gravel shifting as she moved, then he felt her hand on his knee. She grasped tightly, then paused.

She began to scream again.

"You're one of them!"

He seized her hand and put it where she could find his bandaged right arm.

"No, I'm not. I had to fix what you did to me, see?"

She let out a long sigh.

"I can't see anything. The dark—"

"I think it's just night time."

For a long time he tried to get her to tell him what she had experienced. They sat there in utter darkness, unable to see anything but phantom spots drifting before their eyes. Only sound told each where the other was. At first she babbled, unable to form words. Then came syllables, whole words, and parts of sentences. At last, with great deliberation, she was able to say, "You were like a corpse. You didn't breathe. Your eyes were open and they moved, but you weren't awake. It was like some evil spirt inside you, hating me. You glared as if you wanted to kill me, but...I can't explain this...it seemed at the same time you were very far away. I was afraid."

"I was afraid too. Have we been anything else these days? I dreamed I was falling down into a well filled with black oil, and when I got to the bottom there was something kneeling on my chest, covering my face with its soft hands. It was crushing me. I couldn't breathe. Then I felt it reach down my throat and begin to squeeze my heart, but for some reason it let go. After that I woke up."

"You didn't see me? You didn't open your eyes and watch me?"

"No."

"Ginna," she sobbed. "Will there ever be a time when we are not afraid again? I don't see how there can be. I just want to die."

"Kaemen has been with us," said Ginna slowly and carefully. "Perhaps he has been with us all along. There is only one thing to do now. We must find the lady Hadel sent me to find. There is no other hope for us."

"But who is she? What can she do?"

"I don't know. But Hadel was a wise man. And good. He really was. I don't think he's alive now. I miss him. I don't see how he could be alive. Even when he knew what was happening, when he knew the Guardian was spying on us somehow, he told me to seek this lady. It was that important, as if he said it with his dying breath."

"How do we find her?"

"Well, this is a grove we're in now, and I don't see her. There's supposed to be a fountain too. I suppose we go north. The caravan would have reached Dotargun eventually. That's a forest country. What else can we do?"

"Nothing, I guess."

They waited until the darkness lessened before they set out, heading always toward the patch of grey sky in the northwest. Ginna was weak and had to rest often. Amaedig undid his bandage, applied some of the salve she still had with her, and rebound it. Fortunately she had been carrying the salve. She still had her pack. Ginna's had been lost in the confusion at the camp. They had only her supply of food between them, which was little. Before long both were weakened further by hunger.

While they sat by a stream, leaning against a boulder, a wild *kata*, frightened and separated from its herd, came there to drink. They looked at the animal, and it looked back at them for a long time before it went on its way, as if it were reluctant to part from the company of another living creature. This Ginna took for a good omen.

* * *

Again The Guardian lay alone in his chamber, watching them. He did not force Ginna's eyes open this time. The boy was awake and walking through the semi-darkness of day across the desolate country north of Estad. He could feel the rough ground through the soles of Ginna's boots, and it seemed to him that his own forearm was bound in strips of cloth and throbbing dully. He heard Amaedig's footsteps a few paces behind him. He heard her voice when she spoke as if she were standing by the side of the bed. The strangest sensation came when Ginna spoke. It was as if another mind controlled his vocal cords, and he felt the words rising in his throat, but he did not actually utter them. He heard them somewhat removed, as spoken by another.

When he was younger, the experience had fascinated him. Now, the lord of the world, a man of almost sixteen years—he was endlessly contemptuous of Ginna, a boy of the same age, no one of importance, a mere nuisance and curiosity—he had no time for such things. The black lady said the end of all things and the new beginning of all things were coming very, very soon, and he must prepare.

So he watched in earnest to learn what he needed to learn, not for the sensation of riding secretly in someone else's body. He saw the landscape go by slowly. He watched Ginna and Amaedig pause to dig for edible roots and he felt the earth on his hands. He felt their hunger in his own belly, and he listened to their conversation, remembering all.

They did not know when he was there and when he wasn't. The extension of his spirit into Ginna produced some unease, but if he didn't force himself further, there was quite enough else for Ginna to be uneasy about.

So he did not laugh. He did not spit in anyone's face. He was their invisible companion.

* * *

Slowly the rocky plain gave way to gentle hills covered with grass already going white for want of sunlight. The world seemed dead. The air was still and colder than Ginna had ever known it. Only very rarely did he see any living creature, usually a single bird flapping furiously toward that part of the sky which was not wholly dark. On the ground were occasional animals used to darkness, toads and serpents. Worms wriggled up out of the soil, no longer fearing the heat of the day.

Among the hills there were many clusters of scrubby trees with pale, drooping leaves.

Ginna felt faint much of the time from hunger and his wound which refused to heal. At least there was enough water. Both he and Amaedig had never taken off the water bags which hung from their belts, and had had them as they fled. Streams were common in this part of the world. Once they caught a fish by hand, and having no means of making fire, ate it raw. Other than that, neither had eaten anything since Amaedig's meager provisions had run out.

He had no idea how long it had been. Two days, maybe three. Perhaps more. He was losing track of time. The thought came to him that perhaps the sequence of day and night had become disordered and the intervals irregular. Several days might have slipped by in a single sleeping period, presaging a virtually endless night.

Amaedig walked stiffly, deliberately putting one foot in front of another as if she could not consciously plan any action beyond the next step. Both of them had spent their lives in a city where there were no long distances to be traversed and food was always at hand. They were not accustomed to hardship. Both were completely exhausted.

When they paused to rest once more, neither could get up again.

"I guess we sleep here," he said, and she mumbled in agreement. Hills were all around them. The land was rippled the way Ginna imagined the sea must be just as an enormous tempest is beginning. In the twilight the slopes seemed dark and massive, yet fluid. By some trick of the light, they appeared to move as shadows shifted, but he lacked the strength to sit up and watch. The narrow band of almost-light to the northwest was dimming.

He could barely keep his eyes open. He surrendered to the weakness which was dragging him down.

He slept apart from his friend. His last conscious thought was that The Guardian might be watching somehow. He could not touch Amaedig while *that one* looked on. The idea was obscene.

He dreamt he stood in spirit above his body as it lay there on the dying grass. He looked down on himself, and on the girl beside him. He walked over to her and bent low to assure himself she was breathing. She muttered in some dream of her own, turning fitfully from side to side as he watched.

Then he looked back to his body and saw a glimmering black line, like a stream of darkly shining oil, stretched from the side of the head away into the distance. He could not see the end of it. He had no rational way of knowing, but was sure that it reached southeast, all the way to Ai Hanlo.

The night was totally dark, save that one thin strip of sky seemed slightly less so. It would have been impossible for his waking self to see the hand before his face, but his dream-self possessed some other kind of vision.

As he looked closer, he could tell that the black fluid was pouring out of his right ear—that of his body as it lay on the ground. Then the flow stopped, and the end of the stream withdrew like a rope being dragged away from the other end. Somehow his spirit was bound to it, and he felt himself pulled along, away from the two reclining figures, as if he were no more substantial than smoke and a huge mouth were sucking him in.

He was carried over the way he had come so far, over the hills and the rocky plain, past the ruins of the caravan's last camp. He tried to look away, but there were corpses all around him. Finally he found the power to shut his eyes, and he drifted on, hovering above the stream or oil or tentacle or whatever it was. When he looked again the city of Estad was behind him. No torches or lanterns burned among its towers and walls. No voices of the watch called out.

He began to move faster, as if the limb which had fetched him had grown impatient. He raced over a countryside increasingly familiar, along the bank of a river he knew, over fields of failing crops and still puddles of irrigated water. Then Ai Hanlo loomed before him, silent and forbidding, a ghostly silhouette of a city, save for the golden dome which seemed to glow slightly with its own unnatural light. Shuttered houses and empty streets whizzed past, and he was moving up, up into the inner city, into the palace, through courtyards, rooms, and corridors which had once been the whole of his world. The black stream reminded him of a tongue now, and he imagined some toad-like monstrosity crouching in the depths of the palace and reaching out windows, around towers, over walls, across miles and miles of midnight terrain to ensnare—what?

Suddenly he found himself in a dimly-lighted room which he recognized. He had not been there since the day Tharanodeth lay dying on the bed now occupied by an obese, pale form.

Kaemen sat up, spoke a word, performed a motion with his hands, and came out of his trance. He seemed to see Ginna standing at the foot of the bed. At first there was alarm on his face, then surprise, and this gave way to a malicious grin.

"So you followed me home. Are you really there? You must have been dreaming just as I—no, I won't tell you anything more than you already know."

The Guardian wriggled to the edge of the bed and dropped to the floor. He moved more like a festering, boneless mass of flesh than a person. He approached Ginna, reached out a hand to touch him, and the hand passed through. Ginna felt a cold intrusion in his chest.

"Very interesting. The soul cannot exist outside the body except in such extraordinary instances as these. Otherwise there must be a receptacle. But you already know about that. Come with me. I haven't got all night."

Kaemen reached out again. His hand came no nearer than an arm's length away, but somehow he seized him. Ginna felt himself dragged along as surely as if he'd been collared. He drifted lightly. Often his feet didn't touch the floor. The Guardian led him like a kite on a string along many empty, soundless corridors past doors which were either tightly barred or broken open. The open ones revealed empty rooms, sometimes in disarray. Once he thought he saw someone lying on the floor in one of them, twisted into a position no living person could assume, but he wasn't sure. The shadows were so thick. He was past it so quickly.

They came upon a woman dressed in the gown of a high caste of nobility. She had been running stealthily along a hallway, hiding in corners and behind pillars, looking to see if the way were clear, then scurrying on again. She had a small oil lamp to light her way.

She didn't seem to be aware of Kaemen's approach until he was almost upon her. Then, by the faint light of the lamp the look of horror on her face as she recognized him was clearly visible. She screamed briefly, threw up her hands, and Kaemen pointed a finger at her. At once she fell to the floor, dead.

The lamp handle was still hooked around her thumb. Oil spilled out when it hit the floor, burning in a little puddle. This Kaemen stamped out, taking up the lamp. It was still lighted.

"I am not wholly of the darkness yet," he said. "We'll need this to see where we are going."

They came to chambers Ginna had never seen before. Huge metal doors opened to The Guardian's touch, leading to a long, winding staircase descending into darkness. A cold, earthy draft blew up from below, and there were voices, many faintly whispering voices like a million leaves rustling over a dry floor. It seemed to Ginna that the mortar between the stones of the walls glowed a faint, bloody red, while the stones themselves flowed and changed in the familiar pattern of darkness, as Kaemen's own face had, as the things atop the golden dome had. Darkness poured out of the walls and rippled down the stairs over the feet of Kaemen and Ginna. It bubbled and rose up in flabby, half-formed shapes which reached out with feeble hands, which stared with randomly spaced eyes, which croaked and gibbered with lips that flapped and melted back into the overall mass.

A force opposed Ginna's passsage, but it was not quite strong enough to stop him. He moved like a vessel against a stiff current.

At the bottom of the stairs the darkness pooled on the floor of a large, circular room. Kaemen lit several lamps from his hand-held one and the darkness recoiled and diminished. The room was empty except for two larger than human-sized statues of The Goddess, one in black marble, one in white. The head of the white one had been knocked off.

They approached a massive rectangular door set in the curved wall of the place, carven out of the same marble as the statues only somehow mixed, so that the dark and light veins flowed together. Kaemen reached for the golden ring to pull the door open and paused, his hand outstretched, as if he too were meeting strong resistance. Momentary anger turned into terror on his face. He lowered his arm and staggered back as if pushed by invisible hands.

Ginna saw the Guardian's face darkening, losing its shape as it had once before, and it seemed another body was imposing itself over Kaemen's.

It was the black hag with the empty sockets, with fire burning inside her skull.

"No!" she shrieked. "Are you mad? He shall not come any closer. You just wanted to gloat."

At the same time, behind her wavering visage, Ginna could see Kaemen. There was a look on his face he had never imagined possible. The wide, staring eyes he would never forget. Tears ran down the cheeks. The Guardian was trapped, frustrated, both enraged and in despair, afraid and completely alone.

Their eyes met for an instant, but already Ginna was reeling back.

The witch held up her hand like a shadow of Kaemen's.

"*Begone!*" she commanded, and the boy's spirit was tumbling head over heels in a rushing wind, up the winding stairs, out of the palace, and over the open country once more. The wind was frigid. Bitter cold and darkness were all he was aware of. He was moving too fast to see anything but a whirring blur. He was falling, dizzily falling into an abyss without a bottom—

—and awoke motionless in complete darkness. The ground was solid and damp beneath him, but the icy wind was gone. He willed his eyes open, felt with his hands to make sure they were, and could see absolutely nothing. He moved his hands over his body to assure himself he was really there. He touched his right ear gingerly.

Amaedig stirred nearby.

The grass beneath him was wet and the night air was filled with the odor of its decay.

Again the night refused to end. He lay awake for he knew not how long, and there was no change. But then, there was no feature against which to measure change. Feeling and smell were the only senses left to him. When Amaedig was not shifting in her sleep, he heard nothing but the beating of his own heart.

He slept for a while, dreamlessly, then woke again. He sat up and stretched his arms to relieve a cramp in his back, and paused, terrified.

When they had first stopped here, it was an open place. Now he felt something solid and smooth, like a glass wall.

"Amaedig!"

"Huh? What—?" She sat up and also felt the strange thing which had grown up during the night, hemming them in. She began to scream. The two of them leapt to their feet, and as they stood crashed through something so light it seemed only half solid. Fragments of it sprinkled over them like sand.

Suddenly there were crashing and tinkling sounds all around them, spreading farther and farther away. He reached out and felt the barrier crumble to his touch. It was as if an enormous palace, a life-sized model of Ai Hanlo made out of paper-thin black glass, were collapsing around them. They huddled together and drew their cloaks over their heads and fragments rained upon them. Later Ginna pulled his back and looked, and caught a glimpse of distant towers and walls crumbling against the faint light of day. The northwestern sky was a dark grey, but it seemed brilliant compared to the rest.

When they began to walk in that direction, there were no fragments underfoot, only earth and stones and dead grass.

Neither spoke. After what seemed like only an hour or two, the world was again wholly dark. They sat down, unwilling to venture further in that fathomless night, but afraid to sleep, lest some other fundamental change occur while they did. But at last exhaustion returned and they lay down, holding hands to reassure one another of their presence.

Again Ginna did not dream. This time he woke in complete darkness, stared into it for a while, and suddenly beheld a bright speck. He thought it a trick of his eyes. Once when he was a small child, he had wandered into a tunnel which turned out to be much longer and much darker than he had expected. As he groped his way along, red and white specks drifted before him, and he ignored them. Only the steady, unshifting rectangle of light at the tunnel's end had convinced him of its reality.

Now there was this single point of light. It did not drift or grow indistinct around the edges. It was like a star only on the ground.

He nudged Amaedig awake. "Look at that. Do you see it?"

"Yes! A light! We're saved!"

"I don't know about that, but at least it's real."

She got to her feet, stretching stiffened limbs.

"You were thinking it was a dream. Were you dreaming?"

"No."

"I was. I had a funny dream. It wasn't frightening. I was lying at the bottom of a pool or a fountain, looking up through water deep enough to dip your arms in to your elbows. Somebody was moving nearby, but I couldn't see him clearly."

"Then how do you know it wasn't a woman?"

"I don't. I only saw a black shape. Flapping like a cloak."

He decided not to tell her about his dream of returning to Ai Hanlo just yet. There was too much to be afraid of already.

"Let's go see what the light is."

Hand in hand, warning one another of pitfalls, they made their way down the slope of the hill they had rested on. They followed a little valley for a while in the direction of the light. The fact that it seemed near was encouraging. They knew it was not some beacon on the horizon, but a smaller light near at hand. When they walked in the valley it was above them. When they had set out it had been on the same level. This meant it was atop a nearby hill, perhaps the next one over, or one slightly taller beyond that.

They came to a beaten path which rose slowly. Eventually it topped a rise and became a paved road. Now the light was level with them again. It was still too dark to see the landscape.

The road curved and something eclipsed the light. They groped their way to a low, stone hut and pushed the door open.

"Hello?" said Ginna, leaning inside.

Silence. He made a ball of light and let it rise to the ceiling. Before it winked out he saw an overturned chair, a table pushed aside, and broken dishes on the floor.

They found another house. It too was empty.

"Where are all the people?" asked Amaedig.

"Fled, I imagine. Or dead."

Carefully retracing their steps, they found the road again. They walked a little ways and it straightened out and the light was visible ahead once more. It was very close. The pavement broadened out into what must have been a square or market place. In the middle was a fountain in which water still splashed out of carven figures into a circular pool. In the middle of the pavement, a dozen paces from the fountain, a campfire burned untended.

There was a definite scent in the air: meat cooking.

"Food!" gasped Amaedig. She let go of Ginna's hand and rushed forward. He ran too. Both squatted by the fire. Two sticks had been driven into cracks between the paving stones. Horizontally between them, a fowl of some kind had been spitted.

"I wonder why anyone would set this up and leave," Ginna thought aloud.

"Just shut up and eat before he gets back!"

Both of them ate, tossing bones aside, looking over their shoulders lest someone burst upon them at any moment, furious at the intrusion. But when they had finished and still no one came, they ceased to question their good fortune. Both sat in the circle of firelight, wiping grease from their faces with their sleeves.

"I don't think anything *ever* tasted so good," he said.

"No, nothing ever did."

"If only once or twice a day someone could do us a favor like this—"

"Oh Ginna, will things ever be as they once were?" She was sombre all of a sudden, almost pleading. "Or is the world coming to an end? Is this a short reprieve that means nothing when the end comes?"

"I—"

"Well, is it?"

"*How should I know?*" he snapped. Then she began to weep and he was suddenly ashamed. "Forgive me, please. I didn't mean to be angry, not with you. You're the last person in the world besides me for all I know. I'm sorry."

"But—but—you're magical. You should know. You're different."

He folded his hands together and opened them. He watched the tiny sphere of light he'd made vanish into the night sky. It rolled on a faint current of air. Because of the absolute darkness above, it was visible for a long time before it faded.

"If it had become a star," he said, "and I could make stars, or if I could sing a secret song and make the sun rise, then you might be right. Then I probably would know. But I can't and I don't. I don't understand what is happening or who I am really, or why I am different. What few things I know are all terrible. I don't have all the pieces of the puzzle. I'm not much different from anyone else, and I don't have any special way of knowing things. Hadel said I had what some people call the witch sight, and maybe that's why I've had some of my dreams, but otherwise I don't know any more than you do."

"Then what are we to do? We can't go on like this."

"I think you and I will have to find out what is happening. If there truly is no hope, then evil will overtake us wherever we are, whether we sit here and do nothing or move on. So what have we got to lose?"

"*Help me! I can't breathe!*" She clutched her throat and heaved forward almost falling into the fire.

"What is it?"

"Like...drowning...smothered...No! Burning inside." She screamed hoarsely once, then only gasped, unable to draw air into her lungs. She wriggled on the pavement like a beached fish.

"Poison?" was all he was able to say before he felt it too. His vision clouded. He opened his mouth, but could not speak. There was a fire in his chest, spreading throughout his body, as if his flesh were coming loose from his bones and running like hot wax.

Drowning? She had dreamed of being under water deep enough to get your elbows wet in.

The fountain. Suddenly it seemed to thunder like some enormous waterfall.

Almost blind, desperately weak, he forced himself to his feet, staggered the short distance to the fountain, then fell. His head was spinning. Still he drew no breath. Red haze filled his vision. With great effort he grasped the side of the fountain and pulled himself up, forcing his leaden arms and legs to move.

His throat was dry; he made a raspy, wheezing sound like sand ground between ancient parchment. He lurched over the edge of the fountain and his face splashed into the water. He tried to drink, but couldn't swallow. He found himself staring down at a glowing white ovoid. He reached in until he felt the smooth stone bottom of the pool. His arm was wet up to his elbow. Through some trick of the water or a momentary clearing of his vision, he saw the thing below him distinctly enough to tell what it was.

It was Amaedig's head, staring up at him, the eyes wide with terror, the mouth gaping, the lips flapping soundlessly, the skin aglow as if with fire. As he watched the features began to melt and run. Bits of flesh peeled off into the water.

By the fire, on the pavement, Amaedig moaned and coughed. He looked back at her, absurdly, to see if she still had a head. She did. He stood up, looked down at the thing in the water, glimpsed something to the left in the corner of his eye, lurched in that direction, lost his balance, and fell into the fountain. For an instant he seemed to float and the pain ebbed away. Then he was sinking, and the bottom of the pool was rising to meet him. Something else, glowing: his own head, the eyes wide more in confusion than fear. The mouth was shouting. A gurgling sound passed through the water. This head also glowed with its own light and it too was slowly melting. Pieces of it broke off, drifted a short ways, and dissolved into nothing.

He flailed about, caught the edge of the fountain with one hand, the bottom with the other. Steadier, he grabbed the image of his head by the hair and forced himself up out of the water, onto his knees.

He placed the head on the lip of the fountain. Scarcely able to make his body obey him, he moved along the edge, still on his knees, and retrieved Amaedig's head. He put it by the first. Even as he watched the two of them melted, their substance dripping into the water and down onto the pavement. The features were hardly recognizable. Hair fell out as the scalp ran and oozed. The eyes dropped out of Amaedig's sockets, adhering to her cheeks briefly, then falling off into darkness.

He was dimly aware that Amaedig lay still by the fire. It was her head he had there. He couldn't think of it as merely a copy. Indeed, he watched his cheekbones collapse, his face fold in on itself. He put a numb hand on his cheek, his *real* face, he tried to tell himself, and felt nothing.

The two heads were as real as anything. He understood, dimly. It was sorcery of some sort. He had no idea how it worked, but had heard of such things.

Even as he knelt there in the water, hanging onto the edge of the fountain....

His life and hers, running away like hot wax....

Burning with the fire of death....

One of the eyes in his head dropped out of its socket, into the skull. Suddenly, he was half blind.

He wondered if it might not be possible to destroy the heads by another means, to avert the spell. If not, he would merely die more quickly. A matter of seconds ago he had been saying to Amaedig, *what have we got to lose?*

He never knew where he got that last reserve of strength which enable him to take the heads in either hand, to stand up. As he stood his legs slipped from under him, and he fell forward, out of the fountain, all his weight atop the heads.

They smashed on the flagstones like clay jars. There was a burst of foul-smelling steam. He rolled away, his face and hands already scalded, and lay still, his chest heaving, sucking in the cold night air. Then he felt nothing at all.

He must have been unconscious only a minute or two. Suddenly while the remains of the heads were still fizzling, he was awake and aware of hard-shod footsteps approaching him steadily, then pausing. Someone stood over him.

A half-remembered voice: "Very clever. I hadn't thought of that."

He looked up—both eyes were unclouded—and saw a man draped in black bending down. The magician. The one who had banished his roses. The magician from the caravan.

He sat up, but did not rise when he saw that the man held a dagger which was pointed at him.

"You...how did you get away?"

"Yes, it is I," the magician said sourly. "The Zaborman your friend made such fun of. You are surprised that you did not kill me with the others. Since you are about to die, I can tell you my secret. I folded space around myself like a cloak. I ceased to exist in this world for a while, and thus escaped the massacre you brought about."

"But I didn't kill anyone! I barely got away myself!"

"Do you take me for a fool? Reason thus: You are clearly magical. It takes a magician to know. Your tricks with the balls are no mere illusions, but something deeper. You come from Ai Hanlo. The darkness started there. As you move, the darkness spreads. Well you shall move no more!"

The magician lunged with the dagger. Ginna rolled out of the way, fumbling for Amaedig's knife, which was still in his scabbard. He got clumsily to his feet. The man came at him again, and even as he did another familiar voice cried out.

"Stop! That's quite enough of this!"

The magician paused, turned, and confronted his challenger. Ginna stepped back and off to one side, then leaned forward to get a better look. They were a good ways away from the campfire, which had burned low, and there was no other light. He saw a little more than a silhouette, but by the clothing, the build of the newcomer, and his voice, he knew who it was and was faint with terror.

It was Gutharad, headless, both arms hanging limply at his sides; his voice came from knee level; his head dangled by the hair, held in his left hand.

"What are you?" demanded the magician, his voice quavering but slightly.

"Do not harm them. Let them go."

The Zaborman shouted a word of power and began to conjure. But before he oculd do more than raise his arms and point the dagger at the sky, the apparition rushed forward and, expert as a boxer, slammed a fist into his stomach. As it did the whole of its body flowed out through the sleeve and into the magician's abdomen. Empty clothing dropped to the ground. The magician clutched his belly, threw his head back to let out a gurgling scream, and then his mouth was a fountain of blood and pulped flesh. While he was yet standing a black, oily mass forced its way out of him and shot up into the night sky. While he was yet standing he was little more than a ruined, bloody, hollowed-out husk. But he only stood for a second before crumpling to the pavement.

Ginna, still in a daze, thought to look for Gutharad's head. There was nothing, only the empty clothing which had definitely belonged to the minstrel.

He stood for a while, breathing deeply, letting his senses clear. Then he went to rouse Amaedig. He understood more fully now that a game was being played. He was a piece moved across the board without any choice of his own. Everyone, even his dire enemy, wanted him to find the lady of the grove. Whoever she was. Whatever powers she might have.

He appreciated that this time he owed his life to Kaemen. Of course. If he were killed here, mistakenly by some crazed Zaborman, the game would be over.

Light came to the northwestern sky, pale and faint. Ginna always thought of it as dawn, although he realized that it was probably just a part of late afternoon. The sun rose in the east, passed unseen through the region of darkness, nearing the edge late in the day, when a little light came through.

Thus the "days" were getting steadily shorter.

Only by this faint illumination could he and Amaedig see their breath coming out in white puffs. By this light they could make out the dark shapes, the long shadows of a town.

He told her all that had happened. She said nothing. She seemed to be withdrawing into herself.

They explored the town. Windows and doors hung open. Nothing stirred within the buildings. No pigeons roosted on the slate and tile roofs.

There was little food to be had. Mold seemed to grow preternaturally fast in the changed conditions. What few stores they could find had spoiled. There was only a huge block of cheese which he chipped away at, the pieces falling off like chips of wood, until he came to the pure center the size of an apple, What meat hung in smokehouses was ruined. After a while, they gave up their search.

They did find some clothing, though. Each took a heavier cloak, an extra shirt, and blankets. As sunlight became only a memory, the earth and air continued to cool. The mud of the unpaved side streets was beginning to harden. The ground was freezing.

Only once did they find any trace of the inhabitants of that place. The severed hand of a child lay on a doorstep, bloodless and icy white.

Ginna did not try to speak to the unresponsive Amaedig. All the world was silent.

He was glad when they were in open country again, following the main road which passed through the town and went well beyond it. The country air seemed easier to breathe. Since his experience the previous night, he took note of how he breathed. Any pain in his chest caused dread. Each deep, bitingly cold lungful of air was savored.

After a while he thought it best to try to maintain good cheer. He sang and was pleased when Amaedig joined in, but eventually fatigue and a depression he had never managed to dispell made him stop. She did too. His arm had never healed and was beginning to fester. Eventually, if it continued swelling, he would have to lance it or purge it with fire, and the remedy could be as bad as the hurt. His hands and face itched where the steam had touched them. His feet ached. He was still wet from having fallen in the fountain, and his teeth chattered. He held the extra cloak more tightly around himself.

They stopped by a roadside shrine to eat some of the cheese. He noticed that the head of the figure in the shrine, a local spirit, had been snapped off. Small birds had once nested behind the little statue, but the nest was long abandoned and beginning to fall apart. There was an egg in it, which for an instant he hoped would be edible. But it felt like an empty shell, and when he broke it there was nothing inside but a little dust. He was too tired to care if this were an omen, a portent, or whatever.

But tired or not, they continued on in the hours of fading daylight. He was sure now that the days were getting continuously shorter overall, but one after another, there was no regular pattern to them. Some seemed to last only an hour, others three or four hours. Something was wrong with the motion of the Earth.

Both of them gasped aloud one night when the moon attempted to rise in that part of the sky which was not wholly covered over. It was a wonder enough that the moon was rising in the west, but a welcome thing, even if it was only a faint smudge behind the clouds.

They took advantage of the faint light and covered more distance.

"I wonder if it's a trick of our eyes," he said.

"No, it's there. I think it's a good sign."

"I don't know. Let's watch."

And watch they did, walking toward the veiled moon, until a short while later it set in the same direction it had risen.

They came to a hollow in the ground and took shelter there. They lay together, huddled beneath their blankets and spoke of what they'd seen in occasional sentences with long pauses in between, their words like bubbles rising slowly to the surface of a stagnant pool.

"What was it doing rising in the west?" he said.

"Maybe it couldn't get up anywhere else."

"It failed anyway."

She yawned and went to sleep. He remained awake for a half an hour or so, remembering cosmologies he'd seen in musty old books. What if the world had fallen on its side? What if it rolled away from the sun entirely, into the eternal cold and darkness?

The next morning when they came to a stream to drink, they had to break the ice on its surface first.

The moon made no further attempt to show itself.

They came to other towns, all deserted, but in various ways. In one every shutter and door was firmly barred. Thinking someone huddled within the buildings, they pounded on doors and shouted. Their voices echoed back in answer. In another every roof had been removed and dropped into the streets, as if some giant had been rummaging through jars and throwing the lids every which way. The place was almost impassible with wreckage. But no tower had fallen. No house had been smashed. In the midde of a square, a statue of a hero stood undamamged. The giant's touch had been selective.

A village behind a stockade of logs was simply gone. The gate to the stockade was still locked from within. Amaedig boosted Ginna up and he climbed the wall high enough to see over. There were only bare patches where houses had once been, swept clean, without any rubble.

They found it more comfortable to sleep in the open, away from the towns.

Once there was a weasel to eat. Ginna bludgeoned the cold, sluggish creature to death with a stick. They ate it raw.

Now nearly delirious from hunger and weariness, having lost all count of how long they had been journeying, they came to the forest country. The land flattened out quickly, which was a relief, but the open stretches of dead grass or bare soil were more and more frequently interrupted by clusters of the largest trees Ginna or Amaedig had ever seen. When the sky had its faint streak of light in it, they looked like an endless array of black towers, vaster than anything Ginna had seen in the dead places beyond Ai Hanlo. The tops could not be seen at any time. Branches closed overhead like a roof, enclosing the gloom in a new kind of smothering closeness. By the time clearings were few and far between, and the underbrush had given way to the more open forest floor, it seemed they were indoors again, in some endless vault of wooden pillars. Each opening between two trunks was the mouth of a tunnel, part of an entangling maze. Shadows never lessened. Even during the brief days it was often impossible to see more than a faint and faraway suggestion of grey. Ginna though of that grey sky as the last remnant of some body otherwise wholly covered with a cancer. It was dying. The world was dying. Merely to see, when the trunks were a solid wall and he and Amaedig could not pass, he made glowing balls with his hand. When he could, when the branches were not tripping him and scraping at his face, he juggled the balls, but eventually he would miss and they would drop to the ground and burst, or drift up and vanish like the last fireflies expiring in a world grown hostile and strange. He was not cheered by the sight of them. When he could, he preferred to make a single sphere, cage it between his fingers, and use this as a lantern. Amaedig followed him, holding onto his cloak.

Always he would stumble and crush the ball, or his fingers would become numb with cold and it would slip away and go out.

He would always make another one. When the distant grey was gone or hidden behind the trees, when actual night came, he had to have light to keep away the sheer terror of the dark until they managed to sleep somehow—always back to back for warmth, both of them wrapped in the same blankets.

Once he slept fitfully and had a dream. His soul did not leave his body and he did not drift over the landscape, he merely saw with eyes more sensitive than any other creature born in the light. At first there were nothing more than vague shapes against the deeper murk, but then a clearing appeared, ringed all around with trees like the legs of an army of titans. Walls and towers were rising out of the open ground, growing like crystals forming impossibly fast. The walls were vaguely shiny, like hard coal, and they seemed to reflect where there was none to reflect. The outlines were clear. The architecture was wholly alien. What were the inverted stairs for, slowly revolving around the tilted column? Stranger was the solid pyramid, without any means of entry, which seemed to shift and flicker as he looked on it. It was a pyramid, and then it *wasn't*. Some walls were almost horizontal. There were bubbles of black stone rising out of the ground. As the vision became clearer he could see the folk of this place scurrying along the thick, heavy bridges that stretched between the walls. They were hunched over. They did not walk like human beings. Every so often one leapt off one of the buildings and flew.

And then he understood. This was a city of the new world, as Ai Hanlo had been of the old, and the inhabitants were of the darkness, spawned like flies out of a puddle. They were claiming their Earth and taming it in their fashion. Kaemen had created all this. To them he must be a god. To them Ginna was an alien, perhaps frightening. He could not live among them in their world. It would be death. Their world was to come. His would pass away. It was the future he beheld. There had always been prophets, he knew, and he wondered if he were one of them. At times like this the past, present, and future seemed to run together like pigments being mixed. He understood.

Halfway between dream and waking he reasoned thus, and as he drew more out of the dream, the scene faded. When he asked himself, "How am I asking myself anything when I am dreaming?" he was fully awake at once.

The forest was moving around him. A wind blew between the trees with ever increasing fierceness. Branches snapped and crashed down. Leaves struck his face. There seemed to be other sounds besides the wind: chitterings, pattering footsteps, coughings and chatter, as if the very darkness itself had come to life.

He slipped an arm around Amaedig and held her close. She muttered something in a dream of her own, but did not wake. He felt safer holding her, the way a drowning man clings to a log. Indeed they were drowning, scraps and flotsam of the old world sinking in the chaos of the new.

The wind tore at his hair and clothing. A bough fell on him hard enough to make him grunt, but Amaedig slept on. He let her sleep. He envied sleep. He could not sleep now himself, and if he did, what might his dreaming eye see?

Hours seemed to pass. He had never known anything so cold as that wind. It rose into a raging tempest, and all he could do was huddle against its fury.

He was afraid that Amaedig wasn't sleeping, but dead, that she had frozen. She felt cold. He shook her awake, and she sat up and looked around. Her hair whipped around in her face. She huddled with him.

Then the wind brought a trilling, cackling sound, which drew closer and closer, changed direction, and approached again. There were heavy footsteps, the sounds of trees crashing and uprooted, but the thing did not seem wholly defined by direction and place. There was a crash of thunder and something massive, immensely long and heavy, passed overhead, making the night even darker as it cast shadow upon the shadows. Trees bent and snapped. Branches rained down.

He imagined that it was the very spirit of Death passing over, coming at last to remove the remnants of mankind from the world.

He did not imagine that, after it passed, it turned around, very obviously in one place and direction now, and started back.

Amaedig took him by the hand and dragged him through the trees. He groped, allowing himself to be led. He didn't know where they were going and was sure she didn't know either. They went away from the sound, but the thundering was everywhere, and the wind tore at them like an army of ghosts. The trunks were almost a solid barrier, with only occasional and hidden openings. Once through it it was like diving into a raging, bottomless sea.

The huge thing passed overhead again, flapping on enormous wings. They froze against a tree. All the forest trembled.

Ginna found himself detached from the midnight forest, the danger, the flight, and somewhere in the back of his mind part of his consciousness paused to marvel at how much he could hear when sight was denied him. He sensed spirits and powers all around him, the forest closing in like an animate thing, a smothering avalance of rough bark and wood and leaves.

Somehow he perceived, by the sound of the wind passing through the dead leaves, that those leaves and their branches rose up tier upon tier until they formed a world of their own, divorced from earth and sky. He heard the laughter of the thing that followed him coming from every direction. Flight was useless. There was no place to run to when the foe was something not confined to one place. But his instincts and his legs and Amaedig paid no heed to reason. He ran. Amaedig ran.

Suddenly the wind told him that the trees were on one side of him and not on another. Then the ground began to drop and the wind came with less force. The forest had broken. They were running down an embankment until it became too steep, then sliding among mud and stones. Into a valley. A new sound came: water rushing. A river bank. A new terror came with it, the realization that they could not cross the river and would be trapped on its shore.

But then there was a light up ahead and both of them let out wordless cries of relief and astonishment. Ginna saw it as something totally impossible, a miracle, a mirage.

By the edge of the river a large campfire was burning and, even more impossibly, there were clear outlines of many men around it.

"Hey!"

"Hello!"

Instantly there was commotion in the camp. Forms scurried. Metal clanked. When they were close enough to see, they held their arms up to their faces lest they be blinded by the firelight. They could make out twenty men or more standing before them with swords drawn and spears pointed. Many bore shields of polished metal which gleamed in the reflected light.

"Wait!" cried Amaedig. "We're friends."

A massive figure pushed through the throng and stood between the newcomers and the fire. He was a head taller than the rest and wore armor which glittered golden from the fire at his back. His beard was long and white and draped over him like a cloak. They couldn't see his face.

"What are ye that would come out of the darkness?" he barked in a strange accent.

"Two...people. A girl and a boy."

"Or be ye two evil shapes, here to lure us to doom?"

"No, we don't want to lure you anywhere."

"Really," said Ginna. "We don't."

The spears still pointed. None of the shields were lowered.

Behind them, up the bank in the forest, the thunderous passage continued, echoing trilling laughter in its wake. The thing seemed to move up and down the river, passing them, moving on, returning.

"That spirit has haunted us these many nights," said the leader. "Whenever we put ashore it is there, and it calls out to us when we are on the river."

"Then we're safe from it with you?" asked Ginna.

"There's none that be safe from it anywhere, but it will not take us all at once. That is not its way. But it is cunning. What proof have ye that ye be not shapes created and sent by it? We have not seen a true human on these shores for a long time now."

Some of the warriors began a low, droning chant, either a prayer or an exorcism. Ginna looked at the unmoving leader, then at the fire. The fire seemed a wonderful thing. More than anything else he wanted to sit by it. He thought of all the comforting fires he'd known on the road with the caravan and Gutharad by his side, or even in Ai Hanlo.

Tears ran down his cheeks from the hopelessness and depair of all the things he had lost, from being so close to that fire and still so far away.

"Please...you must not send us away...We've come so far and we've been afraid for so long. We'll die if we have to go. We'll do anything you want us to...."

"Come forward, both of you, and come slowly."

Carefully they approached the cluster of men, looking apprehensively at weapons, then at faces, then at the leader.

When they were close enough, that ancient warrior reached out and grasped each of them by the shoulder, squeezing hard. Then he touched their faces lightly. Ginna flinched as the hard, cold hand brushed his cheek. A ring on one of the fingers hit him in the eye.

"Where have you come from?"

"A long way," said Amaedig. "From Ai Hanlo. In Randel-cainé."

"That is a long way indeed."

The men stopped their chanting.

Ginna and Amaedig were led to the fire and allowed to sit. Cautiously they got down, but as soon as he touched the ground, Ginna lost all sense of care, of fear, of everything. Every muscle in his body went slack. His breath came long and deep. He fainted into sleep, crumpling over sideways, his head in Amaedig's lap.

Chapter 9
And Fires Burn
on the Sea

Ginna awoke to a song and the sound of rushing water. They were on the river. He was lying beneath a blanket on a gently swaying wooden deck. Torches were set around him.

He sat up and saw that he was at the front of a long, open vessel with a single mast. The sail hung limply. The wind was gone. Below him, all the company sat at the oars, save for their captain, who stood at the opposite end, holding the tiller. All sang in low voices interrupted with grunts, and the oars moved in time.

"Oh we don't know fear and we don't know greed,
But we're there to die when there is a need.
First a stroke and then a stroke
We are the good companions!"

There were many other verses, mostly about fighting and high ideals, and some he did not understand. After a while he stopped listening. He let himself lie back on the deck. He felt the river flowing beneath him, and the ship leapt forward with every stroke of the oars. He looked at the torches set atop the ship's mast and along its sides. He tried to pretend they were stars. He felt himself dropping off to sleep again.

But then it occurred to him that he didn't know where Amaedig was. He drew the blanket off him, then paused as he noticed that the arms which had been slashed by her knife was now neatly bandaged. There was no pain and the wound felt greasy from a salve put on it.

Amaedig was lying a little ways off. She was awake, and was sitting against the railing, watching the rowers. He crawled over and sat beside her. They watched wordlessly for a while. The song went on. The water rushed past. Somewhere a monster of the river coughed.

"Have you noticed something?" she said at last.

"What?"

"They're all old men. Every one of them."

Indeed, now that he looked, he saw that all of them had long white or grey beards. Like their leader, they wore their hair down over their shoulders, and this too was white or silver.

"Who are they?"

"No idea. I was hardly more awake than you when they carried us aboard."

"How long ago was that?" he said.

"I don't know. Since dawn, I guess."

The sky was pitch black above.

"Dawn?"

"Yes, look." She pointed ahead and to the right—the direction the sailors would call the starboard bow—at a thin line of grey sky. It was the faintest dawn he had ever seen. Suddenly it came to him that it would be the last. The only lights left now in the whole universe, it seemed, were the ship's own.

"I heard of a witch once," he said, "who wanted to kill a man. She conjured his image in a bowl of water, which she kept covered with a lid. Every night she would remove the lid and glare at the image with all her hate. The image glowed with the light of the man's soul, but gradually it diminished, and when the light was gone entirely, he died."

"And?"

"What if the world is like that, and when the daylight is gone—?

"Let's not talk about it. There's nothing we can do now."

They slept after a while. Ginna dreamt that he was a small child again, running barefoot with Amaedig through some vast, dark, damp tunnel, looking for a way out. He was not frightened. They were playing. Their shouts and laughter echoed in the fathomless distances. It was a pleasant dream.

He awoke to silence. The crew had drawn in their oars, and the ship drifted with the current.

"It is well that ye be waked. I watched ye sleep, and know ye to be of mortal flesh."

He looked up, started. The leader was standing over him,

smiling, his thumbs hooked in his belt. He wore a long sword in a jeweled scabbard, which sparkled by torchlight.

Stiffly Ginna got to his feet. He realized his bladder was full.

"Where do you—?"

"Where do you what?"

"Ah... ah...." He gestured vaguely. The man understood.

"Perform a euphemism? Over the side, ye fool! Then join us down below."

He and Amaedig climbed down to the lower deck, where all the men sat among the benches, eating from bowls. A brick stove heated a pot of stew.

They were given food and drink and a place to sit. Ginna looked from side to side uneasily, wondering what was expected of him, but everyone went on as if he were not there. It was the first properly cooked food he had eaten since—when? He'd lost track of time since they left the caravan. It was all a jumbled nightmare.

When the meal was over, the leader clapped his hands once, and suddenly they were surrounded by solemn, hoary faces. Ginna felt sad looking at them. He was not afraid. They reminded him, every one, of a pair of kindly old men he had known and forever lost, Tharanodeth the Guardian and Hadel of Nagé.

The leader sat down before him. "I am called Arshad," he said.

"We are...Ginna and Amaedig."

"Welcome among us, Ginna and Amaedig, for it was revealed to me in a dream that something would happen while we camped at a certain spot along the river. So we did, and ye came. For some purpose, it is certain."

"Yes, to get away from what was chasing us," said Amaedig.

"No, it was something more, perhaps not known even to yourselves. I dreamed it."

"I have had many dreams," said Ginna.

"So do all of us, but were the dreams deep or shallow? Anyone may dream of some little thing, or learn that his sheep are menaced by wolves because he sees it in a dream, but those are petty things. Few have deep dreams of vast import."

"Well I don't know if I do or not," said Ginna, and he went on to relate some of his dreams. Before he scarcely knew what he was doing, one thing led to another and had to be explained by yet another, and he was telling them the story of his life, from the time he had first visited Tharanodeth to those events of the past few days. He omitted, however, any hint of magic in himself, what Hadel had said, or even the fact that he could make light with his hands. But he told of what he had seen at Kaemen's banquet, how his soul had travelled far in the night to confront The Guardian, and what had become of the caravan. He explained how he and Amaedig had chanced upon Arshad and his company by the water's edge. All listened in polite silence. When he was done, Amaedig was the first to speak.

"Now wait—meaning no discourtesy to you, generous sirs, but we have told you much of ourselves, and still we know nothing of you—"

"Fairly spoken," said Arashad. Turning to Ginna, he said, "Young lad, your friend is right. Put not all your gold on one side of the scale before the other has shown any of his."

"But you asked—"

"No matter. Listen, both of ye. We are the Tashadim, a brotherhood formed when all of us were as young as ye are. We heard the call of the great warrior-prophet, Tashad, who had a deep vision, telling him that one day the world would be filled with darkness, and his followers would seek an island of light, the final refuge, and there fall one by one, fighting bravely to the last. All of us who believed devoted our lives to his teaching, waiting for the day. Perhaps ye wonder why we are all so old."

"Yes, I——"

"It is because ours is a hard creed, and not a very attractive one. When the end came, though, we were prepared, while all others were beset as were ye. A few survivors must surely wander about, but in all our long voyage we have met no others."

"Then, has the world ended?"

"Certainly it has changed, never to be again what it once was. Our past is lost forever."

"What became of Tashad?"

"He went to seek the isle ahead of us. He spoke his prophecies as he died, and all of us saw his spirit rise up from his body clad in armor bright as the sunrise, with a golden spear in his hand and a silver shield on his arm. First he rose slowly, then hovered above us. It was a sacred mystery, even then. We fell to the ground, covering our eyes, but he spoke to us, saying, 'Arise and take up my sword and my shield.' When we uncovered our eyes, he was gone."

There was silence for a little while. Ginna could think of nothing to say. The water was silent. They were far out from shore, in the middle of the broad river. Only the ship seemed real, floating in the darkness like a tiny world in the vastness of space.

"And now," said Arshad, turning again to Ginna, "a tale I shall tell to ye. There was a man who built a boat. He put all the planks in place and caulked all the seams, except one. So the water rushed in through that seam, sank the boat, and he drowned."

Again Ginna didn't know what to say.

"That's not much of a story...is it?" he managed.

"No, it is not. The one ye tell is much better, for ye are a seer of deep visions. I know this. But I know also that something is left out of your telling. Ye have not told all."

Arshad gazed at Ginna, patiently but intently. The boy felt himself melting before those eyes. He could not hide anything. This man read his mind like an open book.

Trembling, he brought his hands together and parted them. A ball of light rose, then fell. He caught it with an outstretched hand, bounced it up again, and let it fall onto the deck, where it winked out.

With a speed that brought a startled yelp from him, Arshad bent forward and grabbed both of Ginna's hands, turning them over again and again, scrutinizing them. He pushed the boy's sleeves up to the elbows. Then, just as suddenly, he let go and stood up.

"This is surely a great sign. But I do not understand it fully. I must meditate on it."

He retired to a small cabin at the rear of the vessel, beneath the deck on which Ginna and Amaedig had awakened. The others removed the rope loop which had held the tiller in place, and took the tiller in hand. The two passengers found themselves ignored between two rows of chanting oarsmen. After a while they went up by the helmsman.

"What did Arshad mean when he said it was a great sign?" Ginna asked him.

The helmsman spoke the language of the Guardians, but with an accent so heavy he could scarcely be understood.

"He...be to mean...very holy man not know what mean... but discover out."

They couldn't get any more out of him. So they sat at the edge of the deck, watching the rowers working and the river gliding by. There were two more breaks for meals. Arshad did not reappear for either of them. Then, as most of the men lay down to sleep, the leader came to the door of his cabin, at the bottom of a short stairway, his chest at deck level. All attention was on him, but he said nothing, looked about briefly, and went back into his cabin.

* * *

The faint band of grey on the horizon faded once more, and the sky was wholly black. After supper, all but the helmsman and a lookout at the bow slept, and the vessel was carried by the current. When they woke, the darkness was unchanged. The crew broke fast, then rowed.

When "day" finally came, Ginna and Amaedig sat on the foredeck, chatting with the lookout there. All three peered ahead into the gloom.

"You're lucky you came to the river where you did," the man said. "Here cliffs drop right down the the water's edge. There's no place to land."

The man's name was Yanotas. He was from Laedom, a country of many marvels. Gradually he warmed up to his listeners, and with little prompting told of his homeland.

He was in the middle of a spirited description of a temple built entirely of little golden bells, all of which rang different notes when the wind blew, when suddenly the water in front of the ship began to heave up and churn into white foam.

A wave crashed over the bow, knocking Yanotas off his feet. Ginna felt himself being swept along the slippery deck, but caught hold of the railing and clung there. He looked back to see Amaedig fall off the edge, down among the rowers.

There was much shouting as men were tumbled from their benches by the sudden force of their oars. The ship rocked and began to veer from its course, turning one side to the water which was now bubbling and splashing as if displaced by a mountain rising swiftly beneath it.

Ginna thought of whales. He had never seen one. He wondered what a thousand would be like, breaching all at once.

The sail twisted askew, the crossbar swinging around against the mast. Yanotas was crawling across the precariously swaying deck. The crew was in confusion as oars snapped off in their holes. Some men were down, flattened as another wave caught the oars and broke over the vessel.

Arshad emerged from his cabin, knee-deep in water, bedraggled, but shouting orders. Men raced to obey. Some scurried up the mast to furl the sail. One lost his grip and fell into the river, his scream lost in the thundering of the water. Others wrestled with the tiller. The remaining oars were drawn in.

All this, Ginna knew, had taken place in a matter of seconds. But no more time was needed: with Arshad to lead them, the men to begin to set the vessel right. When the next wave came, the prow sliced through it. The lookout, who had gained the railing next to Ginna, let out a cry. The boy looked forward and he too shouted in astonishment.

He was used to peering into darkness by now. He could see

clearly enough that there *was* a mountain rising out of the water, impossibly huge against the faint glow of the western sky. There was a broad, curved shape large enough to be an island, and then this was entirely above the surface, supported by a thinner but still massive column. He could not fully grasp its size. He thought this moving thing might be as large as Ai Hanlo Mountain, as absurd as his reason told him that was.

Still it rose. *A head on a neck.* Something broke the surface with yet another thunderous wave, setting the ship reeling. The new object rose and fell, its dim form suggesting a flipper longer than the vessel by a good deal.

Arshad bellowed another order. Swords whipped out of scabbards. Lanterns and torches were lighted as best they could be. A man scrambled up from below with a large metal lantern. This was set up on the ship's prow. Torches were set within; when the door of the lantern was opened, the light reflected off its three mirrored sides, and a steady beacon was produced. Now they could see what threatened them. The company stood ready to face the monster.

Monster it was. It was definitely alive. The whole river erupted from unseen bank to unseen bank as the creature's wings emerged. The sky was blotted out as they spread. Their glistening expanse reflected the torch and lantern light. The full length and breadth of them were too great for Ginna to imagine, as was the size of the body, thicker than he could see, rising endlessly up into the sky like an avalance of flesh.

The thing bent around and down. An enormous face was visible for a brief moment, with a gaping mouth wide enough to engulf cities, and round, white patches where the eyes should have been.

The creature was blind, he realized. It was totally oblivious to their torches, their lanterns, their brave sword-waving. Some of the men threw spears at it in their excitement, without visible effect. The neck straightened. The head shot upward out of sight; the body rose like the sheer side of a cliff. Except when a flipper went by (they did not seem to be in pairs) it was hard to tell that the thing was moving. There was another blast of turbulence as a second set of wings, fully as immense as the first, burst forth and unfolded above the surface.

Ginna heard the leader's voice but couldn't make out the words. He was huddled in a waterfall. The railing strained. He felt his grip on it going. He held on with all his strength, but still he was slipping.

Then, suddenly as it had begun, the thundering of the

creature's passage diminished. The waves were less fierce. He looked ahead and saw the tail of the thing tapering down from the sky like a cyclone. Then it was no longer touching the water. Swiftly it rose out of sight. There was a single clap of thunder from above, and all was still.

The river grew calm almost at once. The ship drifted. Only a few of the torches still sputtered. The lantern had been swamped. The torches were relighted or replaced with dry ones.

Amaedig climbed up to where he still clung to the railing. She was soaked and shaken, but the terror had passed, leaving her exhausted and shivering with cold. She sat by him for a while, saying nothing. He was silent too as the sailors went about their tasks, putting the ship in order.

"It must have been a mile long," he said at last. "Longer. I think it was one of those creatures of the new world. We mean nothing to it. Do you suppose that sometime, when the change is completed, creatures like that will look on the remains of what we knew and wonder, as we did, at the ruins? Tharanodeth and me, I mean. What will they think?"

"I don't know...."

"I think they'll remember light, but only as an abstraction. It will be utterly foreign to them."

"I suppose so."

On the lower deck, the men stopped their work. Arshad led a kind of a service. His followers chanted, pointing their swords at the sky.

* * *

The oarsmen were rowing again, singing a low, melancholy song about the hopeless defense of the last tower of the last fortress. "With a sword in my hand and light in my heart till the end," was the refrain. The lookout joined in, as did the other man now stationed on the foredeck to direct the lantern. Even Ginna and Amaedig sang the refrains. Arshad had returned to his cabin. The ship crept cautiously downriver.

They passed two mountains which came to the water's edge. The beacon was played over the cliff faces on either side, revealing immense carvings, bulky figures in armor wearing crowns, a naked superman wrestling a dragon, a school of fishes swirling around a lady with outstretched hands. Beyond the carvings were stone buildings hewn out of the solid rock. Overhead a natural bridge had been shaped to resemble a man-made one. A squat tower stood in the middle of the span. A stone bird was frozen in flight at its top. A gust of wind blew and the bird let out a long, low wail.

No one knew what place this was. Ginna asked Yanotaas if it were all right to call Arshad and ask him, but his sole response was a slightly shocked, "No."

So they watched in wonder and silence as the river carried them under the bridge, past the walls and houses and towers which grew out of the mountainside like toadstools in the morning. When these things had passed away behind, and two wide plains stretched away on either side to meet the darkness, the singing resumed. The song was very simple, and after a time Ginna was allowed to lead. After each of his lines came a response and oar strokes in time with it.

Night came on. The western sky went black. The song changed into something braver, to defend the company against the spirit of darkness.

All paused for an evening meal of biscuits and fresh fish. For all the world had changed, the river was still full of fish. A man was catching them with a hook one after another. Ginna noticed there was no bait on the hook, but did not ask how it worked. It occurred to him that the Tashadim had been very kind to him and to Amaedig, but still they were a mysterious order preoccupied with oats and secrets, and it might abuse hospitality to inquire too far.

As they sat eating a man came to Ginna, touched him on the shoulder, and said, "The master will see you now." He rose at once, and Amaedig rose also, but the man shook his head and bade her be seated, then sat down beside her and joined in the meal. Alone, Ginna went to the cabin of Arshad.

He descended the few steps before the leader's door, hesitated, then knocked lightly. There was no reply, but the door swung inward a crack. He pushed it open and entered, closing it again behind him.

The walls of the narrow cabin were hung with intricate tapestries of faded colors, mostly angular, orange figures on blue backgrounds, a style Ginna had never seen in Ai Hanlo. A single lamp hung from the ceiling on a chain. Shadows shifted with the movement of the river. Everywhere wood was creaking, more so than one heard on deck. There were trunks, leather cases of scrolls, and books lying about. A glittering sword with an immensely wide, curved blade hung on the opposite wall.

Beneath the sword, seated on the bare wood, was the old man, his legs crossed, his back upright. He gazed directly at the youth, still as a statue, saying nothing. He wore a scarlet robe with the hood pulled up.

Ginna stood before him, expecting a greeting or something.

But the man made no response to his presence. He felt awkward and vaguely afraid that he might have transgressed some unknown law of courtesy. He wanted Amaedig at his side. She always seemed to be able to get him out of these situations.

"Nay, your companion cannot be with ye this time," said Arshad in a low monotone. "Your own man ye must become in time, and care for yourself."

Ginna gaped.

"You know what I was thinking!"

Arshad smiled and relaxed.

"There be no magic involved. As I came down the long path into the cabin, I saw ye there, and the rest was plainly revealed. I have watched ye two. She is good for ye, and I think that is why it has come to pass that she is with ye. She knows more of the world than ye and can guard ye from human dangers, while ye are more of the spiritual world and know more of other things. The two of ye are in balance."

"I don't know what you mean."

The Master pointed to a spot on the floor before him.

"Sit there, but first blow out the lantern, that I may behold ye by your own light."

Ginna obeyed, folding his hands together and making a ball of light. He imprisoned it in a cage of fingers.

"Suppose you were to take two of them and press them together? What would happen?"

"When I was little I used to play games with them, and I tried it. They burst."

"Then the first lesson for ye will be to prevent them from bursting."

"Master—they call you that; is it right for me to?—you said you were returning to the cabin, as if you had been someplace else. But I saw you sitting here."

"That will be your second lesson. But let us get on with your first. The creature of the river was surely a sign that there is little time left. For your third lesson, if we ever we journey that far, I shall explain to ye why all seeming coincidences are illusion, linked invisibly by webs of meaning. Consider: if things were random, no man could read the signs or interpret omens. The world would be very confused."

They sat for hours. Ginna juggled balls of light, sending flickering shadows whirling across the floor, walls, and ceiling. Then he remained still, with one ball between his fingers, and Arshad taught him to truly see for the first time. It was as if he had been born blind, and now his eyes were opened. He saw the crack between two pieces of planking as a vast chasm, in which a whole tiny world was contained. A knot in the wood was the center of a whirling storm. And he heard for the first time. The creaking of the ship became a crescendo of voices speaking words he couldn't quite make out.

Then, somewhere in the course of events, of words, of images, thoughts, sounds and shadows, all flowing slowly past him like the river, he was half aware of making a ball of light, letting it rise, making another, then catching the first. He held both of them. He stared at them. He saw them more clearly than he ever had before, as Hadel of Nagé had described them, as worlds, with tiny ghosts of seas and continents whirling around. He concentrated on them, willing them not to burst, to become one, and slowly pressed them together. They merged into a perfect sphere, twice as large as either had been.

But the lesson was not over. There was no applause for his feat. Arshad commanded him and guided him further, teaching him a formula to be chanted over and over until it became a sub-verbal, subconscious rhythm, something which shut out the rest of existence, leaving the mind unfettered for a single task.

He felt power building up in his body. He wanted to stand up, to stretch, to seize the mast of the ship and break it over his knee, all in celebration of his strength.

This feeling passed. After a time he was not aware of his body at all, except for the working of his hands. He made another ball of light, and another, and another. Somehow the first one did not drop to the floor and pop out of existence. It hung in the air, and he was above to add new ones one by one, until he stretched his arms wide and still could not encompass the glowing, spinning globe. The cabin was filled with its light. His eyes were dazzled; he had not seen such brightness since before everything had happened, since last he had seen a true sunrise in a blue sky. The thought came to him that he was building a new sun to be released from the ship, to drift into the air and dispell the darkness.

That was not the old man's intent. He did a most remarkable thing. He reached through the bubble and still it did not vanish. He stood inside it, reached out, took Ginna by the wrist, and drew him in.

They were no longer in the cabin on the ship. Ginna looked up into a hazy sky. Shadows pressed close all around, but the world was suffused with gentle light. They stood on a polished stone floor at the foot of a flight of marble stairs. Each step was easily as high as the boy's shoulders. The staircase had been built for giants.

"Where are we?"

"Wonder! I have never had a student so adept, so powerful. Ye stand where many men struggle all their lives to reach and never arrive."

"But what place?"

"In the realm of the Powers. Ye have climbed a little way."

"Can I go further? It should be easy now."

"No, it will take time."

"But—" And before Arshad could say anything, the boy was running toward the bottom step. As soon as he had moved at all, and was out of the space enclosed by the bubble of light, the whole scene winked out.

They were back in the cabin, Arshad standing, Ginna still running. At once he fell over a trunk and crashed against the side of the ship in a painful sprawl. He grabbed a shelf to steady himself, but it came loose, showering papers.

"Let that be another lesson for ye this day," said the teacher sternly. "Obey always. Do not act rashly. Be glad ye didn't break a leg for your antics. Now go. We have had enough for now."

On deck he found Amaedig sitting among the sailors, helping to mend a broken oar by fixing bands of metal around it. It was well past dawn. No one was rowing. The ship glided slowly on the current. The sail was filled with wind. Most of the sailors sat in groups, talking, working at little chores, or finishing up the remains of a meal. Some were doing something he did not understand, huddled together on a silken rug. They might have been praying.

"Hello," he said, and his words were like bubbles rising slowly from the bottom of the river. He had not realized how tired he was. The world consisted of the chilly air on his face and dimly moving shapes. There was a sharp smell of tar.

He slept.

* * *

When he awoke, the sky was dark. The oarsmen were rowing vigorously in silence. Every few strokes one of them would glance over his shoulder. The helmsman peered intensely into the gloom ahead. At the bow, the shaft of light from the lantern was like a blind man's cane, groping in the endless night.

Ginna sat up groggily and leaned against the mast. It occurred to him that the men were tense. They must be expecting something.

Torches snapped and sputtered. The oars creaked. Otherwise the world was quiet, the water still as oil.

He found Amaedig in the prow, sitting with Arshad. They were playing some kind of board game he had never seen before, with carven pegs fitted in holes to represent ships, castles, and so on. He squatted down beside them.

"So ye are with us again," Arshad said. "I was about to have ye wakened."

"Hello," said Amaedig.

"Hello.... Good morning, or evening...."

"It is evening," said Arshad. He concentrated on the board for a minute, then moved several pieces in a dark strip around the edges. To Amaedig he said, "Behold, and learn a lesson. Ye have taken precautions in the physical world, but in the spiritual world ye are unprepared. Thus I win the game."

"What game is it?" Ginna asked.

"Some day I shall teach ye. But not now." He put the pieces in a leather bag, folded the board, and stood up, holding both. "Come here, ye two."

They went as far forward as it was possible to go, till all three held onto the upright end of the long, curving board which formed the ship's keel. The lantern behind them cast their shadows huge upon the water. White foam churned just below their feet.

"We are on the ocean now. We have left the river behind. In this ocean, not far from the mouth of the river, is the place called the Island of Voices."

"Does it speak?" Ginna said.

"In a way it does. Here it was that men first learned that The Goddess was dead. Long and long ago a ship passed on a dark night, even as we pass, and the wind blew through the limitless caverns which honeycomb the island. The sounds joined together to form a voice which spoke three times, saying, 'She is dead.' The messsage was not understood for a generation, but in time the meaning was clear."

"Does it say anything more?"

"I know not. No voice has been reported, but sometimes ships came too close and are wrecked on its shores, and the ghosts of the mariners call out to other vessels as they pass."

"Oh."

In silence they watched until at last the bulk of the island loomed ahead of them, the texture of its darkness slightly different from the sea and the sky. The current drew them ever nearer. Now the helmsman and rowers went about their work in deadly earnest. Ginna felt a touch of fear as the cliffs towered above them, but as long as Arshad was confident, he was not afraid, and the old man looked on calmly. Amaedig's face was rigid. He could not know her thoughts.

The beam of the lantern revealed gaping caves all along the cliff face. There was no wind, nor any sound but the creakings and clatterings of the ship, and the faint washing of surf at the base of the wall of stone. The island did not speak. In time it slid by and they were alone on the sea again.

"Nothing," said Ginna.

"So it would seem," the old man replied. "The voices speak not. Perhaps it is too late in the history of the world for further revelations."

"Too late! Too late" came a coarse, croaking voice out of the darkness ahead.

Arshad was as astonished as anyone else. Suddenly the fear which had hovered above Ginna reached down and clutched his heart.

"Here! Here!"

The leader raised his hand. The oars rose in unison out of the water and paused. The ship glided. The lantern probed ahead.

"Here!"

Ginna, Amaedig, and Arshad looked straight down. There, clinging to the keel of the ship was a pale, naked man. Only his head and shoulders were visible. Waves broke over his back.

"What are you?" demanded Arshad, leaning over for a better look. At the same time he pushed Ginna and Amaedig away. They stood back.

"What I seem to be. Let me aboard, quick!"

"Foul apparition, ye are no natural thing, nor are ye what ye seem to be, nor shall I let ye up on board. By the name of Tashad I exorcise ye, by the strength of his arm, by the sharpness of his sword, by the—"

Like a whiplash the creature's arm reached out, impossibly far, impossibly fast, seized Arshad by the beard and dragged him over the bow. Ginna could not react. The deed came between heartbeats. But Amaedig screamed, and suddenly he was screaming too.

All around them, the ship was in pandemonium. Ginna staggered back, tripped over something soft and fleshy, and tumbled down onto the rowers. He saw what tripped him. It was like a naked man, pale and deathly white, but not a man, heavy and flat of body, with another set of arms where the legs belonged. Another one appeared, and another, and another, scuttling over the bow like huge, shell-less crabs. They reached out of the water and seized the oars. The sea was alive with them. Ginna had a brief glimpse of rolling waves of limbs and flesh coming at him out of the darkness. There was no sea at all, only millions of deformed bodies. They swarmed over the ship, up the mast and rigging like flames licking up a curtain. The Tashadim drew swords and slashed frantically, but the endless numbers readily replaced the slain.

Ginna kicked one monster in the face, wriggled free of another, and crawled to Amaedig's aid. She was clawing at the thing, forcing her fingers into its eyes, and dumbly it held on to her, insensitive to any hurt.

His hand found a heavy wooden peg in a notch by the railing. The sailors used them to secure ropes. Now he lurched to his feet and rushed forward, holding it like a club, just as the ship shook violently, the sail shredded, and flailing bodies fell onto the deck in a chaos of canvas, rope, and tackle.

He was on top of the creature which was crushing the girl. He beat it again and again with the peg. Something grabbed his ankles and he rolled over, kicking a soft stomach with both feet. Again he pounded on the bald, blubbery head of the thing until it split open. Still the arms held on like an iron vise. It was only when the whole skull was smashed away and there was little more than a pulpy tatter of skin left at the end of the neck that the creature let go. Blindly, it crawled down among its fellows.

The deck was cracking under him. There was a loud snap followed by a perpendicular tilt, and suddenly he was falling. He reached frantically for Amaedig and she for him, and tangled in one another's arms they struck the water. Instantly the cold shock and the silence beneath the surface seemed to convey him into another world. Something was slowly closing down over him, squeezing him out of the world he knew. Then he realized what it was, let go of Amaedig, and swam deeper, struggling to get free of the torn rigging which had almost caught him like a fishnet.

It was only when his lungs were nearly bursting that he turned upward. He broke into the air with a spout of foam, gasping for breath. Amaedig was beside him, splashing to stay afloat.

The sea rolled gently and was quiet. There were no voices, no sounds of the ship's timbers breaking. There was no trace of anything.

Both of them tried to tread water, but it was obvious that they could not last. They were land dwellers. Neither really knew how to swim. They were exhausting themselves minute by minute.

It seemed like a miracle when something solid nudged Ginna's back. He grabbed for it without fear of what it might be, and touched jagged wood. It was a broken piece of the ship's mast. He pulled Amaedig over, and each looped an arm over it.

His legs hung limply down into the water. The cold seeped into him. He tried to move his legs after a time to keep warm, but all feeling had gone out of them. He lost track of time. Slowly he rose and fell with the motion of the sea. His arm was going numb. He switched to the other, but there was hardly any improvement. He put both arms over the mast and tried to pull himself up onto it, but it began to roll and he fell back.

Without a sound, Amaedig lost her grip and disappeared under the surface.

"No!"

He reached down, caught her by the hair, and dragged her up again. Dumbly, coughing out sea water, she resumed her place. He felt a little better for the movement and effort, but quickly the cold came back. His teeth chattered. His ears and face hurt intensely, and then stopped hurting at all. They felt like heavy wax.

He paused to wonder. Tashad had foretold that his followers would die on the island of light at the end of the world, but they had died at sea. Was the ship with its torches the 'island?' Had the end come?

Prophecies and mysteries. The world was full of them. He didn't care. They drifted some more. Darkness seemed to soak into his eyes. His vision was going—

—briefly he had a terrifying inner glimpse of Kaemen, pale and fat, gripping the arm rests of his throne, seated in the great room beneath the golden dome, alone in the darkness, watching—

From far away, Amaedig's voice came to him.

"We'll make it...to the island. Listen for the surf."

The night was still.

"Hang on," she said again, an indefinite time later. "We must keep hanging onto...."

But even as she spoke, dark as it was and dim as his eyes were, he could tell she was losing her grip. With the last of his strength he worked his right arm under hers, so when her fingers finally lost all ability to grip, he had her. She floated with her face barely above the water, while he held onto the mast with his left arm.

When that arm gave out, they would die.

At the very last, after what seemed like many hours, when he found himself dropping into a final, soft, inviting sleep, he cried aloud.

"Do you hear me? This is the end. I have had enough. I am

ready to die now."

And his life moved before his eyes in quick procession, and it seemed mostly filled with horrors. Darkness. Flight. Screaming men and women burning upside down on stakes. Gutharad's corpse dropping from the sky. The heads in the fountain. The child's hand on the doorstep in the deserted village. The few fleeting, happy moments seemed unreal, half buried memories of mirages and fever dreams.

The mast was slipping away. He couldn't move his arm. The cold was in his lungs. He couldn't breathe.

And somehow Amaedig's face, floating on the sea like a film, spoke, "No.... You must keep trying. Do...something. Make a light...."

His mind worked like a frozen thing slowly thawing, dripping into dim awareness.

He remembered the steps in the realm of the Powers. Another place, beyond the world. He remembered the Zaborman magician who had folded space around himself like a cloak.

Amaedig seemed to understand. She was holding him as much as he was holding her. He let go of the mast. They floated on their backs. He held both hands out of the water, empty, coming together as stiff fingers touched. The hands moved without any conscious will on his part, touching, parting, touching again. A ball of light rose over the sea. There was another, and another. He caught one with his right hand, another with his left, missing a third. He pressed the two together. He was entering a trance. The world withdrew. The ocean, the darkness were no longer with him. The pale oval of Amaedig's face was a faint, abstract thing.

The ball of light grew. He held it in his outstretched hands. He wrapped the light around himself like a cloak.

There were other lights on the sea, columns standing in a circle around him, remaining absolutely still while he rose and fell with the waves. They resolved into beautiful figures, tall men and women in shining cloaks, with starry crowns on their heads. Some of them had four arms. Some had wide, delicate wings. They strode radiant and majestic across the heaving sea, closing in.

Ginna heard their soft voices whispering. He held the light close around him. He thought of Amaedig. He willed her to be at his side.

Hands like feathers were brushing over him, and he was drifting in the light.

Asleep, dreaming in the light.

127

Chapter 10
The Watchers

Kaemen, lord of the darkening world, sat in his throne room, as alone as he ever could be. The Black Lady was asleep. Always, always she stirred in his mind like a horde of rats, whispering, scratching, but now, after long labors and conjurings, after making the bones of The Goddess tremble, she lay dormant, perhaps exhausted in some manner he could never understand. She was still there. He could feel the weight of her within himself, but she was no more than a chill, a faint sense of another presence which he had known since earliest childhood.

Only rarely was she thus, and at those few times his thoughts and his sensations were all his own.

He sat contemplating his triumphs, and he was troubled. As she had promised, he was becoming the master of a whole new kind of world. The force which flowed through her like a raging torrent had swept him along also, and by joining with the inevitable, he would be one of the few creatures of human flesh to retain a place after the change was complete. Even she did not fully understand what was happening, save that like a tide, the new universe was submerging the old.

This much he knew. The knowledge had been with him for a long time. He feared no opposition now, but still he was uneasy.

The boy and the girl had disappeared. There was something

magical about the boy, but wholly opposite himself. The idiot Ginna could still make bubbles of light and throw them around, the same as he had when he was a drooling infant. But there was the potential for something more.

Why had they not killed him? He had brought the question up, taking counsel within himself, speaking with the Hag. *No*, she said. *If his role has any meaning, another will fill it after him. Watch and wait. Protect him if you have to. As he was my instrument once, he may become the instrument of someone else. Find out what he is so that he may be combatted.*

He had no choice but to obey. So he watched and waited.

While she slept, he entered into his trance, and beheld Ginna in Arshad's cabin. Sensing a great power there, he had been very careful to remain undetected, interfering not at all. It was like walking on a delicate pane of glass. He had succeeded, and moved with Ginna into that other world, but it was like wading upstream against floodwaters. The very nature of the place repelled him. The strain to remain where he was, let alone advance, became more than he could bear. Just before his consciousness was expelled, he heard the chief of the Tashadim proclaim the boy to be more adept than any other pupil he had ever had. There was a brief chaos of falling, and he awoke on his throne in a sweat, considering the implications of Ginna's coming to understand and use whatever powers he might possess.

"Great Lady, awake. Help me. Tell me what to do." He spoke to the empty air, to the shadows, and his voice echoed through the palace. It was useless to try to rouse her. Never had he any control over her, nor could he speak to her when she did not wish to hear.

And so he panicked. Ginna was learning. He was being taught with alarming speed, gaining strength. In a few days, a few hours even—

Therefore he, Kaemen, Guardian of the darkness-cloaked bones of the dead Goddess, took it upon himself to act, to prevent this disasterous state of affairs from continuing.

He had severed the teacher from the student. That the girl Amaedig had survived was sheerest coincidence. That Ginna still lived was not overwhelmingly important, as long as the process of learning was interrupted. *She* would have understood why he had done what he had done—

To reassure himself, he projected his spirit forth once more. Drifting above the midnight world, above the new cities rising without fear of the sun, he had crossed plains and mountains, followed a great river to its source, then another to its mouth. He soared over the sea, entranced by the vast movements of the waves and currents, listening to the wails and cries of the monsters beneath.

His spirit hovered near Ginna, without any attempt to enter his body, watching, gloating as the boy and his companion bobbed up and down in the frigid water.

The words of despair and final surrender had been especially sweet, but then something happened. There was light everywhere, columns standing on the waves, then figures. He knew them: Bright Powers, once in balance against the Dark, but now all but banished from the world. Yet here, alone, he was far weaker than their concentrated numbers. He felt himself repelled more firmly than he had been from the cabin of the ship. He reached out, like one drowning, for Ginna's mind, struggling to get inside, to see with his eyes, to understand what was going on, but he was yanked away and hurled far. There was a flash of all-encompassing light.

He found himself on the floor before his throne, lying in a puddle of vomit. A spasm in his trance had hurled him from the seat, off the dais, to the very spot where he had had the nurse flogged to death.

Everything was a portent. It probably meant something, but he had more pressing things on his mind. He reached out for a third time, seeking merely to find Ginna, not to touch him, and found him not.

Always, because their lives were somehow joined, he had been able to locate the one he laughingly called his "brother" and spy on him at any time. Not to find him was like waking up after a calm night's sleep to discover oneself deaf and blind.

Gone.

He rose and left the throne room. The corridors and chambers were utterly dark, thick with slithering spirits. No torch or lantern burned in all the city of Ai Hanlo. Those few inhabitants who had not fled and still survived huddled wretchedly in the gloom. Only he could find his way about. He was developing a new sense. He could see without light. The darkness had taken on a kind of texture, dense around solid objects, thin as smoke in mere shadows, forming images in his mind as he passed.

Thus he walked through many deserted hallways. He came to a room in which a certain distinguished lady of the court had spent her last days in madness, where now her skeleton lay twisted among her bedsheets. He entered, took a mirror from her dressing table, and held it before his face. He could perceive the mirror itself all the way down to the pearls around the rim and the ornate silver work on the back, but the glass remained a black oval, without returning the image of his face. Curious, he thought.

The new sense was not like seeing. It was more like projecting his soul across distances and feeling the echo. Like spying on Ginna.

Gone.

He smashed the mirror against the floor. He stirred the glass fragments with his foot, contemplated the skeleton briefly, and returned to the corridor.

He stood on a parapet where astrologers had once stood divining the courses of the stars. There were no stars above him now. Constantly the darkness spread out through the upper spaces, extinguishing them, filling the universe. There was no light on the horizon.

To anyone else, there would have been an endless void beyond the stone railing, but to him with his secret sense, the changing landscape was revealed in all its detail.

He gazed far. He watched mile-long serpents rolling in thunder beneath the sea. And yet Ginna was nowhere to be found.

He leaned over the edge, wondering what it would be like to fling himself into space, to float on the darkness, to let his body soar as his soul did when he projected it, but the darkness itself seemed to come alive and whisper hoarsely and form a barrier against him.

Her darkness, not his own.

He went back inside and descended many flights of stairs until he came to a room he had once known. He had not been there in years. It was dusty and full of books, most of which he had never opened. His nurses had locked him in there sometimes when he's misbehaved, telling him to do something useful with his time. Little did they know he liked the place. The mustiness and solitude appealed to him. It had not even the tiniest window, and in those days it had been lighted by a chandelier set with candles. Now it was not lighted at all. He felt the walls. They were firm and smooth as ever. It was truly one of the oldest rooms in all Ai Hanlo, hewn, as legends told, out of the living rock of the mountain. He had called it his "tomb" and imagined himself the child-king of some ancient dynasty of an earlier cycle of history, waiting for the time when he would rise up and make all the world tremble beneath his tread.

A game, nothing more. Now the world trembled and bowed to darkness, and it was not a game.

He opened one of the books. His dark sense could discern the writing. This was one of the romances he had found exciting and had genuinely enjoyed as a boy. He used to slip them behind his school books sometimes while his tutors droned away.

It seemed that his few moments of happiness and calm were in this room, this "tomb," and now they were buried there.

Certainly he knew no peace now.

He ascended the stairs, emerging into a series of courtyards, then a paved lane between the stables and the guard barracks. He came to a gate through which one could pass into the lower city.

Idly, he approached the gate.

But he could not pass. At once he perceived the darkness becoming almost solid, swirling into shapes: huge, pale, rubbery, fleshy things with hunched shoulders and inverted faces bulging out of their chests like the pustules of a disease. Topmost, flaccid lips dripped slime over the upturned nostrils and blind eyes. Membranous wings whirred and flapped. Hard, talon-like claws clicked open and closed.

Behind them crouched something sloping and rounded, but big as a house. Out of it rose a head with a curving beak easily twenty feet long, opened to reveal rows and rows of teeth. The head twitched from side to side, the beak slicing through the air like a sword.

He raised his hands. He called out words of power. He tried to banish them. They would not go. They would not let him pass.

At last he understood that he was a prisoner within the palace as much as he was within his own body, that it was not his power which mastered anything, that he would no more rule the world than the glove on a king's hand actually holds the scepter.

He wept. He had never been more alone, more utterly afraid. Ginna had disappeared. He, the slave, had acted on his own for the first and probably last time, and botched the task. It was his fault, his poor judgement, his hasty panic.

Within him, the Black Witch began to rouse herself.

Chapter 11
The Wood at the World's End

Dreaming in the light, drifting like the shadow of a cloud, Ginna somehow sensed himself going far, far, in all directions and none, infinitely beyond the ends of the earth and infinitesimally between the angles of space, inside inside, collapsing into a boundless void within himself.

The world was wrenched away. He fell out of darkness, into light, into a place of blue stretching out forever like a flawless daytime sky with no ground beneath it.

The gentle hands bore him into the light, into the sun, the blinding center of all. He saw flames against flames, patterns of brilliance, the outline of a rose as huge as the world, burning without being consumed, slowly turning, rising to swallow him up.

Dreaming in the light—

—his body was nothing but light—

—suddenly dropping into wakefulness out of a higher space, back into material substance, he found himself lying on solid ground. He pressed against it. For a moment it wavered, became like water, but quickly resumed its solidity.

Something dry rustled beneath him as he stirred. Dead leaves.

The air was pleasantly cool. A light breeze brought the scents of damp earth, moss, flowers, of a living world.

He opened his eyes and was blinded by the light, but slowly his vision adjusted. He saw the leaf-covered ground stretching away from him, brown and gently rolling. Above, tall columns resolved themselves into the trunks of trees. He was in a forest, the first he had ever seen in daylight.

Or was it daylight? As he watched, the leaves began to glow one by one, flooding the place with gentle green light. Among them whites and yellows sparkled. He sat up, turned, and saw that in one direction the very air was aglow, as if the sun rested on the forest floor a short distance off.

Around him were wisps and motes of light in the corners of his vision. He could almost see their shapes, but when he looked on them directly, they were gone. He knew them to be the Powers.

And the Powers whispered within his mind, *It is time. She is risen from the dead. Come.*

He got to his feet and followed them as if in a dream, and he was dimly aware of Amaedig at his side, as bedazzled as he. They held hands as they wallked, but spoke not, for no word may be uttered in so rare a dream.

The Powers rushed by them like zephyrs.

He took all this to be a final vision, some last refuge invented by his dying mind as he sank drowning into the sea, but he tried to put that thought aside and lose himself in it, indeed to find final refuge. But the details were too realistic. His clothing was still wet. He was cold, but the air was warming him. He smelled of salt water. Amaedig's hand in his was no illusion.

Thus they went slowly, quietly, as the Bright Powers gathered about them and their light dispelled the light of the trees, and the Powers took on definite shapes, becoming stately lords and ladies, winged, clad in gowns of scarlet and azure, bedecked with crowns so splendidly jewelled they became halos of light.

She is risen.

They came to a clearing and gathered in a circle. In the midst of them the earth opened up, revealing a pit filled with golden vapor, the surface of which lay so still, so seemingly solid it resembled nothing more than some kind of soft, beautiful cloth.

The Powers raised trumpets to their lips and blew a blast, but the sound was faint and faraway to Ginna, almost beyond the range of his hearing.

She is risen, came their litany. *Behold, out of death she comes into life, out of darkness into light.*

And the golden mist parted and vanished away, and standing on solid ground in the middle of the circle, was the figure of a girl child dressed all in flowing green. She held a sceptre of green jade carven in the likeness of a dragon holding a glowing yellow ball in its teeth.

One look to her face was enough to tell she was no child, this being of magic, ageless and untouched by time.

"Come forward," she said to Ginna and Amaedig. As she spoke the Powers lost their shapes and began to disperse, becoming a faint cloud-ring of light.

Ginna, leading Amaedig, stepped gingerly forward, afraid the ground would give way beneath his step.

"You have nothing to fear."

"Who...are you?"

"You possessed the power to come to me and you came, and still you do not know? Who else? I am Assiré Naydata Kamatharé."

He looked at her blankly. An expression of dismay came over her face, and for the first time she seemed human, even though she was an adult or more than an adult in a child's body. All the while Amaedig stared like one bewitched and helpless.

"You mean my name is unknown to you?" the stranger said.

He could find no words.

"You haven't lost your voice, have you?"

"Yes—I mean no...I mean, I am sorry, but—"

"You mean that you are confused," she laughed. "Well you might be, considering. I have watched your progress. My servants have told me much, also."

"I am Ginna. This is Amaedig."

"You are the one who is to come. You are the great counterweight. I am sure of it. Therefore you should know me. I am called the Mother of Light."

He hung his head. "Great Lady, I am sorry, but I do not know you."

"It would seem that your education is sadly deficient, or else men have forgotten much since last I walked on Earth."

"Are we—where are we? I mean, are we spirits now, in the place where the dead go? Is—is, Tharanodeth here? Can I see him?"

"So many questions at once—"

Amaedig let out a grunt as words formed in her throat, but fell back on one another in confusion. After a gasping pause, she was able to blurt out, "Are you *a goddess?*"

"My dear," said the diminutive lady, "there was only one goddess, *The* Goddess. I am not *The* Goddess. She was my daughter."

The words struck Ginna like a physical blow. He leapt back,

let out a startled shriek and tried to run—now he was sure this was some kind of dream, nightmare, that he was going mad—and stumbled and fell over Amaedig, who had fainted dead away.

"I see a lot has to be explained," said Assiré Naydata Kamatharé, the Mother of Light.

* * *

She came to him again in mid-day, when the light was generally diffused throughout the forest. She was no child then, but older, a young woman, even though mere hours had passed. Her voice deeper, her manner stately and grave.

"I suppose I am the lady you were sent to seek," she said. "Your teacher called me what he did to confuse your enemy, but indeed, by the practitioners of the hidden arts I am called the Lady of the Grove and the Fountain. We stand in the grove. Come, I'll show you the fountain."

She raised her hands. Birds made purely of colored light swarmed around her, chirping in a language she seemed to understand. She spoke a word, and they led the way like a weaving rainbow, singing a single, harmonious song. She followed, and Ginna came after, with Amaedig at his side, staying very close, staring wide-eyed.

They went a short way or a long way. Ginna could not tell in this place. Distances were confusing. They doubled back on each other. Space was distorted, like a reflection in a rippling pool. The woods around them were like a deep, green sea, and walking between the trees was as wondrous as somehow swimming to the very bottom of the ocean to view the wrecked argosies, coralled skeletons, all the treasures hidden from mankind. Branches curved above him like the roof of some vast temple. Behind every trunk he half expected to see some secret alcove containing an image, or perhaps some newly embodied spirit there waiting. It filled him with awe, but as long as the lady was with him he was not afraid.

It was comforting to hear the dry leaves rustling underfoot.

They came to a place where any of the trunks would have required fifty men hand-to-hand to encircle it. Above, leaves and branches were all but indistinguishable in the soft light. The birds left the lady and flew upward, and the forest glowed with their passing.

They looked upon a stone fountain in the center of which a carven fish was frozen in mid-leap, an hourglass held sideways in its mouth. Water trickled from either end of the hourglass.

It was the sound of the water running that awoke Ginna's memory. It came to him that he *had* been in a lighted forest before, or at least the image of one, and it had been *this* forest. Hadel had conjured it for him in his study, warning him not to drink the water lest he too become an illusion. He had slammed his face into a stone wall that time, and found himself back in Ai Hanlo.

Now he was in that grove again, entering from the other side, and part of the answer was clear to him: the end of his quest was at the beginning. Yet he wondered, why hadn't the Nagéan merely sent him here if he had the power, or at least told him? Perhaps the matter was not so simple. Perhaps the enemy would have overheard and followed him. Perhaps, for him to come to this place and for it to be real, not an illusion interrupted by stone walls, he had to reach it in his own way, in his own time, and of his own power. It was the difference between the shallow magic and the deep.

The lady sat on the edge of the fountain.

"I used to watch the world pass by," she said. "I could see it all in the clear waters of my fountain. But now the world is dark and I see nothing."

Indeed, the water was clear when it poured from the hourglass, but in the pool there was only impenetrable blackness, as if the water had been turned into oil. Gingerly Ginna put his hand in. He could not see his flesh even an inch below the surface. Startled, he drew it out, holding the wet hand in the dry one as if hurt. The passage had made no splash or ripple.

He went into a fit of abstraction then, forgetting all around him as he contemplated this thing. After a time he was aware that the lady was no longer with him. Amaedig led him away.

* * *

Once they moved with the Bright Powers and were lifted up by them into that great dance which had filled the world. They saw again the rose of fire across which the Powers moved, but at the same time they knew that this rose at the center of the Earth, this realm of the Bright Powers, had been usurped by darkness, and this was but the collective memory of all those beings which had come into awareness when The Goddess fell from the sky and shattered into a million pieces. They viewed the great All, the lakes, the mountain, the castles and rivers of the land of light, which the singer Ain Harad had actually visited many generations before, but now they were only projected images, reverberating with the sorrow of the Bright Powers at their loss.

These things Ginna and Amaedig saw as they soared on the wings of light.

* * *

The lady came to him again at evening, when the light had

begun to fade from the forest and shadows grew long. She was no young woman then, but an old crone, her face withered with the weight of many years, even though mere hours had passed. Her voice was hoarse, cracked, and wheezing.

"I was a mortal woman originally," she said. "I came from Tobar, in the land of Cadmoc."

"I have never heard of these places," said Ginna.

"Our Lord was the Mountain Earl Hadormir."

"There have been no mountain earls for a thousand years," said Ginna. "The last one was slain by Iboram the Scourge, who buried him beneath a cairn made of the skulls of his followers."

"Yes, it has been a long time. I don't know how long. I am very weary. Yes, as I told you, I am the mother of The Goddess. She was mortal too, born to me in blood and agony the way children are. But she had a vision. I told her it was an idle dream, merely vapors in her mind, but she said no, it was more. I told her she must have eaten something too strong for her and her bodily humors were unbalanced. I told her she was in love with some boy and it had turned her head. But it was none of these, and even she did not know what was happening to her. She followed her vision and had another, and gained attributes and aspects, until the earth shook with her passing and her voice was the thunder. Now the prayers of mankind had gone unanswered for many years. The God we worshipped did not hear us. Some claimed he had melted away, like mist rising in the morning. But when miracles happened again, at last I understood. I became her priestess. By the touch of her hand I became more than mortal myself, after my fashion. When she passed into the sky and was no more my daughter than the wind is, she placed me in this pocket of a world outside the world, and here I am to this day."

"Tell me," said Ginna after a long pause. "Did she want what happened to her?"

"I don't think it was a matter of wanting. No one came to her with an offer. It just happened."

Speaking no more, Ginna left the lady and went off by himself. He was deeply troubled.

* * *

She is dead.

It was night in the forest. All the light had faded from the trees. The Powers gathered like pale constellations, bearing the wrinkled corpse of the Mother of The Goddess to the clearing, to the golden pit, where they laid her to rest. Then all of them vanished, like a flock of fireflies breaking up, each going its separate way.

Ginna lay with Amaedig in the darkness, holding her close. He knew fear then, a fear that the lady would not return, would not rise again, that this would be the final night.

He slept and dreamed that he was wandering across the plains with the caravan. He was very happy with Amaedig by his side. They were leading a heavily laden camel. Gutharad was behind them, singing merrily. But when he turned to speak to his friend, the minstrel was not to be seen. He turned back, and Amaedig was gone. He called out, and no sound came from his mouth, and the caravan vanished. He was wandering blindly in the darkness, groping his way through a maze of stones. Then the earth gave way and he was falling.

After a time, when he could see nothing by which to measure his descent, the sensation of falling left him, and he seemed suspended in space forever, helpless, like an insect in amber.

He awoke in a cold sweat, in the light of the trees.

It was early morning. The leaves had begun to glow a pale green, drifting above him like shining moths.

The voice of the Powers came to him again.

She is risen.

* * *

"Did you know," the girl-child told him, "that we are not the original inhabitants of the Earth? There's an old story, and I'm not sure if I really believe it, that some god went mad long ago, and destroyed all life. He wiped the world blank as a clean slate. But when a new god came into being—or perhaps it was a goddess; I think it was—the memories of mankind still lingered like echoes of shouting in a cave, and our ancestors were created in the likeness of those who had gone before, but without their souls, so we can only struggle all our lives and throughout all our history to fill the roles laid down by that other human race, like actors rehearsing parts in a play, without ever really understanding the design or purpose overall. Like I said, I don't really believe this. It's too depressing. But it does explain some things."

* * *

Ginna and Amaedig lay naked by the shore of a rippling brook, in the light of the trees. In the light of the trees the white water seemed a pale green. Their bodies were a soft, greenish yellow.

They held each other and knew each other as men and women have ever since there were men and women, filling roles laid down by their predecessors or not. And when the lovemaking was over, they rested side by side.

He had not known such peace since....

The leaves on the ground and the branches above rustled with the passing of spirits. Ginna laughed inwardly. If indeed the Powers were watching, he hoped to make them sick with envy, if indeed they were prone to such fleshly failings.

He was glad just then to be solid, material, made of living flesh, to be human. He never wanted to be anything else. He turned to look at Amaedig and was silent for a long time, watching her breasts gently rise and fall with her breathing. Lying thus, she was beautiful or nearly so. In his eyes she was special, set apart from all others. Her shoulders were in a slight shrug all the time. It did not matter. Her name, meaning "cast aside," was a malicious cruelty in itself, while at the same time a record of her life, and his, as both had been cast aside to drift in the wild current of the world and come at last to rest on this pleasant shore.

Finally she turned on her side and faced him.

"Are you asleep or what?"

"Just thinking. I don't want to leave this place, ever."

"But we can't stay here. You know that."

"I know that, but maybe if we live just for each minute as it passes, and never try for more than the next minute as it comes, maybe there will be enough of them for us. I know that all I ever really wanted out of life was to be ordinary and unexceptional and live like everybody else. To be a part of the world rather than a stranger wandering through it. I want to love you, and travel as we did with the caravan, and tell people stories of what we've seen and sing songs for them, and earn our keep that way. Is that too much to ask?"

"Who are you asking?"

"I don't know. I mean...it's not like that."

"The world you want to travel through isn't there anymore."

"Then why can't we stay here? What have we got to go back for? Nothing will change here. If someone is really destined to deal with Kaemen, let it be someone else."

She did not answer. Then he was aware she was weeping.

"Hold me close," she said. "I'm afraid that something will happen to force us away from here. I know it. We can't run any more. There's no place left to go."

After a while they made love again. Again they lay in silence. He folded his hands together and made a globe of light, which drifted up a ways, then dropped down onto his chest and remained there. He contemplated it as it rolled with his breathing.

He picked it up and handed it to Amaedig. As soon as she

touched it, it burst.

* * *

He found the lady sitting atop a grassy knoll in the height of the afternoon, surrounded by the flickering Powers. Above her the trees thinned out. Patches of grey emptiness were visible beyond them.

He climbed up beside her and sat down. Suddenly he found himself without words.

"You want me to send them away so they don't overhear," she said, indicating the Powers.

"Yes."

"But that isn't what you've come to tell me."

"No."

"There's no need to send them away. For the most part they have no memories as we do. Sometimes they can recall an event which happened five hundred years ago, but the day-by-day passing of time doesn't mean much to them."

"Still, can't you—?"

"All right, if it will make you more at ease." She raised a hand and spoke a word in a tongue he had never heard before, and at once they were gone, quick as flames snuffed out. "Now, as you were saying."

"I have been thinking about the things you've told me, and what other people have told me. About my whole life. I don't know who my parents were. I don't think I ever *had* parents. I'm not like other people."

"No." she said, "you are not. I know this to be so. Don't ask me how just yet. Go on with what you wish to say. Get it all out or you'll burst."

"I'm not stupid. I can see the obvious. I'm the one who is supposed to put an end to Kaemen, right? Like some hero in an old epic."

She smiled and nodded. "The poets tend to exaggerate, but in essence, yes."

"But what can I do, kick him? He has all the power, all the magic. The only thing different about me is I make balls of light with my hands. I couldn't kill a fly with one."

"In time you will find out what you can do, and do it. I am confident of that. Meanwhile you will conduct yourself with dignity and courage, as befits a hero. You are one, you know."

"*No!*" He slammed his fist into his palm and at once felt it was a silly gesture. He made a glowing sphere, let it drift, then caught it. "I won't fight him," he said. "I won't do it. I'll stay here forever. Let someone else be the hero. If this is an epic, tell the author I

141

resign. I never asked to be a part of it."

She grabbed him by the shoulders and jerked him toward her. The sphere rolled out of his lap and broke against the ground. She spoke to him in a way she never had before, firmly, impatiently, like a sergeant of the palace guard giving orders.

"You didn't ask to be born, did you? Do you ask for your every breath, for the blood that your heart pumps? No, the world takes care of these things, without ever consulting you."

"That's just what Amaedig—"

"If she said that, she was right. Entirely right. Now be still and listen, and I will tell you the story of yourself as I observed it through my fountain before it was clouded. I saw the darkness come into being, and I saw how you were a part of it."

"I—?"

"Shut up and listen!"

She told him tersely, without any mercy, sparing no feelings, the complete tale of his life, how he had come into being, how the witch lay beneath the ground for a day and a night before the demon came to her, how their bargain was fulfilled, and how the demon created him from the flotsam at the bank of the river, giving him the semblance of flesh and the eyes of his mother, through which Kaemen had watched his movements all these years.

He understood everything now, how the demon had climbed up the side of a tower in the dead of night to place him in the cradle, so the witch could be near enough to the one she wanted to possess. Somehow the hag's malice had grown beyond all bounds, until even she could not comprehend the vastness of it. She was a pawn of limitless forces. Her actions were as inevitable and impersonal as the great storms and earthquakes. And he understood one final thing: Kaemen was as innocent as he had been before the evil possessed him. His deeds were not of his own. Had the witch not poured into him, but remained in Ginna, their roles might have been reversed.

His face was pale, He was shaking with fear when he broke in, "Am I really human then, and not a clump of weeds and mud? Do I have a soul?"

The lady's grimness softened a little as she said, "Yes, I think you do, and it is a good soul. What is a soul but a kind of motion, like ripples on a pool when a stone is cast in? Anything which lives, which moves through the years has a soul, and have you not met this requirement?"

"But why me? Why does all this have to involve me?"

"As I said, you were never consulted. You must understand

you are not living in an epic. There is no author. It is more like an avalanche or a tide, a thing of blind nature. Long, long ago, many cycles before any of those we call the ancients were living, before those nearly erased ruins which mar our deserts were built, so far into the past you cannot begin to imagine it, a man who was counted as wise in his era said *forces must balance.* Another, about the same time, said, *for every action there is an opposite and equal reaction.* So it has always been. When the world is tilted askew, it straightens up and comes into a new equilibrium. The universe generates the means. Against the overwhelming darkness, it has generated a source of light, and you're it. It is not even destiny. You are not asked to accept it. It merely *is.* Why you? When a barrel springs a leak, does the hole ask, 'Why me, barrel? Why me, water?' No, before the leak there was no hole. It came into existence for that purpose. You are that hole, my friend, and through you the divine leaks into the world once again."

Throughout all his adventures, he had never known more terror than at this instant. Her every word was sentence and execution. He realized now that he could never have anything he wanted, never wander across the world with Amaedig at his side, never go back to Ai Hanlo and live in quiet obscurity among the dusty corridors.

"But what if I stay here? What if I don't do anything?"

"Somehow you will do something. Even here our skies are beginning to darken. Either this place will also be wholly dark, or it will be cast off from the world, forever beyond the reach of mankind or of powers, or anything. But even then, light will come to counterbalance the darkness. There is no running away. You see, my friend, and I hope I can call you my friend, you say you are smart and can grasp the obvious, the obvious thing is that from you the next god will come. Perhaps you will be like my daughter and speak with the thunder. Perhaps it will come about in some other way. You could sire a god, or one could even rise up out of your death. Yes, it could be that. I shall not hide anything from you. I have conversed with many spirits and studied much during my long years, and I think I know something about how these things work. When the Goddess knew she was dying, she set on me the task of overseeing the transition into the new age. Or she was moved to do so by the forces that made her what she was. So I have watched and waited until you were able to come to me. That is my whole purpose. When there is no deity and all is chaos, the natural balance creates another one. I am merely part of the process."

He leapt to his feet and, without a word, ran away from the

knoll. After a while his voice broke forth in shrieks and sobs. The Powers were all around him as he crashed through the under-brush, into the forest. He ran, stumbled, fell, got up and ran again. Distances and directions were hopelessly confused. His cries echoed back from the spaces between the trees, from all sides at once. He wasn't running from anywhere to anywhere. It was just a thing his body did. His mind was a total blank. It was too painful to think. He just wanted to become something which ran like the wind, like one of the Bright Powers, without memory, without will or consciousness. The forest was an endless green ocean. He wanted to swim to the very bottom, then breathe deeply, and lie there quietly forever. His screams were like flames. He screamed all the more, to be reduced to a fine ash, that he might drift like a cloud. He had no feeling, no sense of actually running. Branches smashed into his face. Blood ran from his nose. His knees banged on stone and earth and fallen logs every time he stumbled, but all these were sensations of the body, remote, abstract, something to flee from.

The Powers were all around him, flashing, chattering. He felt light in the head. His chest heaved and his lungs were burning. He was floating up out of his body as his legs turned to powder and sank down...down....

Darkness rose to receive him, but paused a little ways off.

There was a voice calling his name.

The lady came to him in her old age, in the faint light of the evening, and she found him lying on the ground, gasping hoarse, painful breaths, unable to scream any longer. She stood over him as he rolled and muttered like one in a deep fever. Then she crouched down, put her arms around him, and helped him to sit up.

"It is good to be so human," she said. "You're not some lifeless thing of weeds. I think that somehow you will still be yourself even after you have done what you must do."

"What I...must...."

"You must restore the balance of light and darkness. That is all I can say."

At last he was able to think of someone other than himself. It was a new terror to him that he might have drawn Amaedig into this, that his love-making might have touched her too deeply with his own fate.

"Amaedig. How is she?"

"Why, she is well."

"If I am such a god, can I perform a miracle?"

"What sort of miracle?"

144

"I want to do something for Amaedig. Even if I had no choice, she did, and she chose to come and help me. So I want to help her if I can."

"I don't know that she had any choice," said the Mother of the Goddess. "It was her role to keep you alive and guide you until you reached me."

"You mean it wasn't predetermined that I would? You mean I could have died?" he said bitterly.

"I don't know. Perhaps. Maybe if you had been smothered in the cradle, the movement of forces would have settled on another."

"Please spare me further explanations. I've had enough."

"I'll send for Amaedig." Something like a hummingbird made of pure light hovered before her face. She spoke to it in a kind of chirping and it darted off.

The two of them remained as they were, speaking no more, until Amaedig arrived. She emerged from the forest with the messenger flying circles around her head. As soon as it saw the lady, it vanished.

"Hello," she said, first to the Mother of The Goddess, then to Ginna. She was immediately ill at ease from the look on his face—sorrow, fear, resignation. "What has happened?"

"What had to, I supppose," he said.

"Now what sort of miracle do you want to perform?" said the Mother.

"It's just that. . .it's so unfair that she is like she is, because she is really very beautiful. I want to—"

"Yes, I think I understand."

Amaedig backed away, her mouth forming a wordless "Oh", her hand covering it. There were tears in the corners of her eyes. She looked first at Ginna, then at the lady, then back at Ginna, half afraid, half comprehending.

The lady stood up. Ginna remained seated.

"Come to us," she said, and Amaedig hesitantly approached. "Sit down in front of him." She obeyed. "Ginna, touch your hands to her shoulders, and if this miracle is yours to perform, the rest will come to you."

He did as he was told. The lady placed her right hand on his shoulder. He felt a force rushing through him. Amaedig trembled at his touch, and then, subtly, in a manner his eyes could not follow, his hands were not on her shoulders anymore, but within her body, as if he had dipped them into water. His hands met and parted, and light shone through her back, as if her flesh and clothing had become transparent. Slowly the sphere of light rose, like a luminous fish swimming up lazily from the bottom of a pool, and it passed out of her, into the air, rose a short way, then fell to the ground and burst.

He released her, and it was only after she stood up and turned to face him that he could tell that her shoulders were no longer stooped or crooked. Her face seemed less plain. Somehow he had known it would be so. He felt a deep sense of calm.

"Take a new name," said the Mother of The Goddess. "Be called Tamarel. It is a kind of flower which grows among the mountains of Cadmoc. Its pod is knobby and ugly; its seeds are scattered far on the wind; but when it blossoms it is the most beautiful of all. The name means late blooming."

"This is what I wanted for you," said Ginna.

She seemed about to say something, but could not. She fell to her knees, then prostrate before him in an attitude of supplication and thanksgiving.

As a worshipper would before a god.

Now there were tears in his eyes as he raised her up and gazed into her face. He saw not his friend there, but a girl filled with awe, with wonder, and indeed with gratitude, but the gratitude of the inferior for the unearned gift from the infinitely superior. She was saying, without words, *you're one of them, not like me,* and with that he knew he had lost her, that he never would be a minstrel or any other sort of humble person wandering across the world with her at his side. He had felt that knowledge's icy threat before and rebelled against it, but now it settled over him gently, like a cloud, and all resistance drifted away.

He began to weep aloud, and Tamarel, who had been Amaedig, startled and confused at the sorrow of her god, crawled away from him a distance, then got up and ran into the forest.

He turned to the Mother, who, even as he watched, was growing older. He had never seen a face as wrinkled as hers or a body as frail. The forest darkened.

Weakly she pointed to a staff leaning against a tree.

"Take it." Her voice was a faint croaking. "It contains my daughter's tears. She wept as you did. It will light your way."

He rose and took the staff. At his touch the globe at the upper end began to glow, and he saw that it was the carven sceptre she had been carrying when first he met her.

Powers came to bear her away.

She is dead, they said minutes later, their pronouncement echoing through the forest. All light faded except for the staff, and the Powers themselves, which flickered among the trees.

He was exhausted. He slept, and dreamed of a great wheel taller than any tower. Its spokes were the bones of giants, and out of its rim living hands grew. They came up from beneath the ground as fists, but as the wheel turned they opened, wriggled their fingers, and made strange signs. The thing was horrible. He wanted to run away from it, but was drawn toward it, a sick feeling of helplessness growing ever greater, his legs disobeying the commands of his mind. Unwillingly he walked, one foot placing itself in front of the other, across a barren, muddy plain, toward the wheel, which turned with a sucking, slopping sound.

He was naked. The air was cold. The mud oozed between his toes.

The hands sensed his presence. All of them paused, fingers outstretched, to feel for his approach.

But those which groped for him rose up with the turning of the wheel and were gone; it was a newly arrived hand which reached out quick as a striking viper and caught him by the hair, dragging him up off the ground, dangling like a fish on a hook.

He rose out of darkness into light. The sky above him became a pale blue and he was carried up toward the blinding disc of the sun, the sun he had not seen in so long and barely remembered. Swarms of birds flew past, singing. The blue gave way to brilliant white and he felt the warmth of the sun touch every part of his body. He was near to the uppermost part of the wheel, and no longer dangled, but lay back on the turning rim, among hands which touched him gently. The air was thinner up here, or sweeter, for he was filled with a giddy joy and all terror passed away. He was content to lie still and ride with the wheel beneath the sun, drifting from east to west across the world.

Then the downward plunge began, and his feet tumbled over his head and he was dangling again, dropping downward into the darkness and the sucking mud.

Chapter 12
The Final Encounter

When he awoke, it was still night in the forest. He did not know how long he had slept. The staff had fallen from his grip. He groped around for it, and it glowed again at his touch. There was a hush over all. No Powers moved in the trees. The only sounds were the rustling of leaves as he stirred and the beating of his own heart.

He stood up, holding the staff before him, and began to walk steadily, forcing himself to keep his legs moving and not to shorten each stride until he wasn't moving at all. If he paused even for an instant now, he knew, he would never be able to continue. He fixed his mind on Ai Hanlo, on Hadel of Nagé's study, recalling that day so long ago when he had first glimpsed this wood and heard the bubbling of its fountain.

Onward he went, trying to comport himself with courage and dignity, with resignation, but still with the ability to face his fate like a warrior, to grab his doom by the beard and wrestle. Heroes in epics did it that way. But he wasn't a hero. His life, he had been told, wasn't an epic. Nothing would come out so neatly. He was afraid. He felt like he was walking to the slaughterhouse.

He imagined the trees to be long-faced, sombre old men, with beards down to their ankles, gazing at him as he passed without caring where he went or why.

Ai Hanlo arose in his mind in every detail, every texture.

He passed the fountain. Water no longer flowed from the hourglass. Underbrush grew steadily thicker. He had to force his way through branches and thorns. Then the trees towered over him, standing close together, until they formed a nearly solid wall. Like a worm, he wriggled through the crevices.

Behind him, the forest began to fill with faint light. He looked back and saw the trees silhouetted like the legs of an army of giants. He turned away from the light, into the darkness. He knew that was the way he had to go.

After a while, he couldn't see light anymore. The ground felt less than wholly solid. He closed his eyes once, then opened them with a yelp. He had thought himself falling. He held the dragon-headed staff close to his face, and went on. The darkness and the massive trees closed in around him. He was smothering, but he held the staff like some futile, brief candle and went on. It was as if the whole forest had become one vast, rotted log, and he were tunnelling through it.

He thought again of Hadel's study, and then imperceptibly, as he squeezed through a tight space, the forest became something else. The dark jaws of the earth had closed on him, and he was filled with the paralyzing dread of being stuck there between the forest and the world forever, when he noticed that the tree trunk which pressed against his back was rounded, covered with rough and mossy bark as usual, but the one in front of him was flat, very regularly pitted, and harder to the touch than any bark.

It was a stone wall.

He wriggled through, his clothing tearing as he went, until he stumbled out onto a wooden floor, crashed into a shelf of books, knocked over a lampstand, and staggered to a halt. There was no light. He had dropped the staff. He crouched down and groped around for it, found it, and stood up in its light, looking around. He knew where he was. He had spent many hours in this room, in the inner palace of Ai Hanlo, in the land of Randelcainé.

Something stirred beyond the circle of his light.

He peered in the direction of the cluttered desk, moving forward carefully, holding the glowing staff before him.

Clothing rustled. A chair creaked. There was a frantic fumbling. A bottle dropped to the floor.

"Please! No closer! Take that light away!"

He stopped, astonished.

"Hadel? Teacher?"

"Yes, it is I."

He could only make out the dim outline of a shape behind the desk, and something was *wrong* about it.

"I—I—you can't imagine how glad I am to see you alive! And you speak! How? Did you restore your voice by magic?"

"I speak by a means you soon shall know, boy. I cannot say more just now. I am glad you are here. Please back away a few feet and put out that light. Don't ask me why."

He did as instructed, slipping the staff through his belt. It glowed sullenly, like an old coal. Now he could see little but himself, and his hand in front of his face was a shadow.

"Are you well, teacher?"

"Yes, I am. I am in a better state than I ever have been before. You should appreciate it Ginna. You will be like me before long."

He felt a touch of dread, as if he stood atop a tower which had just shifted half an inch or so, enough to tell him its foundations were being slowly ground to dust.

Hadel's voice was not as he remembered it. The low monotone was emotionless. Sometimes words came out slowly or imperfectly, as if the speaker were unused to the mechanism of mouth and throat, or even the technique of language.

"What happened while I was gone?"

"Much...oh, so much...Kaemen has filled the world with darkness, as needs it must be filled. Yes, that is what he did. I did not see the beginning of the act, though. I locked myself in this room, and he beseiged me, first with his guards, then with... others. His magic smothered me like a damp, stinking pillow. I did my best to hold out against it. I sealed the doors and windows, the cracks between the floorboards, the chinks in the walls. So I did not look upon his great beginning, but I can imagine how it was. One day the golden dome was no longer golden and the sky was dark. I can imagine the darkness flowing out of the inner city like water from a fountain. In the mornings the shadows between the houses did not disperse. More and more gathered each night, joining together, and the feeble days could not drive them away. And...in a way I did not merely imagine this...I came to have memories. But only after I had succumbed to the inevitable. I held out. I fought bravely, but it was inevitable. I am not ashamed...."

Now all Ginna's worst fears were realized. He tried not to weep; he tried to be brave and show dignity, but his voice betrayed him.

"You didn't surrender. No, you didn't give up and over to him. Please tell me you didn't."

"You sound so hurt. Can you forgive the weakness of an old man?...ah!" Hadel let out a grunt of pain. "...it was not weakness. No, I ran out of candles. That was it. I ran out of candles, oil for my lamps, and magic. The room got dark. I was still sealed in, but I dwelt in the darkness for a long time, even as the world did. Yes, yes. . .in time I could feel its currents and the cool, soft textures of the shadows that settled upon me. Darkness was a thing tangible. It spoke to me, first in dreams, but then as I was awake. It mocked me. Then it praised my fortitude. Then it was soothing. And, after a long while I came to love the darkness. I cannot say when. If a cloth is wet, can you tell the very moment has become dry? It was a slow change. That was how I came to speak again."

"*How could you?*"

The chair scraped against the floor. Slippers shuffled, moving around to the front of the desk. Floorboards creaked, as did the desk itself. The old man was leaning on it as he made his way, step by step, slow as a stone statue only halfway brought to life.

"I have just told you how," the flat voice said. "Now believe me that you will understand what it was like when you have gone through it yourself."

Ginna backed away. The wall was solid behind him. No forest, only stone.

"Stay away from me!"

"Why are you afraid?" The dragging footsteps neared him. The voice was very strange. It was not Hadel speaking, he told himself. It was something foul and twisted crouching on Hadel's shoulders, gibbering in this dry whisper.

"Stop! Tell me one thing first. What happened to everybody else? In the palace. In the city."

And the other paused. "Oh, the others? Why they died, or they went mad and then died, or they dissolved into the darkness, I suppose. Only a few of them did as I did and became part of the new world. I only want the best for you, Ginna. I want you to go on living, even as I live."

The footsteps continued, even more unsteadily beyond reach of the desk.

"Don't touch me! I don't want—"

Ginna's hand remembered the staff. Before he realized what he was doing, he pulled it out and the end flared to life. He held it into the face of the one who stood within an arm's length of him.

Both of them screamed, he out of repugnance and horror at what he saw, the other out of agony, like a man burning alive.

Still Ginna held up the light, rapt in ghastly fascination. Hadel, or what had been Hadel, recoiled and cowered back against the desk. Half of the man's head was absorbed in a wet, blubbery mass. It was hard to see its color in the brilliant light as the Nagéan writhed and twisted, covering and uncovering the thing, but there was a suggestion of dung, and another of dried blood.

But it wasn't dried. Still liquid, running, dripping, quivering, it changed shape even as he watched. He saw that the stuff had flowed over the forehead to cover the eyes, but there it ran thin, and the fear-filled eyes glistened beneath a translucent film. The nose was untouched, but the jelly bubbled out of the mouth, down the chin and neck. Now Ginna knew how Hadel could speak, and why the voice was not his own. It was as if a vast tumor had distorted the shape of his head, bulging more to the left than to the right, entirely hiding one ear and not the other; but this was an animate thing. It had two membranous, bony wings on the top, which now flapped furiously in a useless attempt to drive away the light.

Ginna drew his knife. All this had been like a delirious dream of a madman in a fever, but a rational thought came to him. He would cut the parasite away and free his friend, or, failing that, kill him and free him that way.

Hadel dropped to the floor and lay still, his chest heaving. Ginna knelt down beside him, the staff in one hand, the knife in the other.

The wings were a blur of motion. The blade flashed in the light.

"Nahgg—" The teacher sat up and rolled over, pushing the boy away with his shoulder. Ginna fell back, off balance and surprised at the action, still holding the knife and staff. When he recovered, Hadel was under the desk, kicking wildly, burrowing into the debris like some mole dug up by a plough.

Ginna clambered to his feet. He sheathed his knife. He couldn't bring himself to do what he had to do. He had to get out. He ran for the door, and fumbled with the latch. His fingers knew it and worked of their own accord.

He swung the door wide and ran into the unlighted corridor beyond. It gaped like a mouth and swallowed him.

* * *

He heard a woman screaming. He had never heard screams like that before, not even from Kaemen's burning victims. The level of fear and pain in that voice was beyond anything he could imagine.

He followed the sound along corridors, across broad rooms, down flights of stairs, through tunnels. He had no idea where he was. He had lived here all his life but now, in the dark, he was lost.

The place was intensely cold. His breath came in clouds. Through the thick soles of his boots he could feel the icy stones beneath him.

He held up the glowing staff to see where he was and *willed* it to become brighter. To his surprise, it did, and he remembered what he had been told by Hadel—when he had still been truly Hadel—by Arshad, and by the Mother of The Goddess, about whatever he might meet, but then, on reflection, that too seemed a trap. The more he developed strange abilities, the farther he drifted from being himself. He could never forget the look on Amaedig's face when last he saw her. No, now she was Tamarel, changed by his hand. He tried to convince himself that once this was all over, things would go back to normal. But he knew he never had been a very good liar.

The screaming came again, impossibly louder.

He neared a wall, and the light revealed writhing, multi-colored serpents all around him, piled upon one another by the hundreds, their scales glistening. He jumped back, startled, but then saw that they only seemed to wriggle and their scales seemed to sparkle as he moved, as the light from his staff was reflected. He was in a room he had never seen before, the walls and floors of which were entirely covered with serpent mosaics made of tiny, polished bits of tile. In the middle of the room stood a pedestal, on which stood the familiar double image of The Goddess, two statues back to back, one caressed by black serpents, the other by white.

The screaming came. He had no time to consider what the serpent symbolism might mean. Someone was suffering un-speakable torments as he stood there. So he ran, fumbling among the draperies that blocked the exit from the serpent chamber, his footsteps echoing along another hallway lined with empty alcoves. He came to another wide room and skipped gingerly among embracing skeletons which covered the entire floor. He climbed a flight of stairs, descended another, and came through an archway into an open space.

There was no way he could see that he was outdoors, but the air against his face was even colder and there was a slight breeze. The smell of decay and must decreased. The place was less close.

The screaming was right there, heart-stopping, ear-splitting, quite overwhelming any urge to rescue anyone. The screaming was a horror in itself, a tangible thing.

He crossed the last few feet of the yard cautiously, his staff outstretched before him, and he saw the source of the hideous noise. It was a woman's head, the eyes rolled up white, the jaw slack, the tongue hanging flaccid. It was obviously dead. It could not be screaming.

And yet the sound issued forth like acid from a funnel. A dark hand held it above the pavement. As Ginna approached, his light gave the gloom above and around the head form and substance. The darkness trembled with ponderous motion. A dozen hulking shapes were only suggested: here an arm like carven iron, there the long, flabby face of a boneless horse with a single eye like a glistening pustule, there again the immense, toothy jaws of a crocodile on the shoulders of a man, there a blind face covered with bony plates. And again, tree-like towers of legs bent in a crouch, unseen wings flapping like sailcloth, and hard, sharp nails clicking on the pavement.

And here, and here, and here, eyes glowing like red coals opening all at once at a silent command, floating in the darkness asymmetrically. A putrid wind came wheezing out of a dozen mouths.

He held the dragon staff like a burning brand. The creatures spread apart slowly before him, only the one holding the head not moving.

Suddenly he *knew* that face. It was Tuella Marzad, wife of the man who had given him aid that first morning after he and Amaedig had left the inner city. And the screaming, magnified a thousandfold, was her voice.

Sick with revulsion, but angry, he charged the Dark Power holding her, swinging the staff like a club. It was a wild, unthinking action, but he was beyond thinking. The massive shapes scattered like startled toads, making no sound as they leaped beyond the range of his vision.

He was about to bring the staff down on the unflinching monstrosity before him, when it vanished too, and all of them, no more tangible than miasmic vapor, whirled about him, laughing, hissing in his ears. The screaming reached a crescendo.

Just as suddenly the air was empty and there was silence. He looked around, puzzled, and poked the darkness with his staff. He thought himself alone.

And then he realized that something heavy was dangling from the front of his shirt. He brought the light close to himself and looked down.

It was the head, clenching the cloth in its teeth.

He let out a shriek and brought the staff down on it, but missed, for those jaws which had hung slack now worked furiously, devouring the front of his shirt, climbing up him like a ravenous rat.

He was the one screaming when it bit into his chest. He beat on it again and again. He pushed at it with both hands, dropping the staff, and as the pain grew worse he fell to the ground, trying to crush the thing under the weight of his body. But it wriggled beneath him and continued chewing, burrowing into him. He knew its intent. It was after his heart. It would get his heart between its teeth and squeeze and squeeze....

He rolled onto his back, screaming, flopping like a beached fish. He fumbled for his knife and drew it out, stabbing at the thing again and again. Sometimes he missed and stabbed himself, but in the agony of the attack, as his blood flowed freely, he couldn't tell when and he didn't care. He plunged the long blade deep into one eye, then into the other, twisted, and jiggled it sideways, till the bone between the sockets broke and there was one gouged trench.

And still the thing's jaws worked like a machine. He stabbed lower, through the cheeks, cutting away and around until the impossibly snapping lower jaw broke over the edge of his blade. He had hacked the teeth completely out of the mouth. The head let go and rolled off him, then exploded, showering him with blood and fragments of bone.

He staggered to his feet, drenched, his own blood mixing with the other, and he felt the lower jaw, broken off from the rest, still stirring in his flesh. With desperation and hopeless terror, barely able to control his weak and trembling fingers, he groped for the thing, and, careful as a surgeon, extracted it from himself with the knife. He dropped the jaw to the pavement and ground it underfoot until he could feel nothing at all, not even the finest powder under his boot.

Then the pain came back to him, and with it nausea. He fell to his knees, then crumpled forward, but caught himself before he hit the pavement. Leaning on one arm, he coughed and heaved. He felt like he wanted to vomit his whole insides out, but nothing came, and he remained there, gasping, while blood ran freely over his whole torso.

He sat, and tried to pull the tattered flaps of his shirt over the wound, to stop the bleeding with cloth and with his hands. He had no idea how badly hurt he might be.

With all his effort, he managed not to faint. After a while the bleeding seemed to stop. His hands were crusted with dried blood. He was getting stiff. He forced himself to his feet. His heart was beating and he still breathed, so he said to himself, *I guess I must be alive.*

He found his staff and staggered across the yard. He came to a large wooden door inset with iron. This was slightly ajar. He took a metal ring in hand, pulled, and the door swung open on greased hinges. Within, a staircase led up to a level floor. It was another corridor. On either side tapestries billowed from drafts of frigid air passing behind them.

* * *

He had lost all sense of time, and space was closing in on him. The thought came that he had walked in darkness for weeks now, and always the world he had known was still around him, but veiled. He could have walked in that darkness to the horizons he had once seen, and reach Nage, Hesh, Zabortash, Dotargun, or any of the other familiar countries. Now, for the first time, the darkness seemed different. It had swallowed the world. It seemed to him that there was nothing left of the universe except the floor he stood on and the cold stones of the wall he followed with his right hand. He held the staff in his left, making a little circle of light in which he could see the clouds of his breath. That was all. When he turned a corner and came to a stair, it was as if that stair had only then come into existence, and would fade out again when he had passed. Beyond this there were only sounds: water dripping, occasional sounds of wind. The only other real things were the throbbing pain from his chest wound, his numb feet, and the lethargy which was slowly settling over him.

He was forgetting who he was and what he was doing there, wandering lost in the corridors of Ai Hanlo, the holy mountain whose passageways and chambers, some sage once said, were as infinite as the whims of The Goddess.

He remembered the epic recited in the square at Estad, about the hero wandering across the Land of Night at the end of the world for some obscure reason or other. He could identify with the hero now, but somehow the heroics weren't working out.

Spiderwebs broke over his face. They seemed frozen, like delicate traceries of ice.

His staff glowed faintly, like the distant light of the last star in the sky.

He shook his head to keep awake, and as he paused his changed stance tore at his wound, and a warm trickle of blood ran down his belly. The sudden pain woke him up and kept him going.

He noticed peripherally that the corridors were narrower than they had been, the walls closer together, the intervals between doorways longer. The air was filled with ice. The stones were coated with it and slippery underfoot. His fingers ached from touching the wall. His breath came with difficulty. His throat was raw, his head spinning as the frigid air rushed into his lungs every time he gasped to inhale.

His attention wandered from the present into the past. He wasn't in darkness anymore, but in the warm sunlight, basking beneath the sparkling midsummer sky, on a porch high above the city. As a child he often came to that porch, to be alone, to read, to watch the flocks of birds wheeling over the land or the river winding its way to the hazy horizon or caravans diminishing into necklaces of tiny specks upon the desert. He would sleep there sometimes on a couch, or just on the sun-warmed stones, and awaken in darkness with the stars looking down....

...and awaken in darkness with no stars at all, his head jerking up and down by reflex.

He was seated against the ice-covered wall. The staff had fallen between his knees, still held in his limp hand, glowing faintly. He shook his head to clear it and tried to stand up. But his legs wouldn't respond. His whole body was stiff.

He held the staff tightly and produced more light. A small, round room was revealed, filled with ice. Even as he watched, the crystals grew from the walls like some delicate tapestry of glass wrought by invisible weavers. There was ice on his clothing. The latticework touched his legs, his sides, his shoulders. Weakly he leaned forward and found that his cloak was stuck to the wall. In these few minutes the ice on the floor rose to cover his knees, encasing his legs. He could not even feel his feet anymore.

Now fear shook him out of his stupor. He was trapped like a horse in quicksand. He wanted to writhe, to shriek, to give in to panic entirely, but with the utmost effort, he controlled himself. He drew his knife and chipped at the ice around his legs. It was useless. As soon as he broke a piece away, another took its place. The stuff healed like an invulnerable, living thing. It was condensing out of the air. Pale, silvery stalactites grew from the ceiling fast enough that he could actually see them extending downward, touching the floor, becoming pillars. Curtains of delicate flakes billowed between them. He sheathed the knife.

He could not call for help. There was no reason. No one remained in the city who could aid him, who *would* aid him, who would even be likely to reach him before he was frozen solid in an enormous mass of ice.

"*Kaemen!*" he called out, and the ice shivered at the sound. "*I know you're doing this...*" and he paused, feeling ridiculous, unsure of what he was trying to say. He was hardly in a position to threaten anyone.

The ice had worked its way up his chest, between the tatters of his clothing. It touched his wound and all sensation there passed away. This made his head clearer. He worked the staff loose. Ice chipped from his arms as his elbows bent. He moved them constantly to keep them free. His fingers were stiff. His hands were like cement gloves. Only the force of his arms held the staff between them. He touched the sphere containing the tears of The Goddess to the ice and, as he had half expected, the crystals vanished, like lace in a fire. Sure enough, he could "burn" little holes this way, but they filled in as fast as he did. He could move the staff from side to side, and a shower of fragments would come tinkling down. He could stop an icicle from growing. But it wasn't enough. The room continued to fill. The ice was up to his armpits. His lower body was completely numb, and breath came only with immense effort.

There was only one solution. He had used it before. He remembered Arshad's cabin, the swinging lanterns and shifting shadows, the deck rocking beneath him as the ship moved on the great river. He tried to go into a trance, as he had then, but it was hard to concentrate. He began to chant the formula Arshad had taught him, but his grip on it was like that of his hands on the staff. Syllables ran together. His attention was drifting. He was withdrawing from the world, but into sleep. He tried to think of himself as on that ship, to *be* on that ship, chanting.

He let the staff drop. It went out. He closed his hands together, opened them, and a ball of light rose. A little flexibility returned to his fingers. He made another, and another, dropping many, but in time he held an enormous sphere. The ice glittered and sparkled, revealing fantastic shapes as the light filled the room, as the sphere drifted down on top of Ginna. It sank into the ice without bursting, and its soft glow increased to a blinding glare, until he could see nothing but drifting motes of brilliant white against the flaming yellow. He was rising, tumbling in the light—

—and he fell into darkness with a thump. He sat up sputtering in six inches of frigid, muddy water. Rising unsteadily to his feet, he wrapped his ragged, soaked cloak about himself. His chest hurt more than ever. The tatters of his shirt were sticking in the wound. He couldn't tell if he was bleeding or not. His legs burned as sensation returned to them. He tried to clear his throat and the result was a deep, liquid cough.

His floating staff nudged his ankle. He picked it up and held it tightly against his body. The light returned.

* * *

Following the corridor, his hand brushing the wall, he came

to a large room. One minute he was touching the wall, the next he was groping in space. He turned, examined the spot with his light, and saw another wall receding perpendicularly into the gloom. The doorway was a stone arch carven in the likeness of a leafy vine. The top and the other side were too far away to be visible. Walking in what he took to be a straight line, he found the other side after ten paces. It was a very large doorway, betokening a great hall.

He paused. He could either follow one of the walls all the way around, or strike out boldly through the center in hopes of finding a similar door on the other side. In any case he wanted to leave the corridor he was in. He suspected it went around in circles.

He decided to go for the center of the room. He didn't know why. He just did it. The doorway fell behind him like the ghostly shape of a wreck a diver sees on the ocean floor, dropping away as he rises. He walked slowly. His knees threatened to give out. He was very weak. He thought he was bleeding again. Somehow the world seemed even smaller, for all that he knew he was in a large enclosed space. All that obviously existed was a small patch of floor on which he stood. He could discern alternating black and white squares, one at a time. They were two paces across. There was absolute silence except for his footsteps; no echoes, even of those footsteps. If he paused and listened, he could hear the blood coursing through his veins and pounding in his head.

A hand appeared, level with his forehead. His reflexes were ruined to the point he could only stagger back from it. He was too tired to be afraid.

The pale, white hand hung stationary in space. The forefinger was extended and pointed slightly downward. It did not move. He swayed where he stood, leaning on the staff.

"I am...a friend," he said.

There was no reply.

Cautiously he approached. The light of the staff revealed a sleeve behind the hand, of the same pale hue and equally unmoving. Then there was a body, taller than that of a normal man. He reached out and touched the hand. It was marble. The thing was a statue. He held up his light and saw that its head had been knocked off. Using the base of this statue as a reference point, he moved in a straight line beyond it and found another, a barrel-chested warrior in full armor, also headless.

The whole room was filled with statues, all larger than life, all without heads. He sat down on the base of one, between the feet of a lady, and rested. His whole body was stiff. He wasn't sure he could ever get up again. His resolution to do so never quite came. For the moment, he felt safe. At least he knew where he was. It had been the custom of the folk of Ai Hanlo ever since the foundation of the city to carve images of noted persons and display them in a great hall, the deeds of those person inscribed on the bases.

It was just like Kaemen to behead them all.

Ginna had seldom been in this room. Those who actually lived in the palace found the exhibit boring. It was used for impressing dignitaries, wealthy pilgrims, and sometimes officials of the lower town. But he had known how to find this room, and that meant if he could reach certain doors, certain turns of hallways, and a broad flight of stairs that spread out like a fan, he could reach Kaemen's throne room beneath the golden dome. He knew that ultimately he must go there.

Then what? The worst thing was that he never knew what was coming next. If he were flowing with events like a cork in a river, it would have been comforting to know what lay around the next bend. But he was carried on blindly.

Then he trembled, from dread, from pain, from the cold. *Great Goddess, look down upon me in my hour of trial.* The old prayer came to him. He spoke it aloud. When especially alone, especially frightened, he had always repeated it, even though The Goddess had died long before he was born. It never drove the fear away, but it would make it loosen his grip and give him breathing space. Now he looked out into the darkness. A statue stood opposite him like a carven pillar. Now he truly knew, for the first time, that there was no one out there to hear him, that any prayer he might utter would drift and tumble through eternity like a shard of a broken mirror falling through the space beyond the world, turning over and over, glittering, never, never coming to rest. No one heard him. Throughout his life, for all he had been shunned or neglected, there had always been someone he could turn to, one of the nurses, a stable hand, Amaedig, Tharanodeth, Hadel, Gutharad, Arshad, or the Lady of the Grove. Now he was truly alone. Was the Lady watching? If so, he might appear a dim speck moving in the black water of her fountain, but she would not reach out to him, or even speak and expect to be heard.

He wept. *Dignity and courage,* she had told him at the very last. Empty, idiotic words for heroes who strode through epics waving swords and killing monsters. Real quests were much too grim, too full of sorrow, too miserable to be worth telling. If there ever were minstrels again, if ever they sat around campfires and sang the story of Ginna, they would not tell it as it happened, not if they wanted any supper. No one would want to hear of the pain, the loss of all his friends, the end awaiting him that was as strange as death if it were not merely death. No—

Something scurried between the statues. He rose painfully, sluggishly but alert, his knife out. He turned, staff in hand. Shadows flickered as the light source moved. He saw nothing and sheathed the knife.

He started walking, sure he was being watched, through the forest of statues.

The floor trembled slightly. There was a faint rumble, little more than a vibration he could feel with his feet, but then the whole room shook violently with the full force of an earthquake. Statues crashed to the floor. Plaster and stones fell from the ceiling. He ran, one arm raised to shield his head.

Something grabbed his cloak. The arm of a falling statue had ensnared him, dragging him sideways. He was slammed onto the floor hard. Dust and pebbles rained into his face. A stone struck the side of his head. He lost his grip on the staff.

Another statue fell over the first one, breaking off the arm that held him. He sat up. Another stone hit him on the forehead, and he knew nothing more.

* * *

It was like the dream in which his face had floated away. He seemed to rise from the rubble. His body was light. He was drifting on the air. Somehow he felt the statues beneath him as he moved, as if his body had become liquid and were flowing over them. His face was solid, though. It itched with dried blood.

Sometimes his head throbbed and red blobs of light drifted before his eyes. Cold air blasted his face. Vise-like hands bore him up, thumping and jolting with an awkward gait. Voices whispered and tittered in something other than words. There was a smell of damp earth and filth.

Then he was drifting once more. The darkness carried him. It was thick as syrup. Slowly it shaped itself to fill the hallways. It rose to touch arching ceilings, to lift him up to higher levels.

He awoke several times from this dream, if dream it was, and felt himself being lifted. He couldn't tell if he had any broken bones. The thought came to him that only his head was being carried. that the other sensations were ghost-remembrances of his lost body, and he wanted to cry out, to prove to himself that he still had a chest with lungs in it, but no sound came, and again the blackness was there, like quicksand closing over his face, and he was borne on the secret currents to the ultimate pinnacle of Ai Hanlo.

He opened his eyes to a faint light and saw, much to his

surprise, the dragon staff glowing like a faint ember. He couldn't make out who held it. Forcing himself to deliberation, he took stock of his situation. He was lying on rather hard pillows, perhaps on a couch. Yes, that was it. He felt its back to his right, and one arm rest above his head. It had a musty odor.

So he was alive, unhurt, and still in possession of his knife in the presence of someone who squeaked and cackled and grunted to himself, making sounds like a horde of rats, like huge and hideous night birds, sounds which were half words or not words at all, certainly nothing human.

Someone who could make the staff glow, as no ordinary person could.

Someone who, quite suddenly, broke the staff over a knee and crushed the glowing bulb to fragments between two pale hands. The light went out. The darkness was relieved only by the drift of a glowing powder from the wreck of the bulb. Then an ordinary lamp was lighted and a face emerged from the darkness, at first no more than a vague oval, but more clearly defined as it neared him.

Giggling. He knew the voice. He saw the face coming at him like a huge fish rising from the deeps: a tiny mouth set between the bulging cheeks, eyes sunken deep on either side of a pug nose, yellow hair plastered on a pale, dirty forehead. A fat hand held the lamp unsteadily.

The mouth opened, and a chattering noise came out like some tiny animal deep in a cave, and then there were words, and the voice slowly assumed human tones again. More laughter.

"Yes...it is you...how surprised I was...and yet I had always known you would come back."

"Kaemen?"

"Indeed. You can call me Great Lord or something like that. Your presumed familiarity is shocking." More giggling followed, shrill and wheezing. "Ginna, how good of you to stop in and see me. Forgive me if the place is untidy. Hadel told me you were coming, but, alas, there is no one to keep the palace in shape these days."

Kaemen held the lamp up and turned slowly. Ginna could see that they were indeed in the throne room. Light and shadow flickered among fallen masonry. A dark mass stretched from floor to ceiling in all directions. It reminded him of webs spun by enormous spiders, but this was no silky stuff. It was heavy, like flesh, like muscle growing out of the mountain itself. As he watched, sack-like masses throbbed and glistened wetly, and totally dark shapes, man-sized but not manlike, scurried up the membrane, vanishing in the darkness above.

"*By The Goddess!*"

"Yes...I suppose you could say it was by her. How amusing. I didn't think of that. Truly you are miraculous, just as Hadel says."

Kaemen set the lamp down on a table nearby. "You must excuse me for not giving you more light," he continued. "I've grown to abhor the light, just like Hadel, and for the same reasons. I love the darkness, its texture, its touch, the little sounds you hear listening to its distances. It's not the same out there. It's all new." He ran his hands along his body, hugging himself.

"But how—?"

"How else? I hear everything Hadel thinks now, just as I used to see what you saw and hear what you heard, at least when I chose. I could do it any time before you vanished. It was...You know, you gave me quite a shock. Before I do whatever...before ...you really must tell me what strange lands you have journeyed in. As long as you are telling me, and keeping me amused, you shall be my friend. I promise you."

Ginna resolved to tell him nothing. His experience was the only unknown now, his only advantage. He sat up. The other started.

"Don't think you can get away from me!" Kaemen hissed. "Don't think you are more powerful. I am. I can protect myself from any magic. The light of this lamp does not weaken me. It's only for your benefit, so you can see me. I don't need it."

It occurred to Ginna that once he had feared this Guardian, and at another time he had absolved him of all blame, knowing him to be possessed by something vastly beyond himself. Now he feared him again, but it was a different kind of fear. It was like being locked in a room with a dangerous beast—perhaps a mad *kata* which could reduce him to a red smear with a single swipe of its tail. Somehow, for the moment, the beast sat there, staring at him. A sudden action would bring on the attack. He had to be very careful. It was a matter beyond moral considerations, quite apart from blaming. The danger brought him to full alertness.

"Kaemen, why have you done these things?"

"Why. Hsst! Listen! Do you hear it?"

Kaemen stood poised, listening. Ginna heard nothing but their breathing. He knew that things moving in the darkness all around him, but they were soundless. Then there was that faint vibration coming up through the floor that he had felt in the room of statues. He braced himself, but there was no violent quake.

It was like the sound of a huge serpent gliding through the

163

earth miles beneath his feet.

"Ah," said Kaemen. "She moves now even without my bidding."

"What?"

The Guardian winced as the voice echoed back, *what, what, what....*

"Hush, fool...Isn't it odd? Isn't it passing strange? Don't say 'what' again. Consider my question rhetorical. But isn't it curious that we are, you and I, about the same age, give or take a little bit, and I am...myself...while you still gape there like some idiot child? Well then, child, in childish terms, all I can tell you is that sleep and death are alike in a way. The difference is dreaming. I have raised The Goddess up from one state into the other, returning dreams to her. All my magic over the years had been devoted to that end, to make her dream dreams of darkness, and now she does, and she turns restlessly in her sleep. The earth trembles. But the world shall be in balance. You know, light and dark, good and evil, all that. The Goddess is ...incomplete. She shall bring a different kind of balance. She has but one nature now, and when the world is wholly ruled by it, why, there shall be no forces left in contention. I trust I have made this simple enough for you to understand."

Ginna thought only to prolong the conversation. As long as Kaemen was talking, he wasn't likely to *do* anything.

"Why?"

"I fear I have overestimated you. You're stupider than you look. Because *I* will be lord of this new world. The Goddess will dance for me like a puppet. The Black Lady told—" His words were broken off in a grunt, as if an invisible hand had gagged him. His eyes were wide with fear and anger. Once more Ginna saw the frightened, trapped Kaemen of his dreams. He watched intently expecting the other's face to flow and shift. But it did not. If the Hag were there, she did not show herself.

"Why was I brought here?"

Kaemen took several deep breaths and released them slowly, in the way a stutterer does when he wants to make a long speech.

"To get rid of you. So I could decide what to do with you. I tried to kill you, not once, but several times, and things didn't work out. There is something special about you, something very mysterious. I don't know if you are a threat to me, but I can't allow the possibility. I can't believe your entire existence has been a coincidence. No, you're like the white playing opposing the black on the board game. But it's useless. You might as well give up, *because I have already won.*"

"And if I do give up?"

"Then there might be some place for you in the new order of things. There are a few human beings left. I haven't killed them all. They may continue for a while, if I choose to let them, but in a very reduced and subservient role."

Ginna found the reference to humanity as "them" the most terrifying thing Kaeman had yet uttered.

"Kaemen, try to remember who you were. You were human once too."

Laughter returned in a short, nervous burst. "I *was*, yes, but now I have matured. I have risen into something else. It happens, you know."

Yes, Ginna told himself, *it happens.*

"But first," said The Guardian, "before all these great events take place, I want to try an experiment. I want to see if you are still human yourself."

He took up the lamp. Shadows shifted around him. Something like a billowing cape with nothing inside it separated from the shadows and drifted up toward the ceiling.

He leaned over, seized Ginna by the hair, yanked his head forward, and held the flame of the lamp under his chin.

The flesh burned, but Ginna refused to give Kaemen the satisfaction of hearing him scream. He gritted his teeth and tried to pull away, but The Guardian was far stronger than he looked. Kaemen studied him with detached interest, like one cutting apart an insect to see if it has organs.

Below them, The Goddess turned again in her dark dream. Plaster fell from the ceiling.

All right, he wanted to say, *you've proven your point. Now take it away.* But Kaemen did not take it away. The pain increased. The pain moved down to his throat. The fat face floated in the darkness inches away from his own. He looked into the pale eyes. Within the pupils, tiny scarlet flames burned. They brightened. He thought of torchbearers approaching from out of a tunnel.

Kaemen was pulling his face down. The flame touched his cheeks. He gagged as it shot into his nose, and he twisted and pulled harder than ever when his eyes recognized the danger to themselves. Kaemen was in a reverie, fascinated with the very act he was performing. Ginna pounded on The Guardian's arms with his fists, to no avail. He was in the hands of a living, iron statue in the guise of the corpulent son of Tharanodeth. The force was irresistible. His mind told him that all was hopeless, that there was no escape from this single force which would overwhelm the universe without opposition. He cursed the lady of the grove for sending him on this futile mission. He cursed Amaedig for keeping him alive long enough to set out on it. He cursed whoever and whatever had ultimately been responsible for his coming into being.

His eyes watered. He twisted his face. The flame singed off an eyebrow.

And yet, his hand, which was braver than his mind, did something.

Performed an experiment.

To see if The Guardian was human.

The answer was that he was not, and had forgotten simple human devices. He had not taken Ginna's knife away from him. It was a mere artifact, beneath contempt. Now, quicker than Ginna's mind could follow, without conscious thought behind it, his hand whipped that knife out of its scabbard and slammed it into Kaemen's ribs, all the way to the hilt, and drew it out, and then the conscious volition took over. Quite deliberately, Ginna stabbed him again and again, searching for his heart.

Kaemen let out a gasp of surprise. He released his grip, swaying as the stood. Ginna took the lamp from his unresisting hand. Slowly he crumpled to the floor, spouting blood from a dozen wounds. He lay there, quivering like a beached fish. Now Ginna leaned over and held the lamp to his face, not to burn, but merely to look.

The face began to distend, to darken, to bubble and flow. The shape of the wolf was there, snarling and snapping in agony. Rising, like a creature conjured from a cauldron, the Black Hag was there, her eyes glaring in place of Kaemen's. Her head started to separate from his, as if she were about to pour out of him, but then sank down, and once more his pasty-white features were visible. The eyes were wide and watery.

"Please," said Kaemen, and the voice was his and no other's. "Ginna. Help me. Set me free of her. She has been with me always. If I could make The Goddess dance to my will, she did the same to me. She makes me do everything I do. I don't know how much of myself is me and how much is her, but I don't want it to be only her—" He broke into an inarticulate gurgle, coughed, and blood ran from his mouth. He began to scream, rolling his head from side to side, spewing out blood and spittle. "Help me! Set me free! Ginna, you have no reason to do anything for me, but please, kill me!"

Quickly, but with the deliberation of a surgeon, Ginna knelt over the writhing Guardian. He took him by the hair to hold his head still, and cut his throat all the way around, so deeply that he felt the knife blade scrape against the neck bone.

The screaming stopped. Blood flowed from the wound and from the mouth in spurts, then slowed to a gradual ooze.

A wisp of smoke rose from Kaemen's clothing. Ginna had set a lamp down beside him, and now his robe was on fire. He let the flames spread over the body. Soon he recognized the smell of searing flesh.

Below, The Goddess stirred.

He put the knife away, and wrapped himself in his cloak, more for imagined protection than against the cold. The burns on his face began to hurt, and his chest throbbed again. He was bleeding slightly. A warm trickle ran down to his navel. Now that the fury of the encounter had passed, he was very weak. He thought he might faint, but for a feeling of relief that *the whole business of his life was over.* It was too numbing a thought for him to begin to comprehend. He sat down on the couch and stared at the burning body. Around him, dark shapes recoiled at the light given off by the flames. He sat with the lamp in his lap.

As he watched, he saw that the whole business was *not* over.

Two red eyes were rising over the dead Guardian. The witch was pouring out of the wound in his neck like a spurt of blood steaming into oily smoke, then puffing into fullness over him. Silhouetted against the flames, she was a totally black outline, pausing for an instant as if disoriented, then turning toward Ginna, perhaps recognizing him. She edged away. Just before she slipped into the darkness he could see that she was running. Her legs pumped up and down, but her feet did not touch the floor. There was no sound except the crackling of the flames. She drifted like a rag in the wind.

Now he understood that the old lore on the subject was true, and that a spirit could not exist outside of a body for any length of time, unless it travelled that final road along which Tharanodeth might still be walking. Surely the witch had no such intentions. She was going to her grave, to rejoin her own body, and he knew that only if he could follow her there and destroy her once and for all, would the long nightmare be truly over.

Beneath him, The Goddess turned in her restless sleep. The floor swayed like the deck of a ship.

Bearing the lantern now instead of the staff to light his way, he followed the witch through corridors and down stairs, out of the palace of the guardians. She drifted ahead of him, always just out of reach, her eyes shining through the back of her head like twin fireflies. Nothing molested him as he passed. The darkness was empty. He saw skeletons on the floor, a rotting corpse nailed to an overhead beam, but there was nothing moving or alive. His footsteps echoed. Once more the whole mountain shook and debris fell. He was thrown sideways, against a wall, and the two eyes went around a corner, out of his sight. He ran after them and caught up, before the fleeing creature could escape.

His breath came in hoarse gasps. His pounding heart seemed to be tearing his chest apart. His whole body seemed to be melting like wax. At the bottom of a flight of stairs, he missed the last step and stumbled. It was all he could do to avoid spilling the lamp on himself. He thought he would never get up again, but forced himself, and saw the two specks disappearing around another corner.

Tapestries billowed with the frigid wind. He ran to catch up with her. The flame of his lamp flickered and sputtered. An archway gaped. He followed her through and the air was colder still. He was outside. The blast was falsely invigorating, making him aware of every part of his body, but giving no strength.

He was led out of the inner city, into the streets of the common folk, between the ruins of houses. He stalked the eyes as they tried to evade him among the alleys and pitted shells of buildings. Once he ripped aside the curtain of a stall and a young girl huddled there shrieked. He put the curtain back and went on, his quarry still in view.

Some doors and windows he passed were shuttered. Others gaped like the mouths of the dead. His light threw huge shadows of himself against walls, making him a spidery-legged giant picking its way gingerly through the fallen structures, overturned carts, and occasional corpses. For all his haste, he had to move carefully. He was deliberately led over gaping pitfalls which were no impediment to the airborne spirit.

At last they came to the outer wall of the city, to a gate he didn't recognize. It was locked. He saw the two glowing points rising slowly, drifting over the wall.

There was nothing for him to climb. He struggled to move the bar which held the gate. Slowly, with a burst of agony as his wound tore and bled freely from the effort, the bar slid to one side. The gate swung inward. He slipped through and looked up to see the witch descending from the battlements.

She could have stayed up there, or fled somewhere else, had she been a living woman or a Power, but as a ghost she was bound to make for her grave by the shortest route, and he stood in her path. Down she came, passing within arm's reach of him, veering away from the lamp. He followed her a short ways to a barren, open part of the hillside, where talus lay heaped along with rubbish from the city. It was near the base of Ai Hanlo Mountain.

The black hag stopped moving. She hovered above a spot of ground, then began to sink into it. He watched the eyes drop lower. Then he struck out with his knife. The blade passed just beneath those eyes, but did not impede their progress. In an instant the spirit was gone.

Now it occurred to him that he didn't know how to put an end to the witch even if he did catch her. But he could try. It seemed to him that even a magically animated skeleton couldn't do much if all its bones were ground to powder. If nothing else, he could grab stones and batter her. He wished he had a shovel, but dared not leave to fetch one. So he began to dig with his hands, heaving dirt between his legs.

If stones wouldn't work, he would cut off her head. He would nail her into her grave with his knife, and all her evil would lie there with her—

The ground heaved up, and a solid hand emerged, glittering in the faint light, and suddenly the lamp was knocked aside and there was no light at all. Before he could even scream the hand seized his own, and he was pulled down onto his stomach, his face over the hole he had dug, looking straight down as the witch's eyes swam up at him out of the earth. By the light of the eyes he saw the crystalline head, the fires deep in its empty sockets.

Creaking, with a sound like stones being ground together, the head spoke, "*Son, do you not know me? I am your mother.*"

"No! No! Let me go! Leave me alone!" He screamed and struggled all the more. The grip was far stronger even than Kaemen's. His hand was being crushed.

"*I will never leave you alone, not now, not ever.*"

Another hand, another arm broke free of the dirt, seized him by the shoulder, and rolled him onto his back. It locked his neck in its elbow. The first let go of his hand and grabbed him around the body. Now both of his hands were free. He stabbed again and again with his knife at those unseen arms, and back over his shoulder at the face, until the blade broke off.

"*It is useless.*"

Her whole body was beneath him now, wriggling up out of the earth. She locked her legs around his waist, her arms around his shoulders, and suddenly there was a sharp, intense pain as her teeth sank into the back of his neck.

Rise. She no longer spoke. He sensed her words inside his mind. A chill numbness spread from his neck to his extremities. His body was no longer his own. When that voice commanded, his limbs obeyed. He rolled over, and painfully rose to all fours, straining under the weight of his burden. She hung on his back like a huge parasitic slug, becoming every minute more a creature of flesh than of crystal, her substance softening as she drank his blood, drooling saliva down onto his shoulders.

Rise. See. Suddenly he could see with something other than ordinary sight. Nearby shapes were faintly outlined in red, as if etched in fire. He began to move. As her control became more complete, she ceased to issue commands. His legs worked at her will, not his own, and he rode along helplessly, a prisoner in his own body. His arms hooked under her legs to hold her more securely.

Back into the city he went, bent and hump-backed. He saw his way in the strange light, but cast no shadow. He climbed the sloping roads up the mountain, the stairs where the way was too steep, until he came to the inner city. A horde of Dark Powers met them at the gate and followed, just out of reach, mere suggestions of shapes eclipsing the red light from stone and walls. He found he could roll his eyes as he walked and look around, and he saw them, rising and sinking like fish from a murky sea. Some seemed to have bulbous eyes and long rows of inward-curving teeth. Others were blank-faced, but their chests split apart and snake-like tongues shot out. Others hovered on whirring winds.

He came to rooms he knew, to the innermost chambers of the palace, the bedroom of The Guardian. The place was not as he had known it in Tharanodeth's time. There was a headless corpse suspended by the ankles over the bed, and the sheets were a mass of dried blood.

Wind whirled around him, and at least in his mind he saw faces floating in front of him, Kaemen, Hadel, Gutharad, even Tharanodeth and many others he had known or merely met, all of them screaming wordlessly. They vanished like sparks cast out from a fire.

He saw clearly again. His hands pressed a panel on the wall behind the bed. A door slid open, and he stood at the top of a secret stair. A draft smelling of earth and decay rushed up at him. He descended, winding around and around for more steps than he was able to count. He was going deep into Ai Hanlo Mountain. He felt the whole weight of the city above him. Sometimes the passage was so narrow that his shoulders touched either side. He could not turn sideways with the thing on his back. He scraped the tunnel walls as he passed and gravel fell onto the steps with a rattle.

The Goddess stirred once more, and far more gravel fell. The sound of her movement was a muted thunder.

His throat was made to call out a word he did not understand, and she lay motionless, waiting.

At last he came to the bottom of the stairs, to a door which opened into a chamber he had never entered before, but which he recognized. It was large and circular, and empty save for a black statue of The Goddess and a white one, the latter headless. This was the place he had come in spirit, when Kaemen had accidentally dragged him along in a dream. Then the hag had banished him. Now she drove him forward. His hands took up the heavy golden ring on the door Kaemen had not been allowed to open in his presence, which swung forward on silent hinges.

When he saw what was inside he wanted to cry out, to faint, to run away, but he could do none of these things, and so he mutely stood there, staring into the long gallery with jewelled mosaics and a carven ceiling. He beheld what the folk of the city had venerated for so long and only the guardians had ever laid eyes upon: the actual remains of The Goddess.

Her bones were like filthy crystal, long and massive, but surprisingly delicate in appearance, translucent with a faint gleam in their cores. There was a thin flesh stretched over them, like a black guaze, but liquid and flowing.

The floor of the room ended a short ways beyond where Ginna stood. After that there was only bare earth and stone, in which the huge corpse was embedded. Ai Hanlo Mountain had closed over The Goddess when she fell from the sky. The city had been added later, as had this room, in which the secret had been revealed to successive generations of guardians. Ginna felt himself to be an intruder, a blasphemer. He waited to be stricken dead. Nothing happened. Inside his mind, the hag laughed, and pain lanced through him.

He gradually perceived that the gallery was long and rectangular. He could not see to the far end, but the sides were perhaps thirty paces apart. He was inside a huge coffin, like a graveworm. The head of The Goddess was toward him. He could see the skull clearly, imbedded in the ground, curving up like the hull of a capsized ship. Her eyes were vacant caverns. Her mouth hung open like the gate of a castle. Beyond, ribs arched upward like rainbows of pale white, and off to one side a hand lay, palm upward, the fingers curled like crooked, skeletal seige towers.

Closer. Approach her.

His legs obeyed, stumbling over debris, awkward with the burden on his back. He saw that among the fallen masonry there were many skeletons, most of them headless.

Watch. She raised his arms, and cried out with his voice, "Come! Come! All ye shadows, all ye shades, all ye Dark Powers. Come!"

There was a rushing of wind. Again the faint red outlines he saw with his strange new sense were eclipsed, and the Dark Powers came, flowing, crawling, drifting down the stairway like an oily wave. They emerged from the walls, from the ceiling. They brushed him as they passed. They crawled over The Goddess like a million ants, then melted into her to make way for more.

The bones were less visible. Her flesh was being made full. The squirming, flaping things, the things which were no more than dark patches against the great darkness spread over her as a thin film.

Behold how the godhead is reassembled and divinity is reborn.

The Goddess trembled, her body grinding the earth which imprisoned her. Stones and dirt fell from the ceiling. Cracks appeared in the walls. The witch froze him where he stood, and debris rained all around him.

Now, touch me to that which I am to command, and I shall set you free.

"Free?" he said aloud, but there was no hope in the word.

Laughter knifed him again. He made his way forward clumsily, until he could reach out and touch the skull. But he did not touch it. Instead he turned his back to it, until his burden pressed against it, and at that very moment he was released. Blood ran freely as the teeth were withdrawn from his neck. All his weakness came back to him, and he fell forward as she pushed him away. A jagged stone rammed into his stomach. He rolled off it, and looked up at the skull. His night vision was going, but still he could see the huge, curved outline in the red of dying embers, and on it the witch crawling, wholly inhuman in her aspect, like a black insect on the head of The Goddess. He thought of an earwig seeking an entrance.

Exactly.

She vanished over the curvature of the skull. There was a moment of absolute silence. Something flittered against his face and was gone. Visions of his life came to him in his pain. He thought of himself floating gently in a pool of his own blood, and as he floated, as he lay there and knew he was dying, he saw, first, Tharanodeth emerge from the top of the stairs, his face solemn with ritual. He tried to think of the good times, the walk into the desert when he first saw his world from the outside, and suddenly it was all there: the city crouching beneath the moon

173

like a glittering, scaled beast, the sunrise with all its brilliant, subtle colors. He drifted through the sights and smells and shapes of the *kata* stables, watched the trainers trying to ride the wild beasts. He saw Tamarel, who had been Amaedig back when her shoulders were still hunched. He had been closer to her in the first days of their friendship, and innocent enough then to think that only what few people he knew, what yards he walked in day by day, what food he ate and games he played constituted the whole of the world, and everything else was a vague, far away abstraction, like mist rising from the river in the dawn. He tried to reach for those days in his mind, like a swimmer determined to attain the ocean's bottom, to seek release there, to lie forever in the soft mud.

He told himself it was well to die here, in sight of The Goddess, as, to his knowledge, no one ever had.

His sight was almost gone. Only the faintest outline of her head was visible.

There was a sound, a constant thumping like a thousand drummers drumming beneath the earth. No, he *was* beneath the earth, *here*. The travesty of The Goddess was *alive*, and its heart was beating.

There seemed to be motion in the darkness. If more Powers streamed to join into her flesh, he couldn't see them.

He reached out. He wanted to touch that flesh, just to have done so. But he couldn't. He couldn't get up. The rest of his body would not respond. It was hard to breathe, as if his lungs were filled with mud.

His mind was wandering. He thought of himself sinking in an endless, red sea, all his pain dissolving away. His thoughts were all irrelevances, little memories, the image of a bird on a windowsill, the sound of the night wind among the towers of Ai Hanlo, an illustration in a beautiful old book, the first time he had worn shoes and how silly he had felt in them. Gutharad. Wandering on the caravan route between Randelcainé and Nagé. He sank further with an old song.

A Zaborman who can last till dawn, I've never seen before....

Suddenly The Goddess gave a great shout, and all the earth shook. His ears streamed blood, and all sound left him. He saw the stairway *close* like a huge jaw as a single, immense mass of stone fell to fill it.

The Goddess moved. Her hand struck out, and walls and ceiling burst like overripe fruit, spewing the guts of the mountain upon him. He was caught like a leaf in a tempest, tossed about, slammed to the floor, raised again. He rose to his hands and knees, but something hit him between his shoulders like a battering ram. He was down again, pummelled over his entire body with showering rocks. Hundreds of pounds of boulders smashed his legs to a pulpy tatters. He tried to crawl still, propelled by a frenzy beyond any sense or reasoning, and somehow the boulder was broken to powder by another, and he moved a little ways, nearer to the head of The Goddess. Earth and rock broke over her like the ocean over a whale when it breaches.

He had come to his ending. One of his arms didn't seem to be there. He reached up with the other. He touched something soft, something cold, something moving.

The mouth of The Goddess rolled down to meet him.

* * *

There was a flash of pain more intense than anything he had known, as if his body had been wholly consumed in fire, and then he passed through the flame and rose, like smoke, feeling nothing.

Swimming up out of the warm, red sea.

There was a rushing in his ears.

A weight fell away. He was shedding his ruined body like a husk, and yet he was complete in his own flesh once more, climbing upward, out of a tunnel of throbbing flesh, into a broader space.

He was naked. Before him were endless caverns and passageways, not of stone, but of black, dried, brittle matter like fat burned to a crisp.

He was rising out of the earth, without motion, without vibration, but the world fell away around him, silently parting, and he swam up, up, out of the mountain like a whale breaching, the stones and dirt breaking over him like foam.

He was in a closed place.

He was alone on a plain of black glass which stretched to the horizon.

He rose on a column of air.

Running.

Swimming upward through the earth, he felt tons of stone being pushed aside like sand by his arms, his chest, by his feet as he kicked and crawled and scrambled to be free.

He felt Ai Hanlo Mountain rent asunder with his passage, the walls and towers of the city sprinkling over his skin like delicate traceries of glass broken into dust.

He stood over the plains of Randelcainé, all things visible to him, viewing the strange towers raised up without fear of the sun.

And then, for an instant, he withdrew into his tiny body, and was rocked from side to side among fleshy, sticky bands.

He staggered over the plains of Randelcainé, his head roaring inside, his knees buckling.

He spread his arms apart, reaching from horizon to horizon, and another voice called out from within him in something vaster than words, in the very language of darkness, and all the Dark Powers of the world came to him, pouring on his flesh like rain, becoming part of him, filling him with power, drowning that tiny speck of a memory called Ginna in a whirlpool of hatred.

And Ginna felt their unreasoning, endless malevolence, the thundering of their hatred.

And he felt the triumph of the other who shared this state with him.

He became himself again, and he was standing in a vast, curving room draped in black. There were two huge, round windows looking out into darkness, and he knew them to be the eye-sockets of the walking corpse of The Goddess.

He was facing the old, eyeless woman with the flames burning inside her. A bony hand reached out at him. She made a magical sign.

You. Not now. You can't wreck my plans now.

He reached for his knife, but felt only his nakedness. She seized him. They wrestled, her fingers tearing into his arms. He rammed his knee into her and she bent over with a gasp and tumbled, dragging him down on top of her. The flames burned hotter in her eyes. He could feel their heat on his face. She was far stronger than he, like a living statue, irresistible as stone. Her mouth gaped wide, wide, drooling curses.

The world reeled, horizontal to vertical to horizontal. They were thrown against a wall of bone. Suddenly his hands were *inside* her chest, closed together where her heart should have been, and they opened. He withdrew his hands as if from a muddy pool.

The black hag exploded with light. In bursts, in sheets, in showers of sparks, she vomited light out of her mouth, her eyes, her ears. Her body burst asunder in light, the ragged sides flapping and split sailcloth in a tempest. Her arms flailed wildly. She screamed, and screamed, until her screaming was a wind, an avalanche, a force in itself.

Ginna watched, horrified, fascinated. Then, in an instant, faster than thought, many things happened: up became down as the huge body crumpled. The witch was above him, then on him, grasping his back, clawing, locking arms and legs around him like an agonized, dying spider. Awash with light, she scrambled over him until her face was before him, her burning mouth stretching impossibly wide to swallow him, to close over his head like a hood, flooding his mind with thoughts and fears and memories not his own. The two of them fused together like melting figures of wax, losing all shape and form and substance in the great cauldron of light.

There were fires in his eyes. His flesh was hard as crystal, his joints grating as he moved.

Something seized him by the hair, yanking his head back. His arms and legs were sinking into a soft mass. Yes, like wax. It was like swimming in wax as it hardens. He was frozen in place. He felt his body dissolve away; a thousand million voices whispered; a thousand million screamed, and above all the witch babbled an incomprehensible litany in the language of night. His sense of self was rapidly being broken up into countless, tiny particles and lost to otherness. He was sharing his mind with the witch, with the Dark Powers that still screamed to join him, with the lingering residue of The Goddess. He was a silent drop of water suddenly cast into the roaring ocean.

He stopped falling. His knees straightened. He stood up. The witch stood up. That which had been The Goddess stood up. All in the same motion.

The last thing he, Ginna, was able to do as a discrete, if tenuous remnant of his original consciousness, was to move his hands. *His* hands, with bony fingers the size of towers, long arms stretching to the ends of the earth. He brought his hands together; he thought his final thought; and separated them.

There was a burst of light. The witch shrieked for the last time.

A sphere expanded.

Worlds. Hadel of Nagé had said. Those little balls of luminous nothing were embryonic worlds, and now one spread out and grew with all the strength of The Goddess behind it.

And the Earth was reborn. The new age began.

Ginna sought a meaning, a revelation, an answer.

He was not answered.

* * *

It was to Tamarel, who had been Amaedig, that the final vision came.

She sat with the Mother of The Goddess in the afternoon of her life, in the gentle light of the grove, by the edge of the fountain. The water was dark, but the Mother watched it intently. Tamarel looked too, and saw a tiny spark appear like the first star in an evening sky. It was equally far away as a star, only below. Surely the fountain was infinitely deep.

The fish with the hourglass in its mouth stared forlornly. No water flowed.

She wondered what the Mother saw. Did that spark mean that Ginna was still alive? She wondered what it would be like if she were ever to meet him again. She tried to tell herself that their last meeting had been a dream, and he would be his old self.

But dreams tended to be true.

Suddenly the Mother rose and said, "Come."

"What has happened?"

"He has done what he was always meant to do."

The Mother took her by the hand and led her through the forest, away from the fountain. The trees grew nearer together. Even in the presence of the Mother, the shadows deepened.

The Mother raised her arms, and cried out a command in something beyond words, in the very language of light. The Powers streamed around them, forming a glowing vessel which lifted them up on the substance of light. It was like drifting on a cloud made of airy faces and bodies, with lacy wings of fire whirring everywhere. Amaedig felt herself lurch and twist at impossible angles. Then she was falling gently, her senses slipping away, into light.

She came to rest, standing, on hard, polished stones. The blinding light faded into blinding darkness. The Powers hovered around them like a constellation of glowing moths.

"We are in Ai Hanlo," the Mother said. "Look."

Tamarel looked. She saw two red stars high in the sky, far away.

"*Ye lights, ye motes, ye flames of Powers, come to me!*" The Mother cried out, and the air around her burst into brilliance. All the Powers of the grove, all the remaining Bright Powers in existence came streaming to her command. They arched away from where Tamarel stood, over the plain like a rainbow of a thousand suns, revealing in their passing the wide plain, the ruined city of Ai Hanlo all around them, with half its mountain broken away, and beyond the city, on that plain, a colossal figure standing, a thing like a crudely carven stone statue, with red stars for eyes.

The light gathered around it and faded. The world was dark again. The figure stood over the plain, tall as Ai Hanlo Mountain, grey and veined with glistening black and sprinkled with glowing dust.

It folded its hands together and opened them. A sphere formed, brilliantly flaming but delicate, expanding like an immense glowing soap bubble.

The light approached Tamarel like a wave. A hot wind preceded it. For an instant the sky was bright as day. She could see where the side of the mountain had been sheared away. She could see the yard where the *katas* had once exercised, and she knew that she was on a porch just outside Hagel of Nages quarters. She had accompanied Ginna this far many times.

The bubble passed over her. She, and all of Ai Hanlo were within it. Her eyes were dazzled, but when the drifting spots settled to the periphery of her vision and she could see again, she felt a burden lifted from her. She was no longer anxious or afraid. She was more alive.

The stone being was transfigured, its outline softening, growing more human. For an instant she was sure that it had her friend's face. His expression was one of beatific calm.

Something touched her leg. She looked down, and at first did not recognize what knelt before her.

"Help me," it croaked, and she knew the voice. It was Hadel. The thing which disfigured his face hung limp and steaming.

"Take him. Heal him." came a voice, and the broken mountain trembled. Tiles fell from rooftops. A cracked wall nearby gave way into a slide of debris.

The God stood over Tamarel.

"Can you understand it?" demanded her companion. "I can only hear the roaring of the wind."

"Yes, my beloved," said Tamarel, ignoring her.

The voice came like a cyclone, like a great wave rushing over the land, knocking them off their feet. It said many other things. To Tamarel they were words, to the other, only noises.

The Priestess stood. The Mother sat huddled by her as Ai Hanlo crumbled around them.

It was to Tamarel that the vision came. She looked to the east; she saw a face peering up over the horizon, a face half like a bird, but very wise, very beautiful, and she knew it to be a sign that the new age would not be wholly for mankind.

She looked to the God. The stone figure was no longer stone, no longer crude, but graceful, lithe in its immensity.

She saw the God dance the dance of life, juggling stars in his hands, placing them in the sky in new constellations. She saw the God raise a new moon. She saw the God reach to the horizon and bring up a new sun, sudden as thunder, filling the world with light.

She saw the cities of the plain, which had never feared the sun, now vanish away, smashed with the hammer of light.

She saw the God dance across the world, setting it spinning

to a new rhythm beneath the sun and sky.

She saw him increase in size, rushing up into the heavens, becoming more beautiful than the mind can conceive, than the tongues of men can describe, spreading like memory upon the wind.

In the end was the Word, and the Word was Light in Darkness and Darkness in Light, and the Word touched all the Earth and covered it.

Chapter 13
The Avatar of the Dancing God

A million bubbles rose and fell in the foam of time. One of them, tumbling pale and golden, had been called Ginna. A mote of thought came together with another, and another, and slowly awareness grew, and a separation took place, and after a measureless interval, there was something which could name itself "I."

He stood in a meadow beneath a clear blue sky. It was noon. The sun was warm on his bare shoulders. He walked, feeling every blade of grass beneath his feet, every crumpled leaf from the previous autumn, and then the soft, dry dust of a road. A breeze caressed his nakedness.

He juggled balls of light and wandered up a hill and down the other side. He met a traveller on the road, a tall, thin, pale white being with a bird-like head. It wore a cloak of iridescent purple. It regarded him indifferently and went on its way.

From the top of the next hill, he spied a city carven all of coral, like an inverted pyramid, floating above the horizon.

He came to a place of simple wooden huts, where shouting human children ran hither and yon. At the sight of him, they scattered. Then one came out of hiding beneath a basket and approached him. He smiled and let the balls of light drift. One of them burst on the boy's forehead and he flinched, but was not afraid.

A woman came running from a doorway, her face hidden in a shawl. She grabbed the boy and dragged him away.

Ginna created more balls and juggled.

"It's *him!*" someone whispered in a booth behind a wicker screen. "He should go to The Mother."

He let the balls go, pulled the screen aside, and two women and a man stared at him in awe and terror.

"Yes, take me to the Mother," he said. Deep within him, a half-remembered emotion stirred. He savored the sensation.

This was the most beautiful place he had ever beheld, and all its people were marvels, it seemed. It was good to be back.

Hundreds were gathering, making signs with their hands that he did not understand. The crowd parted. A man of stately bearing, dressed in elaborate robes and a plumed headdress came forward. He beckoned. Ginna followed. Keeping a safe distance all the way, the man led him away from the village, through a wood, to a wall, through a gate, along a marble pathway lined with golden images, and into a temple. He tapped a small gong with a hammer, then left Ginna alone.

The polished floor was cold underfoot. He looked down at his reflection, and realized that he was faintly glowing and slightly translucent.

He walked the length of a long corridor, into the heart of the temple. He came to a wide room lit from a skylight set in a dome. There, on a throne, sat an ancient woman like withered driftwood left behind by a storm.

She opened her eyes slowly as he approached, but did not move.

"Oh, it is you," she said in a voice of infinite weariness.

"Yes, it is I."

"You've come for an explanation at last."

"I am still...very puzzled."

"You have a thousand memories, and I have one, and you want me to explain?"

"If you would."

"I have thought about it long, what you would be like if you ever returned."

"And?"

"I think you have become an avatar of yourself, a fragmentary manifestation of a greater whole. But you mustn't delude yourself. You are no more the Ginna that once was than I am...what I once was."

"You helped me once. Now help me again. Bring Amaedig—I mean Tamarel—to me."

"Even as I said, you are not the same. Nothing is. The Earth is a strange place for mankind now. We are few after the darkness. This is not our age. In the eyes of the new creatures, we are quaint and ancient and a little crude, I fear."

"Yes, I saw them. Bring Tamarel."

"Ginna, don't you know me? *I* am Tamarel. The Mother of the Goddess died long ago, as soon as her task was complete. But you touched me and commanded me, and I obeyed, and lived, and five hundred years went by. Everyone thinks me divine. I'm still your priestess."

"But...they called you The Mother."

"When you were.... You touched me, as a man touches a woman, and I found I was filled with your seed. I gave birth, in great pain and greater joy, to most of the forebears of present mankind, and to the...others. The world was repopulated through me, through you. I have earned my title."

"I wanted to love you."

"I wanted to love you too."

"But it was impossible."

"Now I only want to rest. Do you really need a priestess?"

He reached out and touched her, and in the blinking of an eye, only her faded clothing lay in a heap upon her throne. He felt her spirit drift past him.

Later, he came out of the woods and looked over a plain. He saw a broken mountain standing, pocked like a face wasted by disease with the ruins of a city. He thought of the towers he had seen standing in the desert, built during the world's noon. They were gone now.

He reached out and touched the mountain, cleansing it.

The world was wholly strange to him now, wholly new, and he had no place in it.

A brave and pious man followed him and, when he at last examined the spot where he had stood, he found that he had made no more impression on the ground than the passing shadow of a cloud.

183

Lightning Source UK Ltd.
Milton Keynes UK
UKOW03f0020221013

219514UK00001B/234/A